UNDUE INFLUENCE

UNDUE INFLUENCE

Priscilla Masters

**SEVERN
HOUSE**

First world edition published in Great Britain and the USA in 2023
by Severn House, an imprint of Canongate Books Ltd,
14 High Street, Edinburgh EH1 1TE.

Trade paperback edition first published in Great Britain and the USA in 2023
by Severn House, an imprint of Canongate Books Ltd.

severnhouse.com

British Library Cataloguing-in-Publication Data
A CIP catalogue record for this title is available from the British Library.

ISBN-13: 978-1-4483-0983-2 (cased)
ISBN-13: 978-1-4483-1007-4 (trade paper)
ISBN-13: 978-1-4483-1006-7 (e-book)

All Severn House titles are printed on acid-free paper.

Typeset by Palimpsest Book Production Ltd.,
Falkirk, Stirlingshire, Scotland.
Printed and bound in Great Britain by
TJ Books, Padstow, Cornwall.

PROLOGUE

When my parents named me I don't know whether it was intended that I should follow in the Lady of the Lamp's sterling example. They've never told me and I didn't ask. I didn't plan it, but sort of fell into nursing after spending a summer working in an old people's home and rather liking it. When my A-level results arrived (better than expected), I was welcomed into the local university hospital to train as a registered nurse.

And that was it. The beginning of my life as a nurse.

ONE

Question: is a nurse ever really off duty?

One of the penalties of living in the town where I work is constant encounters with patients who don't recognize that there are times when I am off duty. On my days off, even when I am wandering up the pedestrianized high street, idling at the stalls set out, weighing up whether to splash out on a plastic-lined beach bag or treat myself to a pot of flowers to stand outside my front door, they approach me for a consultation.

'Nurse.'

I pretended I hadn't heard but jutted my chin out as though pondering this very important decision.

'Nurse.' This time harsher, more insistent. I sensed it was not going away however hard I 'pondered'. I half turned into the plump, earnest face of Annette Parry, whose pale, sweating features were practically touching mine. I backed away as she hissed peppermint into me. 'It's me piles. Ask the doctor to leave out a prescription for some cream, will you?'

I headed up the usual track, verbally finger-wagging at the request. 'Now, you know, Mrs Parry, the doctor can't prescribe without an examination.'

She huffed out her disapproval and I put a conciliatory hand on her arm. 'Just to make sure it's not something more serious.'

That alarmed her – as it was meant to. 'You're saying . . .?' Her voice trailed away miserably as she contemplated an awful diagnosis while her face flushed with embarrassment as shoppers who might eavesdrop on the subject matter filed past.

I offered another salve in a soft, intimate tone. 'You can always see one of the lady doctors.'

She bit her lip but nodded and turned away. I watched her for a moment, wondering whether she would take my advice or duck away from the possibility of ill health and buy an over-the-counter remedy – as many do – before resuming my dilemma between the beach bag and the terracotta pot of late-spring flowers. I still couldn't make up my mind when I was distracted – again. Out of the corner of my eye I saw Ryan Wood sliding something into his pocket.

Ryan Wood, age twenty-three, was another of my patients. He wasn't a bad lad but, to quote Olivia Newton John (in part), he was hopelessly devoted to drugs. The product of a violent, drunken father and a mother who also had an alcohol problem combined with the morals of an alley cat, Ryan was, thank God, their only offspring. We couldn't have dealt with a nest of vipers in such a small, polite, middle-class town. Ryan had tried them all – pot, monkey dust, skunk, MDMA, fentanyl, spice. He'd smoke a cabbage leaf if he thought it would give him a buzz. Really, he should have been confined in a young offenders' institute years ago, but Ryan was blessed with a pair of wide, blue, innocent eyes (inherited from his mother before *her* baby blues had practically disappeared beneath the puffiness of boozy bloating). When Ryan looked a magistrate or a judge in the eye and assured them (quite sincerely at the time of speaking) that he'd reformed, he got away with it – again. For all the legal teams' natural cynicism they were taken in by a straight gaze from a pair of guileless blue eyes. How *could* this disadvantaged, innocent youth be guilty? And so, time and time again, his defence wheeled out his past and he got away with it. Again. He'd got used to it now and the town had got used to him (sort of).

Now Stone is, in general, a pretty, peaceful, law-abiding and civilized market town with most of its inhabitants working for a living. It boasts a high street (now pedestrianized, lined with shops which have survived the death of other retail businesses) which slices up its middle. On a Saturday, as today, it boasts varied stalls on the wide pavement. They sell almost everything from local farm produce to clothes, handbags and household items. A van pervades the streets with the scent of frying onions and sells mouth-watering burgers, and in hot weather, like today, another van tinkles out the unmistakable invitation to ice cream. It has a farmers' market once a month, street markets three times a week (except in January) and is sliced through by the Trent and Mersey canal with its flight of locks. It boasts historic buildings such as The Crown Hotel and is surrounded by the usual new-build housing estates. It is not a town of villains, thieves and felons, but a safe and pleasant place surrounded by undulating farmland and chocolate box villages and is a Stone's throw (ha-ha!) from the M6, one of the country's main arteries when it is not clogged up – not with plaques of sluggish fat like some of my patients' arteries but roadworks, the aftermath of accidents and, well, just traffic.

Ryan was an exception here rather than the rule and the town recognized but tolerated his weaknesses. He was a petty thief who had had a 'dreadful' start in life, they reasoned, and forgave him. He'd been entered into no end of drug rehabilitation programmes and Mark, my policeman ex, said the main reason he still walked the streets was that he had no history of violence. 'No real harm in him, Flo,' Mark had said, arm around me in the days when we were together and the best of friends. 'Bit of a wimp, actually,' he'd added, and I'd agreed. There *was* no real harm in him. He was not all bad. Not rotten to the core. I'd seen him pick up an old lady's shopping without nicking a single item when she'd gone head over heels and her bag had broken, spilling its contents all over the place. He'd chased oranges and apples along the street, laughing, had rescued a split Tetra-pack of milk and helped the lady to her feet. I'd seen him patting a dog upset at being tied to a post when the owner had vanished for too long inside the pub. He even booked, periodically, into my anti-smoking clinic, perhaps believing I had a magic bullet to cure him of his habits. But there was no real intent there. Ryan was a waster, a drifter. But Mark, with his benevolent and forgiving policeman's instinct, was right. There *was* no real harm in him. In fact, it was easier to like him than to dislike him or make critical judgement on him. I watched, arms folded, as he pocketed another trophy, this time a cheap but flashy watch, temptingly set out at the front of one of the street stalls.

'Put it back.'

Someone else had spotted him. Not the tradesman – he was too busy heatedly discussing the faults of the prime minister with his next-door tradesman, arms waving in a fury, voice raised.

No. It was a policeman.

I knew the uniformed officer too. He'd been in school with
my boy, Stuart. His name was Rob Pantini. It was easy to
remember his name because Stuart had, rather cruelly but
predictably, along with the other boys in his class, called him
Pants. I smiled as I pictured Stuart (aged around eleven) telling
me 'Pants' was calling round later so they could do their
homework together.

Pants had grown into a tall, bulky boy with an impressive air
of authority about him as he witnessed the crime. His hair was
already thinning and judging by his uniform he had joined the
police force.

I wondered what road he'd taken to be in the police. University
fast track or had he worked his way up? He'd never struck me
as a particularly clever boy. But he had the stolidity and literal
honesty which matches well with a PC on the beat.

I watched as he tapped Ryan on the shoulder and wagged an
index finger in admonishment. I continued to watch curiously,
wondering what the outcome might be this time. Sheepishly Ryan
slid the watch out of his pocket, returning it to the stand (still
unseen by the trader who was continuing to sort out the country's
problems and on the verge of appointing a new PM – *in your
dreams*). But the outcome disappointingly lacked drama. As Pants
watched, Ryan sidled off, probably planning on filching something
from one of the other twenty or more stalls at the street market.
I was preparing to renew my acquaintance with 'Pants' when I
saw her. Another of my patients. A thin figure, standing in the
middle of all the hustle and bustle, people streaming past her
while she stood stock-still, an island of confusion in a sea of
strangers. And yet she shouldn't have been. These were not strangers. Having lived in the town all her life, she would know many
of them. And these surroundings would be as familiar as her own
home. But I sensed she didn't have a clue where she was.

I watched, puzzled, for a moment longer before approaching
her.

'Nora?' Though I'd spoken softly she startled, hands flying
up in defence like someone woken from a nightmare. But it
wasn't that that troubled me. It was her look of utter confusion.
Not only did she not know *where* she was, I realized she had no
idea who *I* was.

I put a hand on her shoulder. 'Nora, it's me, Florence. The nurse from the surgery.' I tried a smile. 'The one who does your health check. Gives you your flu jab.' I tried another smile and repeated, 'Nora. It's me, Florence.'

Her confusion was clearing but dispersing as slowly as morning mist on a windless day, until she managed a smile which, disturbingly, still lacked recognition. She was doing a reasonable job of pretending, with a watery, quivery smile, but it didn't convince. Besides that, she looked strange today with a clownish gash of orange lipstick distorting her mouth and tired eyes as dark and empty as the button eyes sewn on a teddy bear. She'd lost weight too. Her clothes hung loose. My concern was compounding. I recognized sickness whether mind or body.

'Are you all right, Nora?'

That was when the fog finally did clear as she at last registered who I was, but she met my eyes now with a barrier of hostility. ''Course I am.' She was miffed now. 'Why wouldn't I be?' Her lips were thin and angry. Then she jabbed my arm, hard, with a finger. 'That's the trouble with you health people. You see someone over seventy and immediately think they've lost their marbles.'

I was taken aback. This aggression was new too. Nora and I had been more than nurse and patient. We had been friends. I was quick to mollify her. 'No. No. No. You just looked a bit—' I was preparing to say lost but didn't get the chance. She pre-empted me.

'Well, I wasn't,' she snapped, index finger still poised. 'I wasn't. I was just recalling my *entire* shopping list, every' – *jab* – 'single' – *jab* – 'item, deciding which shops to visit first and whether I needed to take some more cash out of the ATM.'

She produced the phrase like a trophy.

In the early stages of dementia, folk, particularly intelligent people like Nora, are apt to cover up discrepancies, clumsily darning the holes in their memory or smothering outright gaffs with spirited aggression used as a means of defence. I'd seen it a hundred times before and would see it a thousand times more before I retired.

'Fine,' I said, backing off. 'Fine.' I stepped away but she was still glaring at me, waiting for *me* to retreat further. I turned away, pretending to study the second-hand book stall behind me, searching for titles from my favourite authors – I like crime. But my mind was firmly fixed on Nora Selleck. Why hadn't I picked up on this before? That her mental agility was deteriorating?

I'd seen her only a few months ago for her over-eighties and thyroid check-ups and she'd been her usual bright, intelligent self. I recalled our exchange following well-worn tracks: politics, the pandemic, our families, the weather. Which meant her confusion now could be a sign of rapid-onset dementia, which was doubly concerning. I checked my memory. It must have been around February when I'd last seen her.

There'd been no sign of confusion then. Or had I missed any clues because I'd been too busy racing through my consultations, trying to squeeze my patients into the allotted ten-minute appointment time? Had my mind been deflected by the demands of the pandemic, failing to pick up on nuances? Or had I been guilty of being distracted by my own private thoughts, the fleeting Christmas visits of son and daughter who'd barely concealed their anxiety to leave, managing the shortest possible duty visit? It took me until spring to leave Christmas behind. I recalled chatting to Nora while I'd raced through the usual checks for hypertension and hypothyroidism, alert to the fact that she was pre-diabetic while noting some arthritic bulges in her hands. As I remembered I had had some concern over her nutritional state and had been reassured that she was having meals delivered by a local supplier named Tasty Foods. I'd made a mental note to myself to check her weight in another couple of months. Nora had been thin then with a BMI at the lower recommended level. Now, I reckoned, she was thinner. I had the perfect excuse to invite her in for another check.

Perhaps hoping for a sale, the owner of the book stall was watching me. Or maybe he thought I might be another light-fingered Ryan as I picked up a book with a promisingly lurid cover, a man being held by the throat by an enraged assassin. I pretended to scan it while I peeped over the pages to study my patient now she was less aware of my scrutiny.

She was still standing in the middle of the walkway as though she didn't know which way to turn. I picked up on her indecision now rather than confusion. Nora was of medium height, thin as a stick, with sagging dry skin, wrinkled as a prune, and bony arms. Her hair was thin enough to see every lump and bump of her scalp. Long ago it might have been ginger or auburn, but now held only faint traces of pepper with the salt. Maybe once it had been curly and lustrous but now it was lank and frizzy. God only knew when it had last been cut professionally. It looked to me as though Nora had hacked at it herself with a pair of blunt scissors. Her fringe was lopsided, unevenly cut, giving her face and entire head an asymmetry I hadn't seen before. On this warm spring day she was wearing a loose, multi-coloured cotton skirt with an elasticated waist, straight out of the seventies, and a T-shirt which was inside out. I could see a mirror image of large black italic letters. Her legs were bare, with ghostly, blue-veined white skin, but her feet looked comfortable enough in a pair of grubby sandals. Across her shoulder she'd threaded a hessian bag-for-life which sagged and looked empty.

You might consider her ensemble bizarre but no one, apart from myself, appeared to be taking any notice. But I knew Nora well enough to recognize she took pride in her appearance and normally looked smart, her hair regularly trimmed. Stone is a tolerant town. If someone wants to shoplift to support a habit the inhabitants try their best to ignore it unless it impacts them directly. If someone appears less than immaculately or traditionally dressed, that's OK too. Nora was well known enough to fit in with the natives – sort of.

I watched her for a few more minutes as she still stood, marooned again in the sea of shoppers, and I made my plan. I would have a word with her GP. Maybe I would alert her son, suggest he keep an eye on his mother. In the meantime, I had the perfect excuse to invite her in for another health check with the pretext I needed to check her weight. I would ring her next week and call her in. I could assess her mental state then and take appropriate action.

Problem solved – or at least addressed.

I turned away from the book stall, too distracted now to buy either the beach bag, the pot of flowers, or even the lurid-covered book. I reached the top of the high street and continued along the road towards my house.

Still bothered about my patient.

In a small town, a nurse is never really off duty.

TWO

Monday 17 May 12.30 p.m.

I kept to my resolution about inviting Nora into the surgery for 'a check on her weight', telling myself her thyroid function levels were due anyway and I should keep a check on her fasting blood sugar which in the past had been high. The truth was over the weekend I'd thought of little other than my patient, picturing her bewilderment and that peculiar sense that she was disorientated. In a town where she'd lived almost all her life, it made no sense. And so my concern had bubbled away, like a pot of stew simmering on a low heat. I had to intervene. It was my job.

Because . . .

Nora had been more than just a patient. She'd been a friend. I'd been round to share a cup of tea on a few occasions when I'd had problems of my own. Her appointments always overran because we'd have so much to say to one another, chattering through subjects as garrulous as a pair of monkeys. I'd felt a real connection to her, closer than the one I'd shared with my own mother. Maybe it was because she had lost her husband at around the same time that I had 'lost' Mark; both of us having had our dreams of shared companionship stretching into the forever snatched away. Hers through Peter's sudden death with a heart attack, mine through infidelity confessed in a misguided 'heart-to-heart'. For some unfathomable reason Mark had thought it best to break the news of his affair on a night out in a Thai restaurant which had, up until then, been my favourite. These days even walking past it made me feel nauseous. Duplicating my response on that grim grey January evening. I had stared at him across the table, paralysed by his revelation. I'd realized he'd appeared distracted recently, but I'd put that down to a recent case he'd been working on. One of his colleagues had been seriously assaulted, knocked off his bike in a hit-and-run. They hadn't tracked down the driver and the current thinking was that it might have been deliberate, connected with the recent conviction of a violent criminal, a case which the officer had been heavily involved in. The accident – or assault depending on how you viewed it – had left the officer with life-changing injuries. In this case the tidy, neat phrase hid paraplegia. He would spend the rest of his days in a wheelchair instead of running marathons for charity. He would need care from his wife and would never walk his daughter down the aisle. And they still had no proof that the officer, who had been a particular friend of Mark's, had been an intended target or simply that horrible cliché: in the *wrong* place at the *wrong* time. Mark had been terribly upset by it and the subsequent investigation had thrown him right into the path of the predatory PC Vivian Morris – a goofy-toothed siren with an attraction I could never fathom. The only point she had on her side was youth. An extra ten years of it. I could still remember my gaping, nauseous astonishment over the Thai red curry served with fragrant rice which had suddenly tasted like rust smothering sand. Mark, my middle-aged, middle-spreading, quiet, unassuming husband, who so long ago had been my Adonis, had been cheating on me for the past eight months and I hadn't picked up on it. Any abstraction or uninterest in sex or even physical closeness I'd put down to The Case. So when he'd dropped his bombshell I'd been floored, unable to decide between eating my curry and risk puking it up later, or asking for a doggy bag and hopefully recovering my appetite sometime in the future when I would be able to breathe normally again. I couldn't decide and so had sat, motionless, fork hovering halfway to my mouth, while he confessed in far too much detail about romps in the squad car and her wonderful 'understanding'. In the end I ate half and gave up before I was sick and walked home in a swamp of incredulous misery, hardly noticing Mark's quiet, softly ashamed steps at my side while bleating out the lamest of excuses. He'd been devastated by what had happened to his friend, fearful for the future, knocked off balance.

Nora had been my first patient in the following morning's surgery and, sensing my distress, she had sympathized, held my hand and made all the right noises, echoing the platitudes I'd made to her only weeks before in response to her bereavement.

So a bond had been forged. We were connected.

As I drank my morning coffee I dialled Nora's number, already wondering in what state I might find her. It rang and rang; there was no answering machine. I was about to hang up when it was picked up and, her voice still sounding quivery, she spoke. 'Hello?'

'Nora,' I said, feeling genuine relief. 'It's Florence.'

Silence.

'Florence Shaw. Nurse Shaw. From the surgery.'

'Oh – hello.'

I got the impression she still hadn't placed me. Yet there was no real curiosity in her tone. It was flat and weak. So I altered my own voice, deliberately making it authoritative, professional and business-like. 'You need to come into the surgery for a health check, Nora. I need to weigh you and take a blood test, check your blood sugar. I can make an appointment now, if you like?'

I waited.

Silence.

'I also need to check your thyroid levels – make sure you're on the right dose of thyroxin?' It was the perfect subterfuge because it was true. Her last samples had been on the lower edge of normal. Even then I'd recognized it should be checked, maybe her dose increased.

'Oh.' Uninterest.

'And I thought, when I saw you on Saturday, that you might have lost weight.' I paused. 'Have you?'

No response.

'So,' I said enthusiastically. 'When can you manage?'

'I – don't know.' She sounded tired, words dragging out of her, a contrast to her normally brisk tone. 'I-I can come in next week, I suppose? Some time?' She still sounded dubious and worryingly vague. Disconnected.

I responded with even more forced jollity. 'Name the day, Nora, and I'll sort out an appointment time.'

Silence.

I improvised. 'How about next week? Tuesday the twenty-fifth? Eleven o'clock?'

'That'll be all right, I suppose.' Her voice was limp, listless, and my concern grew wings and sprouted roots. This was not the Nora Selleck I'd known for years but a wraith, a shadow, with vibrancy and intelligence erased. I filled in the appointment on the screen but was far from convinced she'd turn up. I pressed ahead anyway, trying to imprint the time and date on her mind. 'Eleven o'clock next Tuesday then. A week tomorrow.'

'All right.'

I put the phone down, still planning. If she didn't attend, I could pay her a home visit, check how she was coping. If she was starting to run into trouble we could keep an eye on her. If we were concerned the next step would be to get in touch with her son and involve Social Services. I would talk to Nora's GP at lunchtime.

But thereby lay a hurdle.

I work with five GPs: two women who job share and three men, all of whom work full time. The two women, Gillian Angelo and Suzie Carter, both trained at Birmingham and were friends before they joined the practice. Both are public-spirited and family orientated. They do their work efficiently and go home as soon as they can. The senior partner, Morris Gubb, is around seventy, but as sharp as a needle and there is no mention of his retirement, partly because he was widowed five years earlier. It is patently obvious to us all that the practice is his life now. Without it I fear he would deflate like a pricked balloon. He lives a solitary life with Doric, an aged black Labrador.

Sebastian is the junior partner and sandwiched between them is Dr Bhatt, a softly spoken, ultra-polite Indian doctor who does his work diligently and without fuss, then goes home to his wife (a radiologist) and their five children who all attend private school and must be costing them a fortune. Dr Bhatt came to the surgery about the same time as I did but I can't really say I know anything more about him than what I learned on that first day when we were both introduced as newcomers. I'm not sure if he is shy or it is part of his culture not to socialize with members of staff, particularly women. He keeps himself to himself.

Sebastian Timor is the exception, a beam of light which shines right through the practice. He is charismatic and handsome, tall and slim, with a mop of curly dark hair. He is also the life and soul of the place, full of fun and with a sharp sense of humour. We all adore him, and I suspect one or two of us fantasize about him. But he is married to a rather beautiful but distant woman, Hannah, who runs a beauty salon on the high street. I've never been into Scheherazade, but from the board outside and the flyers Sebastian scatters liberally around the surgery, it offers everything from manicures to Botox and a wide variety of facials guaranteed to give you a flawless complexion and which, from the few times I've met Hannah at retirement dos and the Christmas party, she looks as though she must use night and day. Out of my price range, I'd thought, as I'd scanned the prices and studied, enviously, the photographs of perfect-looking models which decorated the windows before scuttling round the corner to a more age-appropriate salon which charges half the price. Though, in general, when I'd stood outside and watched the front door of Scheherazade open and close, the women the salon extruded were nearer my looks and age than the beautiful model girls in the photographs. Dr Sebastian Timor felt as far above us surgery staff as Daniel Craig or Brad Pitt. Still, as we all know, a cat may look at a king. Or a nurse at a doctor. He and Hannah had no children. In my cattier moments I imagined that was because she wouldn't want to spoil her figure.

So . . .

Nora's registered GP was Dr Gubb. On the upside Dr Gubb is a sweetie, a gentle, experienced doctor who listens carefully to patients' symptoms and nurses' concerns. He is one of those gifted doctors who has a real instinct for unearthing the truth; sharp, knowledgeable, instinctive and empathetic. But there is a steep downside. He veers away from believing the worst of anyone. He is trusting and unsuspicious, an optimist who anticipates positive outcomes and wants a peaceful, untroubled life. His attitude borders on naivety in spite of the years he's spent in general practice and the riff-raff he must have come into contact with. I had known him trust people he should not have done, believing their stories of intractable backache (which resulted in prolonged sick notes) and everlasting tiredness (in spite of those very people having been spied out in the town, carousing in the early hours of the morning). He believed in all the unprovable illnesses: ME, Lyme disease, myalgia, and he made excuses for aberrant behaviour when asked to provide a reference to the courts for a patient who was undoubtedly a miscreant, in order to avoid conflict. He was prone to missing drug or alcohol abuse and, on one notable and tragic occasion, domestic abuse, because he believed the husband's far-fetched explanation for his wife's injuries. In my opinion Dr Gubb was too trusting, too anxious to avoid conflict, and that made him a potential accomplice. But the practice rule was that if you had a concern about a patient you *must* first discuss it with their registered doctor. If I was truly concerned that Nora might be showing signs of early, rapid-onset dementia, I would need to discuss it with him and back up my case with indisputable evidence. And for that I needed to make a proper assessment.

I did have one other idea. Nora and I had both discussed our offspring at length, wishing we saw more of them. Jack, her son, was her pride and joy, a clever boy who had left home a few years back to go to university. Her walls were decorated with framed photographs of 'her boy' in cap and gown. But I didn't know where he was now, whether near or far, or even in the country. I searched through Nora's computer records for Jack's details, arguing with myself that if my concerns about Nora were founded it wouldn't hurt to open a dialogue about her management. I hadn't met him for years and didn't know how close they were since she'd been widowed. But Nora's personal details hadn't been updated for some years and still had Jack listed as living with her in Swynnerton. So that was a bit of a blind alley.

I wandered out to the reception area, scouting for Dr Gubb, hoping I could alert him to Nora's apparent deterioration, form a plan of action with him. But out here all was activity and noise, the receptionists hardly looking up from their screens as I stood in the doorway, watching them. There were the familiar background noises: the click of computer keyboards; printers spitting out prescriptions; and the ring of phones that were no sooner answered and the handset replaced than they began to ring again.

All was busy, busy, busy.

Through the window I watched the GPs' cars slide out of the car park, among them Dr Gubb's Peugeot.

I'd missed him.

Lunchtime.

Jalissa O'Sullivan called daily with a basket of sandwiches and cakes so we didn't lose time trailing up the high street for our lunch. Jalissa was a black girl, one of the few people of colour in the town which was a static little pool of middle England. Her presence was the result of a diving holiday taken by electrician Brett with his mates in Jamaica, eight years ago. He had fallen for the café owner's hot snacks, her dreadlocks and quite fantastic way of speaking (patois) as well as (he'd confessed to me when I'd checked his holiday jabs six months later) the tantalizing swing of her shapely hips. He had returned to Stone, dumped his local fiancée (who'd never got over it and lobbed insults from time to time) and courted Jalissa at vast distance and expense, marrying her less than a year later. They had two of the prettiest children I have ever seen in my life: Petronella, six, already sporting her mother's corn rows and curly eyelashes, and Charles, who had the sort of dignity you rarely find in a four-year-old. He strutted behind his mother, chest out, chin up, a stance he preserved even when having his MMR. He was like a beautiful, brave, clockwork soldier and did not take kindly to my efforts to pick him up, pat his head or tap a kiss on his cheek. He even turned down the proffered jelly baby. One day, I swore, this dignified little boy would be a politician. And a good one. I liked his bravery, his steady gaze and firm chin.

As I chose my sandwiches, I remembered something else about Jalissa. Not only did she deliver to our surgery and the other group practice in the town, she also delivered Tasty Foods to many elderly who found it difficult to get into the shops so stocked up their freezers. One of those customers was Nora.

'Jalissa,' I began. 'Do you still deliver food to Nora Selleck? Out in Swynnerton?'

She fixed her eyes on me, hand on hip, head to one side. 'Why you wantin' to know?'

I glossed over the truth. 'I saw her the other day and thought she'd lost weight.'

I could see from Jalissa's face that she wasn't convinced of this lame explanation. Petronella was tugging at her hand while Charles stood still and regarded us, black eyes flicking from one to the other as he mused through the subtext. Until Jalissa smiled. 'You sayin' my food not good enough? She losin' weight because of that?'

I smiled too and shook my head, waiting for the answer.

'Well,' Jalissa said, realizing I was not going to rise to the bait. 'It's not my food that is to blame, because she don't have it no more.'

'Really?' I worried now that maybe Nora was facing hard times and couldn't afford it.

'Since when?'

'A month, two month.' She raised her eyebrows. 'Maybe three.'

'Did she say why not?'

'She say she don't need it anymore. She got herself a friend who's cookin' for her.'

'Oh.' I wondered who that could be.

'So if she needs bulkin' up a bit, Florence,' Jalissa continued, 'you tell her to pick up the phone and place an order.' Flashing me a smile, she picked up her basket and waited while Charles opened the door for her, the perfect little gentleman.

When he'd seen his mother through he turned back and faced me, met my eyes and said in a worried tone, 'And I don't like him.'

They were gone before I could ask him anything, and I brushed the comment aside.

I finished off my clerical work as I ate my sandwiches. I often worked through my lunch hour, filling in the consultations on the computer, updating patients' records, writing out prescriptions for the dressings and drugs I'd used during the morning; today I was doing this with my door open watching for Dr Gubb's return. Our surgery doors were conveniently opposite each other, both opening out into the corridor, and I knew he would be back. He had an afternoon surgery while I would be busy with childhood vaccinations. I checked the fridge for the batch numbers and expiry dates in readiness.

My afternoon would be full: injections to give to babies who might squawk a bit but soon forgot once they were picked up and cuddled (my favourite bit), and the older children who were, quite frankly and understandably, terrified at the sight of a needle but soon quietened with a jelly baby. (If they were allowed. Some parents are very strict about sugar intake.)

The afternoon passed with some wailing and some glee at the jelly babies, mothers' anxiety turning into gratitude. I dished out advice (Calpol) and warned them to expect a couple of grizzly days.

At three thirty p.m. I opened my door to see Dr Gubb passing and intercepted him.

'Can I have a word?'

His smile was instantly beatific and attentive. 'Of course, Florence. What is it?'

I explained the encounter on Saturday as well as I could – Nora's apparent confusion, her dishevelled appearance and defensive attitude. 'It's so unlike her.'

The smile he gave me back was sad. '*Anno Domini*, Florence, catches up with us all.'

I could only nod in agreement, even though I couldn't put all this down to such a convenient excuse.

He put a kindly hand on my arm. 'So what do you think we should do, my dear?'

That was another thing I liked about our senior partner. What do you think *we* should do?

'I've invited her to come in next week for a blood test – she's due anyway – and I can do an over-eighties check at the same time . . .' I was smiling now, on familiar ground. 'Slip in a few cognitive checks, I thought.'

'Good idea.'

'If she doesn't turn up, I can go out and check everything's all right at home.'

Dr Gubb was frowning now at another problem. 'Why wouldn't she turn up? She doesn't have a habit of skipping appointments.'

'No, but . . .' I let the comment drift away.

'Who's her next of kin? Her husband died a few years ago, didn't he?'

'Yes. She has a son but I don't think she sees much of him. She hasn't mentioned him in a while.'

'Oh dear.' Dr Gubb took on his mournful basset hound sagging look. 'So sad.'

I realized the AD comment as well as the absence of Nora's son resonated with his own life. But underlying his sympathy I also sensed relief that I was taking on the responsibility. He even went so far as to pat me on my shoulder. 'Good work, Florence,' he said. 'Excellent. I always know I can rely on you.' It was a throwaway comment, backed up by his following words: 'Let me know how you find things.'

'I will.'

He'd already turned towards his surgery door while I sensed conflicting feelings bubbling up inside me. I felt warm towards this elderly doctor who, having given his life to his patients, now faced an empty and lonely future – apart from Doric. But I also had a sense of frustration that the initiative had been firmly placed on *my* shoulders. As though to emphasize this point his door had already swung closed.

'Right.' I was speaking to myself.

A GP might have a list of 3,000 patients, a constantly shifting population as people move, are born, become sick, die. Men, women, children. The elderly, patients with disabilities, the chronically ill, and others who believe they are, need constant reassurance and soak up a disproportionate amount of a doctor's time. Each one of those 3,000 patients has the same rights, the same demands and the same expectation: nothing but the best medical care. It can be a tall order.

THREE

Tuesday 25 May, 11 a.m.

I'd worked my way down the list of patients, dealing with their needs and problems until I came to her name and saw from the screen that she had not yet arrived. An 'A' appears to the side of the name when a patient logs in to the surgery either on the waiting room screen or with the receptionist. The side of

Nora's name was still blank. I sat, eyes fixed, already worrying a little, willing the screen to register her arrival, while at the same time I acknowledged that I hadn't really expected her to come. The old Nora would have sounded brisk and business-like at my phone call, already scribbling the date and time on her calendar. Not this vague acknowledgement of a phone call. Already, I realized, I was accepting the change in her. And as the minutes ticked by, the conviction mounted. She wasn't coming. But still I watched the screen obsessively, willing the 'A' to appear. Nora, or at least the Nora I'd known so well, was, by nature, polite. *That* Nora wouldn't have simply failed to turn up. In my mind I was already notching up the symptoms of dementia. At eleven twenty-five a.m. I rang through to the main desk and asked the receptionists whether Nora had cancelled her appointment but received the expected negative answer.

My next two patients had arrived and were waiting. A quick blood pressure check and a blood test. All over in a few minutes.

11.40 a.m.

And Nora still hadn't arrived. I worked my way through my morning surgery until lunchtime, trying to suppress the tinge of guilt I was feeling. Maybe I should have done more when I'd seen her on the high street, made the appointment then, alerted Dr Gubb earlier, emphasized to him how out of character her appearance and behaviour had appeared. Maybe I should have said I would visit her at home instead of inviting her into the surgery. I felt responsible and knew I had to act.

Swynnerton was an outlying village a little under four miles from the surgery. Nora didn't drive. Like many women of that generation, she'd left 'all that' to Peter. They had been one of those couples with clearly defined roles. Hers included housework, cooking, shopping and the front garden, while he dealt with all the insurances and paperwork connected with their home, house maintenance and the vegetable patch to the rear. She'd told me in the past that she'd never had a driving licence. There was a bus service into Stone which passed their cottage but it only ran every two hours. Maybe she'd missed it. I was still searching for a rational explanation for her non-attendance.

Anything other than the fact that her cognitive function was disintegrating. I tried her number again but this time no one picked up. It was left to ring with that prolonged, hollow tone that communicates you are ringing an empty house. My concern was compounding and I felt fidgety and vaguely guilty. I should have done more. And now? She'd fallen. She was injured. She was wandering somewhere, confused.

I had an hour's break for lunch. I could be there and back before my afternoon clinic began at two.

Nora lived in a pretty, white-thatched cottage on the edge of the village along a quiet lane which ran at an angle to the main road. Whatever it had originally been called, she and Peter had renamed it The Beehive because of the way the apex of the roof faced the front while the walls appeared to slant inwards towards the roof. The illusion was furthered by the fact that they had painted it a rather stark white but left the front door the rich yellow of honey. She and Peter had renovated it, she'd told me, almost thirty years ago. They had moved in and named it once the renovations were complete, standing back in the garden and coming up with its name. It was a quirky, attractive place. Peter and Nora had felt justifiably proud of it and loved it like a second child. Every inch of the house and garden had been lovingly restored and cared for by them both, almost as proud parents.

I pulled off the road and parked on the verge, behind a green van, sitting for a moment, unable to work out why my feeling of apprehension was compounding when The Beehive looked peaceful. It was a quiet moment without passing cars or any but distant sounds and even those were not human. From far off I heard only a buzzard's shriek and a barking dog. I tried to focus. Perhaps my subconscious had registered that something was not quite right here, something subtly out of kilter. It took me a few moments and careful scrutiny of house and garden to analyse what it was.

Nora was a keen and precise gardener. She did not tolerate weeds, digging them up with the ferocity another might have reserved for an enemy. The front garden consisted of a narrow concrete path bordered both sides by a lavender hedge already sporting spikes. But between each plant now grew dandelions and ragwort, buttercups, even a thistle or two. The small lawns either side were long and unkempt, like a head of hair that badly needs a trim. And it wasn't just the garden. There was something different about the house too. I climbed out of the car and locked it, which was another symptom of my unease. I had never done so before. This had always felt a safe, country environ. So why this change of habit, this sense of a threat nearby? What else was my subconscious registering that my conscious had yet to catch up with?

I strained, trying to catch a sound besides the ripple of a blackbird in the beech tree but now I heard nothing. Except an ominous quiet. The dog had stopped barking and the buzzard had, presumably, flown away to seek out distant prey. And, of course, that was something else that I'd caught up with. Nora almost always had Radio 4 playing in the background, from the time she woke, she'd confessed to me once, to the time she went to bed, disliking that ominous and heavy silence which made her feel alone. Indoors she had a digital machine. Out of doors she tended to carry around a battery-operated radio and listen while she hoed out weeds or tended plants. But however hard I listened I could not hear the sound of voices. That was it. It was too quiet. Even the traffic that ran through the village only yards away seemed to have abandoned it. I strained to hear the hum from a distant hive of bees but heard nothing. I opened the wicket gate and dropped the latch behind me. Each step forward felt wooden, reluctant, heavy, taking me some-where I didn't want to go. Inside. Because I worried what I would find there. Nora on the floor? I searched for something that would tell me all was well, really, but all that registered was that the curtains in the front window were carelessly, untidily, half drawn.

My knock to a closed front door sounded hollow. So I called out. The elderly, particularly those with impaired hearing and perhaps limited eyesight, do not like to be surprised.

The 'Hello?' bounced straight back to me. I called again.

Something creaked inside the house. I pushed the door open straight into the sitting room and breathed in alien smells. Cigarette smoke? Beer?

To my relief she was sitting in a chair, her back to me, fingers pleating and re-pleating a woollen blanket made of multi-coloured knitted squares that lay across her lap. As I moved into the room she turned her head and saw me.

'Nora,' I said, moving forward, glad at least to have found her alive, apparently unharmed. My relief was diluted when her eyes fixed on me, polite but vague and uncurious.

I dropped to my knees, mindful to keep accusation out of my voice while I probed for the truth. 'You were due in the surgery this morning.' I smiled, trying to turn my words into a tease. 'Did you forget to write it on your calendar?' There was no response. I touched her hand. 'Did you have a problem getting in, Nora? Miss the bus, maybe?' With no answer I again tried to turn my probing into a joke, my voice hearty. 'Well, as you can see, as you didn't get to see me I thought I'd pop out, take a drive in the country and say hello. If the mountain won't go to Mohammed, et cetera et cetera.' I gave another friendly laugh at my pleasantry while tucking in a mild reproof. 'You could have phoned, you know. Cancelled the appointment. We could have arranged transport.' I was still smiling while inside I felt a chill, knowing something was very wrong here. The house *felt* wrong. To fill the silence, I rambled on. 'Not exactly a Rolls-Royce, I agree – but . . .' I realized she wasn't taking any of this in so I finished with a lame: 'One of the volunteers would have fetched you.'

We have an army of good-hearted volunteer drivers who bring patients, who have difficulty accessing appointments, into the surgery. And she knew that. She had used them before.

But she was pressing her lips together, staring ahead, avoiding my eyes, her own eyes stony and cold as though we were complete strangers. When she did turn to look at me, she was again in that argumentative mood, ugly and defensive. 'I didn't need to come. I don't know why you told me I should.'

I resented the use of the word 'told' as though it had been an order rather than an invitation. I'd wanted her to see the appointment as an invitation. I tried to retrieve my stance.

'You needed your annual test for thyroid antibodies and a . . . health check.' I substituted the description 'over-eighties' for 'health check', thinking it was less antagonistic.

'*He* said,' she spoke aggressively, spittle in her mouth and a witchy hostility, 'I didn't need it doing.' Her voice was stubborn, uncompromising. 'He *said* I didn't need to come.'

I didn't like this. 'Who said? Jack?'

'No, not him.'

'Who then?' I was disturbed now, feeling unsettled by this angry lady. Did she mean Peter, her dead husband? Was she being influenced by a ghost?

She turned her head and looked at me, triumph illuminating her face as though she stood over me, the victrix. 'Ben.'

'Ben?' I scrabbled around in my mind. Neighbour? Friend? Relative? Contact? And found no one. 'Who's Ben?'

She smiled, a self-satisfied smile now, which chilled me even more than her confusion.

'Who's Ben?' I said again.

One of her hands stopped pleating the blanket to creep across to mine and pat it, almost patronizingly, as though she pitied me.

'Nora,' I said, really worried now. 'Who's Ben?'

'He helps me out.'

'Is he one of the neighbours?'

She shook her head very firmly and I tried again.

'When you say helps, do you mean a sort of odd-job man?'

'Sort of.' She ducked her head, a jerky, angry movement as I pursued my quest.

'So he helps you out, does bits and pieces around the house?'

'That's right,' she said triumphantly, and in another sudden turn of attitude she spoke again. 'Florence,' she said, having apparently recovered my name, '*you* know how lonely it can be on your own. And difficult managing a house.' She looked around her. 'Especially one as old as this one.' She gave a girlish laugh. 'And I'm no spring chicken.'

I should have been glad that she had struck up a new friendship, someone who would help her with everyday problems, support her. But, looking around me, I couldn't see any improvements.

So, I was not reassured and returned to my main concern, the supposed reason for my visit. 'I need you to come to the surgery to . . .' I didn't finish.

Her eyes were alight and she was smiling and patting my hand again. 'Ben is just wonderful. A real friend. Family. Kind and so helpful, Florence. He does all sorts of things around the house. You wouldn't believe how helpful he is. How glad I am . . .' She stopped abruptly. Her next words chilled me. 'He advises me on things as well.'

I didn't like the sound of this. 'What sort of things?'

She looked almost girlish, pink coquettish cheeks. 'General repairs,' she said airily, 'insurances, business stuff. The sort of stuff Peter used to do,' she said comfortably.

Disquiet was ringing softly in my ears. 'But surely Jack helps you with that?'

She shook her head. 'Jack is . . .' Her eyes were sad until she picked up. 'Jack has his own life now.'

I was silent for a moment, empathizing with her until I felt I should delve deeper into this new friendship. 'How did you meet him, this Ben?'

'What does that matter?' she snapped.

'Nora. Who is he?'

She pressed her lips together and tilted her chin upwards like a defiant teenager.

'Nora,' I said, really concerned now. 'Who *is* he? Is he a relative perhaps? The son of a friend?'

'He is my friend.'

'But who is he? How did you meet him? Where does he come from?'

In a sudden change of mood, she gave my shoulder a playful punch. 'Oh, you,' she said, laughing now. 'You sound so old fashioned. You might be my mother. "Where does he come from?"' She wasn't doing a bad job of mimicking my voice. It might be a joke to her but I wasn't laughing. This person was a stranger to me. And she hadn't answered my question.

'Nora,' I said sternly. 'Who is he?'

'What do you want to know for?'

But it wasn't her voice.

FOUR

He was standing in the doorway, blocking it. A big guy. Dishevelled, bulky, unshaven and I could smell the beer and tobacco from across the room.

Nora half lifted herself from her seat, trying to jump girlishly as though to greet her sweetheart. 'Oh, Ben,' she said, smiling and laughing. 'There you are.'

'Here I am,' he said, his words parodying hers with a harsh tone. Which made me realize, this was no friend. He turned his full attention to me. 'Who are you?'

I stood to my full height (five feet seven inches), lifted my chin and met his eyes with a challenge of my own. 'I'm Florence Shaw, the nurse from the surgery,' I said, dignified and formal, not even hinting at a smile. 'Nora is my patient and she was supposed to come in today for a blood test and a general check, but apparently . . .' I let the sentence drift where it would.

'It were just a check, weren't it? Nothing important.'

'How do *you* know?'

He surveyed me with a pair of dirty blue eyes. There was ice in the irises, blue flecked with grey. He didn't even try to answer my question but leaned back against the door jamb, smirking. I didn't even try to disguise my antagonism and mistrust towards him. Only my fear.

The three of us stayed like that, unmoving, like a tableaux, Ben and I glaring at one another, trying to achieve some dominance, Nora twisted round towards us both. It was she who broke the impasse. 'Oh, Florence . . .' She was fluttering like a debutante now as she tried to keep the peace by appealing to me. 'I'm sure it wasn't important, was it, Florence, this appointment? I can come another time, can't I?' She was trying to appease both of us and succeeding with neither. After a swift glance in her direction we'd resumed our face-off.

Nora looked from one to the other and back again, perhaps

absorbing the hostility that hung in the air, and I sensed her fear. Feeling protective, I took a step towards Ben to challenge him. 'Who are you, exactly? What are you doing here?'

He was ready for me with a response as sharp as a flick of a whip. 'I'm Ben Evans. And I'm doing what you should be doing, Florence Shaw, nurse from the surgery. Keeping an eye out for an elderly lady. Watchin' over her.' He grunted. 'Doin' stuff around the house. For her,' he added.

I hadn't seen much sign of it. But I kept that view to myself.

And again, it was Nora who tried to keep the peace. 'See, I told you, Florence. He takes care of me, don't you, Ben? Helps me out with things.'

He ignored her but stared me out coldly. I took in his sagging jeans, the denim jacket thrown over the top of a blue T-shirt, a tattoo snaking down his right arm, the forked tongue, licking the knuckles of his third and fourth fingers. I tried another angle of attack. 'Do you live near? Are you a local?'

In a small town those four words can be the key which unlocks an entire identity, past and present, as well as pinning intent for the future.

'Not exactly.' He was giving nothing away but I was not going to let go so easily. I toned down the aggression, adopted my coffee table, polite voice. 'So how are you two such friends? How did you meet?'

A veil dropped over Nora's face.

But Ben had an answer ready. 'Bumped into her at the street market,' he said casually but with a hint of a challenge tucked in. 'She looked a bit . . . lost.'

Just as I'd seen her on the Saturday, I thought, while mentally replacing lost with another word.

Vulnerable.

Nora grabbed at the word like a lifebelt tossed to a drowning person. 'Yes, lost.'

'I asked her where she lived and gave her a lift back here. Realized she could do with a bit of help. A couple of jobs that needed doing.'

As if I believe that!

'So kind,' Nora said, nodding to herself.

They both waited for my next question. Which I addressed to

Ben rather than Nora. A fact that I realized later was significant. 'Nora does need to come to the surgery for a review.'

Ben chewed his lip before speaking. 'Then I suppose I'd better bring her,' he said gruffly.

'Good. Thank you. Thursday. Ten o'clock.' I smiled – a peace smile. 'And you say you'll bring her?'

'Course,' he said without looking at me. Then he stood aside, no longer blocking the door, but holding it open, a shallow bow sending out a gesture of mockery.

As I left, I could hear her voice behind me, thin and uncertain. 'Thank you.'

That was the voice I heard all the way back to my car.

Where I had an idea.

FIVE

1.45 p.m.

On the opposite side of the road, slightly elevated from The Beehive, lived an elderly couple, Tobin and Orpah Hudson, also patients of mine. I'd performed their new patient screen a few years ago when they'd moved into the area from Blackpool. I'd wondered why they'd chosen Stone and asked them.

It had seemed a question they either couldn't or wouldn't answer, but had looked at each other, confused. They hadn't friends or relatives down here, they'd told me without enlarging, but had selected Stone on a random whim, as though they'd stuck a pin in a map of the UK and ended up here, purely by chance. At the time I had puzzled over it. But as I hadn't seen them since their initial screen, I hadn't had a chance to probe a little deeper and satisfy my curiosity. Mark had once commented that I was too nosey about my patients' private lives. The comment had stung.

Orpah looked apprehensive when she opened the door to my soft knock. Maybe she didn't recognize me. Even though I was in uniform she'd only met me the once. But the sight of a nurse in uniform, any nurse, even one wearing the friendliest of faces, makes patients instantly feel guilty, recalling instances when they had neglected their health; in some way breaking the NHS rules.

I was quick to explain and reassure her. 'It's Florence,' I said with my widest, friendliest smile, watching some of her unease melt, but not quite all. She still looked wary, a faint shadow on her thin face. So I followed that up with further reassurance. 'It's OK. There's nothing to worry about. Really.'

I wondered why she looked so seriously apprehensive. For a moment my curiosity was diverted away from Nora. What was Mrs Hudson up to? I wondered, recognizing the cloud of guilt while peering past her into the house in search of a clue, while my mind rolled around the possibilities: drinking too much wine in an evening; having a crafty fag out the back; not taking enough exercise; forgetting her tablets; scoffing sugar? The list was long but that was not why I was here.

Orpah was standing quite still, her head slightly tilted at the angle which suggests an enquiry. She was a slim woman in her fifties, with dyed dark hair which emphasized her sallow complexion. She was dressed casually in black jogging pants and a loose blue T-shirt and was wearing no make-up. Obviously not expecting a visitor. Her feet were bare, with unpainted toenails, and she was waiting for me to speak, needing an explanation.

'I wondered if I might have a quiet word with you?'

Far from allaying her fears, she looked even more anxious. 'Of course.'

I stepped inside after glancing back over my shoulder. Across the road Ben Evans was standing in Nora's front doorway, watching me, his hostility and suspicion beaming across the road. No doubt wondering what I was up to. And I cared? I gave him what I hoped would be interpreted as a withering and disdainful stare. The body language equivalent of 'Fuck you!'.

'That man,' I said, still focused on him. 'How long has he been hanging round Nora's?'

Orpah put her hand to her throat. 'I don't know. I haven't taken particular notice.' Her next words chilled me. 'He's her son, isn't he?'

It took me a minute or two to process her statement. I

eventually answered, 'No. He's not Jack. Jack lives in . . .' Then I realized I didn't know where Jack lived. 'You mean he's *living* there?'

'Well, he seems to be there a lot of the time. We thought he *must* be her son. Tobin and I thought how lovely it was, that he's so attentive.'

I shook my head. 'He's not her son.' I'd met Jack once or twice, a quietly spoken, polite, intelligent teenager when I'd last seen him. And he'd been at his father's funeral, his arm around his mother's shoulders, a tall, slim man, in a smart, navy-blue suit, with an air of authority. No way had he morphed into *that* uncouth person. I turned my back to Ben knowing he was wondering what I was up to, maybe guessing my intent.

'How long?' I repeated.

She seemed flustered. 'I don't know exactly. A month. A couple of months? Is something wrong?'

That put me in a dilemma. Nora, in her current state, appeared to welcome her guest. She certainly hadn't expressed any wish for him to go or seemed aware of any threat. It was I who sensed the threat, convinced that this man was a wrong 'un. Why was he here? What was he planning? What was in it for him? Far from seeming a handyman, helping around the house, the cottage – and its garden – had seemed more neglected than usual. And that was without considering Nora's deteriorated mental state, which was currently confused at best. At the moment she seemed passive. A red flag to me. I knew her. This was far out of the character I was so familiar with. She'd been a teacher, a professional woman with intelligence. Sure, she'd relied on her husband for many things and Peter's absence had made its mark. But she was not this confused, muddled, dependent elderly woman allowing a stranger to take over her life, make decisions for her.

I gave Mrs Hudson a bland, friendly smile, bordering on conspiratorial. 'She's one of my more vulnerable patients, Mrs Hudson. And living out here . . . I wonder if you'd just keep an eye out for her. Ring me if you have any concerns?' I tried my friendliest face on her, but it didn't get me very far.

Orpah still looked uncomfortable. 'I don't know about . . .'

She needed convincing, so I pushed a little harder. 'Nora's elderly. She's a widow. Her son works away, I believe, so is

unable to keep an eye on her.' For some reason I was diverted
into trying to remember what family the Hudsons had, who *their*
next of kin was, but I couldn't quite reach an answer. Another
piece of another puzzle which I tossed aside.

Orpah clearly wasn't convinced.

I tried the disarming look next, strong on appeal and a sense
of public responsibility. 'I can't be here all the time . . .' And
then I stepped on to the thinnest of ice, practically hearing it
crack under my feet as I spoke. 'I'm really fond of her. I'm
worried . . .' Oh, how to choose the right phrase. 'His presence
might not be as welcome as you think.'

Now Nora's neighbour looked confused. 'I haven't seen any
sign . . .' Her voice trailed away, sagging with uncertainty.

'Well . . .' I reverted to my brisk but friendly, professional
district nurse tone. 'If you do notice anything that concerns you,
perhaps you'll get in touch with me?' I kept it professional,
sensing I'd already taken a step too far. 'At the surgery.'

She was glad I was going. Her shoulders dropped, her face
lost the tension and resumed some animation. She saw me to the
door and closed it as soon as I was safely through.

I'd read her mind. The nurse was asking her to *spy* on a
neighbour?

That hadn't done any good. She'd almost looked panicky at
the thought. Frightened even, which didn't make any sense. But
as I'd walked away from their house, I'd realized their property
was elevated so from their front-room window they could peer
right into Nora's living room. It was the ideal place to spy from.
Mrs Hudson might be reluctant to play the part, but she was in
prime position. Maybe alerting her would be enough.

Back in the car, as I drove back to the surgery, I ran through my
options and found another possible avenue to explore.

At the surgery we have a community psychiatric nurse. Kelly
Spears might be only twenty-five years old but she had a natural
talent and almost mystical intuition which, combined with her
training, made her a valuable asset in the treatment and management of our patients with psychiatric problems. Her workload
consisted mainly of sufferers with depression, but she could cope
with it all: bipolar disorder; schizophrenia; narcissistic personality

disorder; and anything else we cared to throw at her, including dementia, for which I now recalled she'd had special training a year or two ago. The course might only have been a week long but she would be a good starting block and a valuable ally.

For me to initiate any intervention in what I was now calling 'a situation' I would need a professional to back me up, someone with mental health expertise. And Kelly was perfect for the job. We could then liaise and work together. If Kelly deemed Nora vulnerable and her mental abilities compromised, we could take steps to intervene.

True, they would be slow baby steps. Little in the mental health services moves faster than a tortoise on sedatives, but it was the best option by far.

I planned a joint consultation for Thursday. Whipped along by a sense of urgency, I didn't want to waste any time. While I was doing the physical stuff, taking blood, checking Nora's blood pressure, monitoring her blood sugar and checking her height and weight etcetera, Kelly could be making an assessment of her mental state. She could ascertain whether there was a level of coercion in this new 'friendship', which was what I strongly suspected. At the same time *I* could do a bit of digging into Ben Evans: who he was; how she'd met him; where he'd come from; how he'd slithered into her life as well as her home; work out how much influence he had over her; and lastly whether there was a sinister angle to this partnership. Some people with dementia have heightened suspicions; others are dangerously too trusting. Both responses are frequently misplaced. I suspected that Nora's capacity for rational judgement was compromised. The Nora I knew would have kept her distance from a roughneck like Evans, smelt a rat at his proffered help. Never have allowed him to slurp his beer and smoke in her house. Never even have allowed him inside her home.

I wondered if Jack knew.

Once Kelly and I had assessed and agreed on a course of action we could move forward. Speak to Dr Gubb, involve Social Services, contact her son, even seek intervention from the courts. My nurse's instinct was telling me I had to put some distance between my patient and the intruder, but I had a nagging fear that I might have trouble persuading Morris Gubb to share my view. I reasoned that Kelly would be the conduit to persuading him to take the situation seriously.

I found Kelly in the staff room, filling in patient records while drinking what passed as coffee. One day, I'd vowed on many occasions when I'd drunk the muddy sludge that masqueraded as coffee, when I'd won the lottery, or a patient remembered me in his last will and testament, I would donate a posh coffee machine to the surgery making sure my name and generous gift were engraved on the side. So every time anyone enjoyed flavoursome coffee instead of the stuff we endured, they would bless me for my generosity. But for now that was a dream inside my head.

Kelly looked up. 'You OK there, Florence?'

I dropped into the seat by her side.

The first thing anyone noticed about Kelly was her hair, which she regularly dipped into dyes of various colours of the rainbow. Cut short in a sixties' bob, today it was orange. A beautiful, vivid orange as bright as a flame. And she had lipstick to match. I grinned at her and, as succinctly as possible, un-ravelled the situation while she listened, her face tilted to one side, remaining impassive. Kelly was a good listener, neither interrupting nor asking any questions until I finally stopped for breath. I guessed she'd heard a strange tale or two before.

'So what do you want me to do?'

'See her with me, make a proper assessment of her mental capacity?'

She didn't answer straight away but spent some time thinking before responding. 'It's a tricky one, Flo,' she said. 'If Mrs Selleck doesn't seem to object to this man being there and he says he's helping her out, there's not a lot we can do. Unless we can be certain that this is a result of a compromised mental state. And . . .'

And . . . I waited, my mind diverting. Finally she picked up. 'And,' she continued, her face deadly serious now, 'he crosses a line.' Now she looked more like a double agent masquerading as an anarchist.

She drew a large A5 diary out of her floppy leather bag and opened it to the page marked with a ribbon while I kept my fingers crossed that she would have some free time. She looked up and grinned. 'I was going to be in a meeting,' she said, grin spreading, 'all day. But it's been cancelled. Hallelujah. So, day after tomorrow? Thursday, you say? Ten o'clock?'

I nodded and felt relieved. I believed I had an ally.

I only had to hope that this time Nora turned up to her appointment. Then, armed with ammunition, I could speak to Dr Gubb about his patient. Between the three of us we could decide on a course of action.

SIX

Thursday 27 May, 10 a.m.

Kelly and I sat, looking at each other, waiting silently. I could tell she was sifting through a series of questions in her mind, the best ones to expose Nora's mental state and focus on any coercion in this new relationship she'd formed.

I ran my eyes over her, always enjoying Kelly's colourful and imaginative sense of fashion. Kelly had her own interpretation of the word and her current outfit might look strange to me, a tartan pinafore dress with a white blouse underneath, black tights and clumpy boots, but it was probably the latest craze. She looked like Morticia Adams in a posh school uniform. It was a change from her usual outfit – skinny jeans and sweater or shirt depending on the weather. The tartan of the dress, predominantly red, clashed with her orange hair, but that was probably part of the effect too. Tomorrow her hair could be blue or purple or green or any other colour. Kelly was fond of ringing the changes. Sometimes she looked more bizarre than the patients she was seeing. But she was my best hope. I had faith in her professional qualities.

I gave her a tentative smile which she returned even as we both glanced towards the door.

Ten o'clock, the time of Nora's appointment, came and went and I grew anxious. Not only was I wasting Kelly's time, but it crossed my mind that I was losing my sense of perspective because of the close relationship I'd had with my patient. I felt hot under the collar, embarrassed and increasingly angry, not only with my patient, but also with myself.

At ten forty-five I finally met Kelly's eyes, aware that she had more than enough work to get on with, as did I. My patients would also be lining up in the waiting room. I'd allowed half an hour for this joint appointment, half an hour that was being wasted. In that time I could have seen three patients. Finally, at ten fifty, steaming with anger, embarrassment and frustration, I picked up the phone and dialled Nora's home number.

He picked up on the first ring. He'd been waiting for the call. 'Hello?'

I could hear the light, mocking note in his voice, sense his enjoyment.

'I need to speak to Nora.' I heard the fury in *my* voice which I wasn't even trying to hide. Gritting my teeth, I added a polite, 'Please. She had an appointment with me this morning.'

He knew just how to rile me. 'Who is that – the hairdresser?'

I could hear the barb in his voice and before I could stop myself, I snapped out, 'You know perfectly well who this is.'

He continued to play his game. 'Sorry?'

I had no option but to play it by his rules. 'It's Nurse Shaw from the surgery,' I said, trying now to disguise my fury with a dignified tone. 'Mrs Selleck was due here for a health check this morning and some blood tests.' I turned the tables on him. 'You *said* you'd bring her in.'

'Oh, so I did.' His response was as smooth as silk and as fake as a ham actor slapping his hand over his forehead in a scene of self-blame. 'So I did. I am *sooo* sorry. I *completely* forgot.'

Kelly was meeting my eyes now, warmed with perceptive sympathy which the twist in her mouth also tried to convey. Perhaps her expression also held a hint of warning. But my blood was up. I was too angry to absorb it. And I still had a card up my sleeve. 'If she doesn't come in, Mr Evans, we may have to stop issuing her prescriptions. And that could mean a hospital admission.'

Which will put her out of your reach.

But my threat only provoked a snort of laughter. 'Not sure the stuff's doing her much good anyway, *Nurse* Shaw.' I picked up on the derision in his voice. This was practically open conflict now. So I dropped any pretence at politeness.

'Mr Evans,' I said, managing to sound patient – just. 'Nora is elderly, a potentially vulnerable widow. She has complex health needs and multiple co-morbidities. She needs *all* the medication she's prescribed. Every. Single. Pill. If she didn't need them we wouldn't be prescribing them, but she does need careful monitoring on them. Or else . . .'

Silence at the other end as I felt a rising triumph.

I shot my last bolt. 'I'll be discussing her case with her GP. As well as her failure to attend the surgery on two occasions now, which could be an indication of a compromised mental state. You, however, can't claim that. And it was *you* who promised to bring her in.'

There was a brief silence followed by another grunt which I interpreted as a shoulder shrug. He may as well have said, 'Do what you like'. But he didn't quite dare. Like me, he could only go so far.

But then I overplayed my hand with nothing but righteous indignation as an excuse. 'If we think Nora is potentially "at risk" we will remove her from her home, admit her to a unit, and assess her condition and needs.'

Kelly was frowning and shaking her head even before I dropped my heaviest hint. 'Her safety is our paramount concern.'

Evans made a feeble attempt at placation which didn't get anywhere near fooling me. 'She's perfectly safe here,' he said, calm and controlled now. '*I* keep an eye on her.'

Head-to-head, then.

I took a couple of virtual steps back and tried to regain my footing. 'I don't know who you are, Mr Evans. You're not a relative. I don't really know how you came to know my patient. Yet you seem to have stepped inside her life . . .' I paused. 'Somehow.'

Apart from his heavy breathing Evans gave no response so I ploughed on, wrapping my threat in gauzy placation. 'Maybe your intent is good, Mr Evans . . .' Had I imagined another derisory snort? I continued smoothly anyway. 'But it's our job, our responsibility, to make sure our vulnerable patients are safe.'

He challenged that. 'You think she isn't safe here, with me keeping an eye on her? I'm here nearly every day.'

I could almost hear the ice crack as I stepped back on to it, responding as carefully as though I was being recorded, choosing every word with regards to the Nursing and Midwifery Council's directive on patient contact, treatment of relatives, et cetera, et cetera. 'With all due respect, Mr Evans, she's missed two appointments now, so it doesn't seem like she's being well-cared-for to me. I was concerned about her when I observed her home circumstances.' I turned the assault on to him. 'And you've displayed some scepticism about her need for her medication. Added to that Nora is elderly, vulnerable, and doesn't have family nearby to keep an eye on her.' I fired my last salvo. 'We don't know anything about you.' I let that sentence hang in the air, a sticky flypaper for anything questionable to stick to. As well as an opportunity for him to produce his pedigree, his origins.

The silence told me he had no response to this except reluctant capitulation. In a clever voice, schooled Teflon-smooth, he said, 'Why don't I bring her in this afternoon then?'

'I'll see if there's a free appointment.'

I smothered the mouthpiece with my hand, Kelly's shaking head already registering.

Tomorrow? I mouthed.

She nodded. 'Eleven.'

I was smiling as I turned back to the conversation. I had him now. 'It'll have to be tomorrow, I'm afraid, Mr Evans, at eleven o'clock. I don't have a free appointment this afternoon. Also, we need some blood samples and they are dispatched to the hospital lab at lunchtime, so it needs to be a morning appointment.'

'Tomorrow then.'

It was a very minor victory but one which had found its mark. I'd sensed grumpy resentment in his response, even in this minor defeat. And in a final attempt at domination, he put the phone down. Hard.

I hadn't liked the guy before. Now, added to the dislike, I felt mistrust bubble up like marsh gas from a swamp. I took a deep breath, trying to steady my heart rate. 'He's up to something, Kelly. I really don't trust him.'

She opened her eyes, raising heavy false lashes and meeting

my look with a warning of her own. 'We need to be absolutely certain what the situation is before we can take any action, Florence. You know that.' We both knew how tightly bound we were by the rigid rules and no less rigid guidelines of our profession.

'Just wait until you meet him, Kell,' I countered. 'Then you can make up your own mind. But my opinion is he's a shady one, probably emptying her bank account as we speak. Odd-job man, my foot. There was no sign of any odd jobs done, inside or out. Whatever he's doing at The Beehive, it isn't odd jobs. So why is he there? Wait until tomorrow, Kell. You'll see.'

SEVEN

Friday 28 May, 11 a.m.

Another tense few moments looking at Kelly, whose hair today was a rather fetching blue, waiting for Nora to arrive. But Evans played a clever card. Nora turned up alone for her eleven o'clock appointment, arriving promptly and tidily dressed. She eyed us suspiciously from the doorway, mildly hostile towards Kelly as her eyes took in the ID badge which read, quite clearly: Kelly Spears. Community Psychiatric Nurse.

Nora spent a moment reading the words. Only then did she give me a sad, questioning smile, a brief nod, and sat down without uttering a word.

Today, as though to further refute my suspicions, she was tidily dressed in a dark skirt which, admittedly, hung loose, but was still smart, and a clean, white shirt. She had flat leather loafers on her feet; her legs were bare and her hair was neatly brushed. She wore no make-up. She looked what she was, a retired school-teacher. I could see her through Kelly's eyes. There was little evidence of the confused, bewildered woman who had stood in the middle of the high street, not knowing which way to turn, as though she hadn't known where she was or how she had arrived there.

My heart sank. There was no red flag here for Kelly, who was giving me a puzzled look. Ben had got the upper hand.

Nora regarded me coldly, which was as hurtful as a knife wound. As if our friendship had melted away. Now we were strangers, on opposite sides of a fence.

She said nothing as I took her pulse and blood pressure, lined up the syringe and blood bottles, tightened the tourniquet and found a vein.

All the while Kelly, perched on the examination couch, was chatting idly, as though to a friend she had just met socially. But I recognized her subtext.

'I take it you've had your booster vaccine?'

There was only a little hesitation before Nora responded. 'Of course.'

Kelly studied her nails as she shot out another question. 'So, how's the garden these days, Nora?'

This provoked a stronger response. Nora swung her head around to glare at her. 'Why are you asking me all these questions?'

Kelly batted this away with a casual: 'Just making polite conversation, Mrs Selleck.'

But now Nora had clamped her mouth shut. Kelly eyed her for a moment. Now she was frowning, puzzled, but she did risk another question. 'How's Jack these days, Mrs Selleck?'

Nora's response was unexpected. Jack was – or had been – her pride and joy. Her clever boy, she'd always referred to him as. But today, her response to the enquiry was a shrug and a pursing of her lips. 'All right, I suppose.'

Kelly straightened up. 'When did you last see him?'

Nora stared at the floor, frowning before finding a response. 'I don't see him much these days.'

I was still taking blood at the time but glanced up to study her face. She seemed to be struggling to supply a suitable explanation, which finally came: 'He's busy. Living his own life.'

Nora looked from me to Kelly and back again. 'Why is *she* here?'

'It's part of the health check.'

'No, it isn't. She's never been here before.'

'It can be helpful to have an extra person.'

She was unconvinced, so I changed the subject as I stuck the labels on the blood bottles and filled in the forms. 'How did you get in today? Did you catch the bus?'

At that point she was searching her memory, puzzling to find the answer before she looked up at me, as though I would provide it. I felt a snatch, not only of concern, but also of pity. 'Did someone bring you in?'

She shook her head, still puzzling, until she found the answer. 'I had a lift,' she said slowly. 'He brought me in his car.'

'Who brought you in his car?' Kelly had asked the question, slipping it in so softly it was like stroking velvet. Nora looked from one to the other, lost, while I felt the temperature in the room plummet. 'He said you would' – her eyes flicked over to Kelly and back to me – 'ask things.'

The trouble with dementia is the mental capacity is not constant. It fluctuates between memory and memory blanks. The mind fills the emptiness with spurious events, rogue memories and explanations.

I diverted her by leading her to the height chart before checking her weight. 'You've lost eight pounds, Nora.'

'I eat well.' But her voice was now abstracted. We'd lost her.

'I understand you don't have Tasty Foods delivered anymore.'

'Who told you that?' The response was sharp and suspicious.

'Jalissa. You know she delivers our lunches here.'

'You've been gossiping about me?' She practically spat out the comment.

'No. She just happened to mention it. Did you cancel them because you didn't like them?'

'No. I didn't need them anymore.'

'So . . .?'

'*He* does my shopping.'

I read between the lines very quickly and arrived at an obvious deduction. *He had access to her money.*

I said nothing. I daren't make unfounded allegations. They would achieve nothing, only land me in the soup with the NMC. At the same time, I sensed the antagonism between Evans and myself was out in the open, which meant it could well be turned up a notch by either of us. In which case I acknowledged, sadly, that Nora would probably take *his* side. I listened intently, watching her search the floor for answers to Kelly's probing questions, all the while worrying at her lips with her teeth.

I filled in her weight loss on the computer and drew up her prescription record. 'Still taking . . .' I rattled off her drugs.

She shook her head. 'I don't need all of them. I take the ones I need.'

I logged that on the computer. 'So which ones do you omit?'

'I told you,' she responded crossly, obviously lacking the answer. 'The ones I don't need.'

I had to pursue this. 'I need to know, Nora. Which ones are you taking and which ones have you dropped?'

'Oh, I don't know,' she said. 'He puts them out for me.'

Alarm bells clanged a warning, loud and clear. 'I think it would be a good idea if we got the pharmacist to put them in a week-long container marked off day by day, don't you?'

'That's not necessary.' She was still frowning while her eyes still roamed the floor.

I responded smoothly, 'I think it is necessary. I'll arrange something.'

She pursed her lips at this, like a rebellious child, but said nothing.

I made a mental note to speak to the pharmacist while flicking down the computer to see whether she'd picked up her prescriptions regularly. They had been picked up, but that didn't mean she'd actually swallowed them.

Kelly slipped forward, ready to speak now. 'Mrs Selleck,' she said, 'who exactly *is* Ben Evans? What is he to you?'

For an instant Nora looked panicked, her head jerking back. But once she'd had time to consider an answer she came back with a dignified reply. 'He's a friend, as I expect you know.'

Kelly moved off the couch and took the seat next to her. 'How do you know him? How did he come into your life?'

Nora frowned, searched her mind for an answer – and didn't find one.

Kelly shot a meaningful glance at me and I felt exonerated.

Nora looked frightened. She put a hand on my arm as though pleading with me to stop these questions.

'Is he perhaps the son of a friend?' Kelly prompted.

Nora shook her head. She drew in a breath as though to tell us, but she exhaled and said nothing. But I was left with the impression that she had been about to give at least some explanation.

'So, how did you meet him?'

'I think – I think – I think I met him . . . in town.' The words had come out quickly before stopping abruptly. 'Or somewhere.'

'When?'

'I don't—' She stopped and the defensive anger was back. She was addressing me. 'I don't know what it's got to do with you. Why don't you mind your own business? You have a' – her eyes drifted over Kelly's name badge – 'psychiatric nurse here. Do you think I'm mad?'

I tried to soothe her, putting a hand on her arm. 'No, Nora. Of course not. We're just concerned.'

'Well, don't be.' She stood up. 'I can look after myself. I don't need you poking your noses into my affairs. It's nothing to do with you. Who he is, how I met him. Anything,' she finished.

I tried to retrieve the situation. 'He said he does odd jobs around the house?'

'Yes.'

Kelly was watching her very intently now.

I wanted Kelly to be the one to ask whether she was paying him but she stopped me short with a little shake of her head. Just as Evans had classed *me* as an unwelcome interferer, Nora Selleck was resenting Kelly's presence.

The room felt silent, each of us with our own thoughts. Evans was a bum and a sponger. I'd already decided that. What was worrying me now was what else was he? How far would he go?

I couldn't stop my mind churning over the same questions: what was he *really* there for? Where had he come from? Nora was no pushover. Was the fact that she seemed to have accepted Evans into her life a result of her waning mental acuity? How had he slipped into her life, gained her trust, seemed to have free passage to her home, probably her bank account too, and been able to come between her and me? He played games, promising to bring her in yesterday, then deliberately keeping her away. And she wasn't even curious, wasn't raising any objections?

Kelly was looking equally thoughtful, chewing on her lip and frowning.

Nora's apathy worried me even more than her apparently fragile mental state. And I sensed there was another facet to this, something that bothered me even more, a subtext she was anxious to conceal. She was looking away from me and it was deliberate.

As I'd checked her pulse and blood pressure, taken the blood samples, I'd picked up on concerning physical signs too. Her pulse had been slow, her skin dry and cold and something in my mind lay dormant, a sleeping knowledge which I would reconsider later.

I met Kelly's eyes, jerked my head towards the door and she got my meaning. I wanted her to see Evans for herself, make her own judgement.

She stood up. 'I'll walk you back to your car, Mrs Selleck.'

As expected, Nora got to her feet. 'No need for that,' she said, with a touch of her native dignity. 'I can see my own way out thank you *very* much.'

Kelly had her answer ready too and produced it smoothly. 'It's fine. I'm going that way anyway.'

She held the door open, gave me a conspiratorial wink, and followed Nora through.

EIGHT

S he was back minutes later, closing the door behind her and flopping down into the chair with a soft exhalation. 'What a creep,' she said. 'And he stank of beer. He's as dirty as a—' She broke off with concern. 'Who is he, Flo? What's he up to?'

To that I had no answer but my own opinion. *Nothing good.*

She put a hand on my arm. 'I think we should get her properly checked out at the memory clinic at the hospital. And have someone else to keep an eye on her. Maybe get a home help to pop in a couple of times a week?'

12.40 p.m.

In our practice the rule is that we address any concerns to the patient's registered GP – in this case Dr Morris Gubb. Had it been any one of the other doctors things might have turned out differently, but fate is fate, written in the stars and unalterable, dependent on sometimes small decisions, sometimes on pure chance, the consequences of which can be as devastating and far reaching as the butterfly effect.

I hovered outside his door while he saw his last patient, who left leaving the door ajar. Through it I could see him bent forward, shoulders rounded, glasses perched on his nose, as he peered into the computer. I knocked and he looked up, taking a brief moment before he recognized me, and his expression changed to a welcome.

'Florence,' he said. 'Come in.'

I was struck at the change that had happened to him inch by inch since he'd lost his wife, Sylvia. Ten years ago, when I'd first joined the practice, he'd been a lively, intelligent man with a head of thick grey hair, piercing blue eyes and a well-honed sense of humour. Always smiling, it had seemed. A happy man. There had been days when the practice had rung with the sound of his boisterous laughter. But from the moment Sylvia had been diagnosed with ovarian cancer, we had noticed the change in him, almost overnight. One of the penalties of being a medic is that you have no straws to cling to when a loved one receives what you know to be a terminal diagnosis. No one can pull the wool over your eyes, feed you platitudes and disguise the truth with euphemisms or offer you the slender reeds of chemotherapy, radiotherapy or even complementary therapy. From the first you see the shattered glass, the brutal hard truth, the stony road ahead and its inevitable terminus. So the laugh was gone; the man shrunk. It was cruel, as if half of him was in that diagnosis with her. He and Sylvia had been skin close. They'd met when Morris had been a medical student and she a student nurse, and they had married as soon as they'd both qualified. They had one son, Tim, who was also a doctor. Medicine often runs in families. Dr Gubb's father had been a GP here before Morris took up the reins. But Tim had chosen another path. He worked for Médecins Sans Frontières, so was rarely in the country, let alone able to support his dad with frequent visits and fill the gap created by his mother's death. Charity might begin at home but for doctors the word charity can encompass the whole world, not just their immediate and close family. Morris could have done with his son being a little less charitable. They'd always been close, and I knew our senior partner would love to have seen his son carry on the tradition and take over the practice; although he would have denied it, instead focussing on the wonderful work Tim did for the disadvantaged of the world. So Morris had been left alone with his aging Labrador. There were other signs that indicated the loss of his wife. Morris was a boy lost, in odd socks, his shirts missing buttons, sometimes buttoned up wrongly and badly ironed. His hair was thinner now and cut less frequently. He went through the motions of life and work without any real direction or pleasure. When he attended the practice Christmas party he smiled, he drank, he laughed, but it was unconvincing. He was giving me one of those brave smiles now and waving me to a seat, knowing I must need to discuss something with him. I sensed he was glad to have someone to chat to – even if it was just about work. His face had warmed, become animated, but just for a second.

'What can I do for you, my dear?'

I'd thought carefully about this, lining up my sentences in a manner least likely to sound histrionic, but a structured professional concern about a patient I perceived as vulnerable.

'It's about Nora Selleck.'

'Nora? Oh, yes. Did you call her in?'

I nodded.

'And?'

'She didn't come, so I visited her at home.'

'Good.'

This was a bit trickier. 'It seems some guy is hanging around.'

'Some guy?' Then he came to the same conclusion that I had. 'Her son?'

'No. He seems . . .' I was having trouble finding the right words. 'I didn't really like him.' There was no other way to say this. 'He seemed a bit of a roughneck.'

Morris Gubb smiled. I could see he was thinking I was being a snob.

I had to put this better. 'I think he's sort of . . . controlling her. He said he'd bring her in to the surgery.'

Dr Gubb waited, sensing there was more.

'I set up a joint consultation with Kelly.'

'Good idea. What does she think?'

His eyes were puzzled and I knew he thought I was being overzealous, seeing a problem where there was none.

'Again, she didn't come.'

Dr Gubb was frowning now and I continued with what even I felt was a poor version of my concerns.

'He brought her in this morning instead.'

He smiled and put a hand on my arm. 'That's all right then, Florence. If he's helping her out, surely that's a good thing?' He smiled fondly as he continued, 'If I remember rightly, there's quite a bit of garden at her place. Peter used to do it. She must be finding it hard work at her age. Probably glad of some help.'

He wasn't getting it, or rather I still wasn't putting it across very well.

'Kelly suggested we refer her to the memory clinic.'

Dr Gubb was still smiling. 'Not surprising at eighty-four.' He tried out a misguided quip. 'How many of us will be in a similar position, I wonder?'

He really wasn't picking up on my concerns.

I tried to make my point again. 'I think he's taking advantage of her.'

'In what way?'

I knew I'd missed my opportunity because I'd used the wrong word. I should have said 'influence'.

'He's doing her shopping.' It was too late to backtrack. I tried to get him involved. 'Maybe you should see her, judge for yourself?'

He dived for the easy route. 'Certainly, if you think I should. I'll get one of the receptionists to make an appointment.' He was logging off from his computer at the same time, distracted. 'If you think that's necessary.'

'He seems to be discouraging her from taking her medication.' Even I wondered then whether I was being overdramatic, making work for an already busy doctor, seeing shadows where there were none. But I had to trust my instincts. I tried to move away from my imaginings and shift to something more tangible.

'I suspect she might be hypothyroid. I've sent some blood off for the usual screening.'

'Good.' He was on familiar ground here. 'Well, we'll take a look at those then, shall we? And I'll review her tablets. Maybe she doesn't need to be on all of them. Perhaps we can reduce some.' He was sounding hearty now. Sure-footed. He had his hands on the arms of the chair, preparing to lift himself out of it.

I took the hint. I would leave it with him, wait for his verdict. He was, after all, Nora's GP.

Two weeks later

Unfortunately, appointments for routine consultations can be as rare as hens' teeth and Dr Gubb had some annual leave, rumoured to be visiting his son in Ethiopia. He would have returned from holiday to an avalanche of emails, test results, items marked urgent, appointments backed up and a myriad of other problems all demanding his attention, so the consequence of this unfortunate timing was that it was mid-June before he actually saw Nora face-to-face. I too had been busy in the meantime, decorating my front room, and then the kitchen looked shabby, so that had been next. I'd also had to provide figures for an audit on our follow-up appointments for asthmatics, so I'd been distracted. Having passed the baton to Nora's GP, I suppose I'd tried to focus on other things.

On Wednesday, the sixteenth of June, I noticed that her name was down on his morning surgery list for an eleven o'clock appointment. I kept an eye out for her but missed seeing her. Dr Gubb must have realized I would want to hear his impressions because at lunchtime he joined me in my clinic room. 'I saw Nora this morning,' he said, sitting down and looking relaxed. 'She did seem a bit vague. Slower than usual but nothing really concerning. And . . .'

'Did she come alone?'

'No. She had her friend with her . . .' He was still smiling.

'She describes him as the odd-job man. He seemed perfectly pleasant to me.'

I've experienced this so many times. You meet a patient, their relative or a friend, who is rude to you, offhand. And then they go and see the doctor. On their best behaviour they give a totally different impression. So Ben Evans was playing this game, was he? Jekyll and Hyde. Well, I had seen the other side of him. I gave a puff of annoyance at Evans's slick deceit.

'What about her blood tests?'

'All good except TSH up, T4 a bit low. I've increased her dose of thyroxin and she's a wee bit anaemic so I've prescribed some iron tablets. I noticed you'd registered she'd lost weight. Told her odd-job man who, incidentally, also seems to be her personal chef' – he swallowed a smile at his witticism – 'that he should bulk her up a bit.' He put a friendly hand on my shoulder. 'Nothing to worry about, Florence. No dark secrets there.'

Maybe a trickle of my lingering doubt reached him so he felt he should say more. 'She's been widowed a few years, hasn't she? Probably just lonely and her son's working away so she's latched on to this fellow. Lucky he's there.'

We were looking at this situation through different perspectives. I saw darkness while he saw light. To me, Evans was a problem. To Dr Gubb, he was a solution.

Dr Gubb then bent over my computer and flicked a few keys, read the information on her next of kin and cleared his throat before turning to me. 'Maybe we could have a word with her son, suggest he pops in, sees his mum.' He frowned at the screen. 'Do we have current contact details for him?'

'Only those out-of-date ones.'

He harrumphed. 'Best get that sorted out. See if Nora can give you current contact details for Jack.' He straightened up and I knew he was passing the buck. And so responsibility twists and turns, and was passed between us like the baton in a relay race.

I tried to press my case before he disappeared altogether. 'So you had no concerns about her mental state?'

'No more than any other octogenarian.' He patted my shoulder.

I'd wanted to insert the word 'coercion' but Dr Gubb was already heading towards the door, turning round to say, 'Stop worrying, Florence. She's all right.' And possibly to allay my fears as well as reassure me that *something* had been done, he finished with, 'I did increase her thyroxin. That should help. Maybe boost her cognitive function a bit.'

It was only later that I understood the significance of this last, throwaway sentence.

'Perhaps,' I inserted slyly as he reached the door, 'it might be a good idea if *you* paid her a visit, saw the lie of the land at home?'

I was watching him out of the corner of my eye, alert to his response to my suggestion. Anyone of the other doctors would have resisted a home visit on such a flimsy premise, particularly when the patient was able to attend the surgery, but Morris Gibb was an old-fashioned doctor. He was used to visiting patients at home, in person. The pandemic had hit his style of practising hard. He liked people – face-to-face not mask-to-mask – and he was the one partner who disliked video consultations – not that Nora would have managed one anyway. Dr Gubb's patients were largely, like him, elderly. Apart from newcomers into the area a GP's list ages at the same rate as the doctor, with the result that many were not computer literate, and if they had a mobile phone they used it 'for emergencies' (to save the battery, bless this frugal generation). If you rang them on a mobile phone they sounded slightly shocked. And that's if it was switched on in the first place. Things were changing. But slowly for some. Technology was leaving these patients stranded.

Dr Gubb looked back at me and smiled. At the time I assumed it was a sympathy smile shared between two people who felt more at home with their old-fashioned values, doctor and patient. But I was too distracted to give it much thought. I'd forgotten that smile; we saw it as rarely as winter's snow these days. I felt suddenly grateful to this tired-faced man who had given his life, his kindness and loyalty, to his patients. I felt an urge to lighten his burden. Not increase it. I felt guilty.

'I've always been fond of Nora,' I put in. 'Why don't I go and have a cup of tea with her? We can swap stories and I can get Jack's current whereabouts.'

I could feel his relief like a balm.

NINE

I drove towards Swynnerton through undulating farmland, looking around with pleasure. All was as it should be. Cows, sheep, crops in the fields, the sky blue. Peace reigned.

The day was warm but not hot. I had the windows open in spite of the visitors who flew in, buzzed for a while exploring the interior of the car, and just as quickly buzzed straight out again. I hadn't warned Nora or her Ben that I was coming. I wanted to 'surprise' them.

All the way there I'd been wondering how to play this. What I wanted to do was warn Ben off, let him know I was on to him, that I was watching his every move. I would protect my patient.

That was the exact moment when I began to doubt myself. What if I was wrong? What if Ben really was helping her? He was uncouth, rude even, and resented my 'interfering', but what if I had misjudged him? What if Morris Gubb had read the situation more accurately and Evans was her guardian angel in the absence of her son? Maybe I'd exaggerated the deterioration in Nora's mental state. Perhaps she wasn't suffering from early dementia but was just a bit vague? We had to wait for a proper assessment. I couldn't put all my patients into a cardboard box. Things weren't always simple, neat and tidy. Edges were blurred and my judgement possibly impaired. Mark had always said I was too involved in my patients' lives. 'You're just their nurse, Florrie,' he'd said on one occasion when I'd voiced some concerns about a family.

With these thoughts in mind, prepared to look afresh, I climbed out of the car, locked it, pushed open the gate and threaded my way along the path bordered by a lavender hedge and towards the front door.

Before I even reached the door, it opened and he stood in the doorway, hand on the lintel. Instantly I knew my instincts had been right. He was staring at me and there was no disguising his hostility and malice. Even as I took another step towards him, I felt my heart begin to race. What was it about this guy? Today he was dressed in baggy shorts and a plain black, armless vest which displayed bulging, gym-honed biceps and the full length of a snake tattoo as well as numerous other animals on both arms and legs. His drum of a belly was displayed proudly as a trophy. His feet were bare and slightly grubby and it looked as though he had no intention of shifting, just as I knew I could hardly barge past him and insist on seeing my patient. My dislike of him, mingled with fear, caused bile to rise in my throat. I felt my face tighten. Had I been a dog I might have growled, hackles up, and bared my teeth, threatening. But I might just as surely have dropped my tail, whined and slunk away. Two steps away from him, I managed to stand my ground while fingering the mobile phone in my pocket.

He spoke first. 'So, it's the nosey nurse from the surgery, is it? And what do you want today?'

To my credit I stood firm and my voice sounded decisive. 'I need to check up on Nora as her medication has been changed. Dr Gubb was going to come, but as he was busy I said I'd attend myself.' I even took a step forward, my eyes not dropping from his face, waiting for a sign that he would shift. The truth? My heart was yammering now inside my ribcage, causing it to rock. I wasn't a dog with sharp teeth to dig into those thick ankles. More truth? He frightened me. He was of a type I recognized and feared. With his big, sweaty, heavy body and the tattoos that ran up and down his arms, patterned his legs, his presence, like his animal scent, was overbearing and threatening.

He didn't shift. Not one inch, but stood, arms folded, an immoveable object blocking the doorway. 'Why? She saw the doctor. She's fine.'

'Who changed her medication.'

For a while we stood immobile, each challenging the other however much I was quaking. I was trying not to look into his face, not to see the determination in his eyes or the sheen of sweat on his forehead and cheeks.

He shifted slightly and I pressed home the advantage I was sensing.

'We regularly check in on all our over-eighties who live alone. Make sure they're taking their medication properly, especially when it's changed or been tweaked. Check there are no side-effects.' I continued, 'Prevent trips and falls, no health hazards.' I finished brightly and quite untruthfully.

He still stood, considering my statement. Was I going to have to shove him out of the way?

'She's fine,' he repeated, his voice a little softer now, almost conciliatory. Then he followed that up with: 'You can save your time, nursey. Go visit someone who really does need your attention. *I* will keep an eye on your patient.' He leered at me and I noticed one incisor was broken. In a fight? Then he scratched an ear with a large, gold sleeper threaded through it.

I stood my ground. Our eyes met. I looked away first. I thought he wouldn't move but after a pause he stepped to one side and gave a mock flourishing, Regency bow.

I felt the bulk of his body, sticky and pungent, as I squeezed past him, trying not to breathe in beer and cigarettes which combined with another scent, a strange odour, one I couldn't place, not then, anyway. I stepped inside. As before, the interior of The Beehive was fusty and stale, cigarettes and something sweeter which I recognized from the sole spliff I'd experimented with in my student days. In spite of the warm day the sitting room felt damp and chilly. Airless. Nora was again sitting in the front room by an electric fire which radiated warm air but did nothing to alter the atmosphere. She didn't turn to greet me and showed no curiosity as to who had entered. All I could think of was why wasn't she outside on what was a breezy summer's day, kneeling at the flower beds as she dug out dandelions and buttercups and grass that had strayed from the lawns? The picture I had was of her always busy in the garden, wellies on, cardigan drooping from her shoulders. Why was she huddled up like this, shoulders rounded, staring into the fire and doing nothing? This figure was in stark contrast to the Nora I had always known, who was always doing *something*: gardening, reading, listening to the radio, cooking, cleaning. Never, *nothing*.

I'd been right to worry.

'Nora?'

When she turned to face me I realized how deep the change

was, accelerated in the weeks since I had last seen her. She looked blankly at me, her eyes hollow. Her skin appeared dry and she seemed weary. She turned away from me, uninterested. I knelt by her side and touched her chilly hand, hardly knowing where to begin. 'Nora,' I said, unsure now how to talk to this 'stranger'. 'You know who I am, don't you?'

She angled her face towards me. There was a film over her eyes and I realized it wasn't so much that she didn't know me, it was more that she didn't care who I was.

I had seen this before, patients detaching from their surroundings, from reality, gradually letting go of the world around them and all they had once held dear. It is often a predictor of death because if you don't care about anything you have nothing to tether yourself to life.

My concern compounded. But I couldn't blame this situation entirely on Evans. Dementia creeps up mainly on the elderly, uninvited, unwelcome, but nobody's fault.

I tried to tug her back. 'You know me. Right? It's me, Florence, from the surgery.'

Her head dropped, chin on chest. I was unsure whether it was a nod or whether her head felt too heavy to support it. Had Kelly been sitting here she might have diagnosed severe depression. But, recalling the results of Nora's blood tests, I was wondering something else. Hypothyroidism has many, many manifestations, as one would expect from a gland which controls one's metabolic rate. One of the signs and symptoms lesser known than the commoner ones is a part loss of the outer third of the eyebrows. I stretched out my hand, noticing she did not wince or draw back, and touched the outer aspect where her eyebrow should have reached.

'How many of those little white tablets are you taking?'

He was standing in the doorway now, watching me, smoking a roll-up. Nora coughed as he puffed out a cloud of smoke and gave a little huff of laughter. 'Satisfied? Told you I was keeping an eye on her, didn't I?'

I shook my head, turned to my nurse's bag for the sphygmomanometer, took her pulse, blood pressure and temperature, all the while studiously ignoring him. As I'd thought. She was slightly hypothermic and bradycardic.

Nora gave me a ghost of a smile. 'Still alive, am I?' Her voice was croaky. Her hand grabbed mine, nails sharp, digging into me. I felt it meant something.

I repeated my question. 'Are you taking *all* your medication, Nora, and the extra tablets Dr Gubb prescribed?'

'Am I?' She swivelled her head towards Evans.

He couldn't hold back a gloating smile. 'Are you?' he mimicked. ''Course you are, love.' He skewered me with a glare while he spoke to her. 'Every single white, red, blue or yellow little piece of poison prescribed by the *nice* nursey and her colleagues. Mrs Obedience. That's you, innit, love?'

He followed that up with a question to me. 'Happy now?'

I stood up. 'Not exactly. No.'

I put a hand on Nora's shoulder but she didn't respond. I bent down and spoke softly, only to her. 'How about we get you into the cottage hospital? Take care of you and then get in touch with Jack, suggests he visits?'

She looked at me blankly.

I pressed my point. 'Do you have his current address so I can contact him?'

I shouldn't have done it. I knew that almost as soon as the words had left my mouth. I sensed it from a sharp movement in the doorway. I should have left the threat unsaid, tiptoed out of there, smiling pleasantly, all the way back to the surgery where I could have spoken to Kelly and Morris, and persuaded them that Nora was too vulnerable to be left to the mercies of Evans whom we did not know. Together we could have rescued her. But I'd shown my hand and it was too late now. Nora was staring ahead, her head dropping. She was almost asleep, while behind her Evans was looking thoughtful, plans already formulating. I looked down at her. Sometimes when I look at a living patient I already see their dead face imprinted, the bones underneath the skin. This usually happens in a terminally ill patient. You know they are sliding out of life and will last less than a day – maybe two. But this was Nora. She wasn't terminally ill. But I still saw her dead face as clearly as if I had just read a scan or seen a tumour on an X-ray. I backed away, chilled and frightened. And then I was angry. He had done this and I thought I knew how. The signs had been there in the blood I had drawn weeks ago before the change in her medication. TSH – the thyroid stimulating hormone – was raised, trying to generate the important hormone. Her T4 was down because she wasn't even taking the initially prescribed thyroxine let alone the increased dose.

I might know how; I had yet to discover why.

Evans was chewing his lip, obviously waiting for me to go, but standing in the doorway so I would have to squeeze past him to escape. I moved towards him while feeling as though I was abandoning her, leaving her to an uncertain fate. My visit had made things worse.

I could only think of one thing. 'We may have to take Nora into the cottage hospital,' I said. 'Some of her blood tests indicate' – I fell back on a useful euphemism – 'her medication dose may need careful refining.'

He saw through my pathetic attempt at deceit and laughed. 'Adjusted again?'

I continued to hide behind trite phrases, avoiding anything that could later be quoted in a complaint. 'Sometimes it's a bit of trial and error.' I even managed an accompanying smile.

Nora turned her head at the words. 'Trial?' she queried.

'Trial and error,' I repeated.

But something had upset her. She was shaking her head. 'You don't know me,' she said. Then louder. 'No one really knows me.'

I stood and faced her. 'Of course I know you, Nora. I've known you for years.'

But she was shaking her head sadly. 'No one does. I'm not what people think I am.'

I couldn't work out what she meant.

I decided to leave. The sooner I left the sooner I would be back at the surgery and could plan my next move. As I passed Evans, trying not to inhale his scent, I looked him straight in the eye. Had I caught the faintest sign of sympathy? I looked again and thought I must have been mistaken. This time the expression was something else. And now I worried that even mentioning admitting Nora to the cottage hospital as well as summoning Jack might have foiled his plan. Had I flushed him out?

That thought bothered me as I drove away.

TEN

I headed straight back to the surgery hoping to speak to Dr Gubb again, to emphasize my misgivings both about Nora and her 'carer'. But he had only seen her two days ago. He might be difficult to persuade. Besides, he might already have finished his surgery and gone home. Instead, I came up with an alternative.

My solution of admitting Nora to the cottage hospital had not been an idle one.

Cottage hospitals can be a GP's answer to many problems: a minor injuries unit; respite for patients with a terminal diagnosis whose family need a break; a halfway house for elderly patients who need an escalation of their care package; somewhere to park patients waiting for residential care to be arranged. Arranging residential care takes time and the magic word is funding. Everyone argues about it. No one wants to pay. Funds are always short. I thought I could wheedle Nora's admission by arguing that her medication had been adjusted. But really my reason was that within those walls she would be safe, out of reach of whatever plan Ben Evans had for her. I imagined he purely wanted to fleece her out of funds. Maybe when he realized we had him in our sights, he would back off, find someone else to cheat out of their life savings. We could involve Jack, who would surely be able to protect his mother's interests, and then maybe, with a care package, people *we* had appointed – a home help and regular home visits from myself and Kelly, as well as reinstating Jalissa's Tasty Foods – her condition would improve. But there was one problem. Empty beds in a cottage hospital are as rare as the proverbial hens' teeth. I had known patients wait weeks for an available space. A magic wand would have been useful. But who has one of those?

It was now late on a Friday. The surgery would be preparing

to shut down for the weekend. When I arrived back most of the staff, except the duty doctor, had already left, including Dr Gubb.

Which suited me.

The duty doctor was Sebastian.

I caught him as he emerged from his clinic room. He looked knackered, tie loosened, top button on his shirt undone, chinos crumpled, and I caught a whiff of irritation. No one likes this shift, the time when patients start to panic. No doctor, except the relief service, until Monday morning.

I tried my best to give my request calm justification, without bias for a favoured patient, or against a man I disliked and mistrusted. But somehow, even though I emphasized that some of Nora's symptoms were due to hypothyroidism and that the support she had at home was 'questionable', it came out muddled and prejudiced and I knew I'd got it wrong.

Sebastian was frowning as though he was struggling to understand and certainly not seeing any urgency. I knew how very wrong I'd got it when he put a hand on my shoulder. 'Calm down, Florence. Doesn't sound like an emergency to me.'

I'd omitted primarily using Evans as a reason, putting the emphasis on Nora's frailty. Now I wondered if I'd got that wrong too. 'I think she really does need admitting, Sebastian.'

He pulled back and blew out a frustrated breath. And said again, 'I don't see the urgency, Florence.' When I didn't respond to that he moderated it to: 'So you really think . . .?'

I nodded sagely and returned quickly with my prepared answer. 'If we monitor her mental health and medication as an in-patient in the cottage hospital, adjust her dose of thyroxin, I think we'll avoid a crisis in the future.' What I left out was: and remove her from the influence of the 'odd-job man'.

I watched his face, my hope slowly fading, as I picked up on his doubts. 'Just for a night or two?'

His mouth twitched. 'To keep her away from the big bad wolf?'

I knew then just how wrong I'd got it. I had painted too dramatic a picture, made Evans sound like the villain of children's stories, and I forced myself to calm down. 'I was thinking more about her mental health,' I said with dignity. 'Involve Kelly in further assessments; adjust her medication until we've got it spot

on. I suspect at least some of her confusion is due to her hypothyroidism. It's possible that her symptoms will improve if we
admit her.' Now I was focusing on the medical aspects, I thought
I could win him over, and I was right.

'I'm going over to the cottage hospital later,' he said, 'to check
up on a couple of patients. If they don't have an empty bed
maybe there's someone I can discharge, if you like.'

I knew he was mollifying me, but it was the best we could do
between us. 'That'd be great.'

I would have liked it 'sooner' rather than 'later'. But however
pressing and urgent decisions feel to the person on the front
line, they do not happen in an instant.

If there were no free beds at the cottage hospital we were out
of alternatives. To send Nora into the A&E departments, whether
Stafford or Stoke, would see her peremptorily discharged
with an adjustment to her medication and a snarky discharge
summary back to the surgery. This was not an emergency – except
to me. We were pedalling uphill.

I thought that even if we couldn't admit Nora today it
would be OK. I thought she would be safe for now. Nothing would
happen over the weekend. Again, I'd almost handed over the
baton. But not quite.

I returned to my clinic room with a sense of purpose. I flipped
Nora's paper notes out of the Lloyd George envelope. While her
summary was computerized it was possible that, hidden in the
pages, there might be some information that would prove useful.

And there I found a slim straw to clutch at.

Buried in recent past consultations, in among the health
checks, blood results and other paraphernalia was an email
address for her son noted when she'd had flu two years back.
Jack had requested that we keep him informed of his mother's
condition. It was worth a try. So I could console myself that I
had done something, however ineffectual it might prove, I typed
out a brief message, beginning normally, but ending with a share
of my concern.

Hi Jack, it's Nurse Florence Shaw here from your mother's
surgery. I'm a little concerned that a man called Ben Evans,

who claims to be an 'odd-job' man, appears to be having some influence over your mother and, according to the neighbours, might even be staying there on occasions. I have visited her twice and both times have felt unhappy about the situation as well feeling concerned at the deterioration in your mother's mental condition. It'd be great if you could perhaps visit her?

Just in case he wanted to contact me I added my personal mobile number.

I pressed Send and felt very slightly better. Inertia can seem the easiest route. I hadn't done *nothing*. I had done *something*. I shut the computer down with a sense of correctness. Actually I don't know what I expected from Jack. He'd probably just get angry with us – as people do. Their mothers and fathers are *our* responsibility, not theirs. That's what nurses and doctors get paid for. If I'd heard it once I had heard it a thousand times.

But I had handed over responsibility. Now I could try to relax.

ELEVEN

Saturday 19 June, 12.30 p.m.

Flaming June and it was raining. I looked out of the window to rivulets streaming down the glass and felt trapped inside my own home. I live in a semi-detached house at the end of a cul-de-sac. It's a modest house but at least I own it. When Mark succumbed to Cupid's arrow, he felt guilty enough to let me keep the house, provided I let him keep most of his pension pot. I wasn't too worried about that. I had my own NHS pension pot and I could, with care, manage on my salary, though I might have to work beyond my planned retirement age. The house has three bedrooms, one large room downstairs (a knocked-through living room and dining room) and a half decent kitchen – Formica tops with pine-fronted cupboards. I'd considered bringing it up to date but actually I was well content with my home and enjoyed doing my own decoration. I see little point in paying money to a decorator when I can do it myself. The house isn't large but it is plenty big enough for just me. Stuart and Lara haven't been near the place since Christmas. Somehow when Mark had left, the family had disintegrated. We had ceased to exist as an entity. We were now four separate people whose paths and lives had diverged.

My neighbours know I am a nurse with the result that, unlike many on a housing estate, we are all on speaking terms – sort of. I am adopted as their private nurse available for consultation twenty-four seven. Which has its disadvantages.

Mrs Miller (Eve) lives in the adjoining house with her husband and baby. She looked as though she was going to miscarry late one Sunday night with abdominal pain and some bleeding. Her husband, Johnny, had knocked on the door. I told her to go to bed and stay there for the next few days. Amelia is now two years old and Eve is 'indebted', almost as though I had conceived, carried and delivered the child myself. Every time she sees me she tells me how indebted she is. Which can get a bit tiresome.

Mr Ford lives in the house beyond them. He's in his sixties and is, I suspect, a closet homosexual. His wife walked out after twenty years, having confided in me that they had not had sex for ten years before that, asking me whether that was normal. *Hello?*

I love it when my neighbours confide their secrets to me and ask for my advice, which I give freely. I kept the closet gay theory to myself and said to Mrs Ford that men had varying libidos.

She walked out a week later.

The house to my right is inhabited by Darryl and his partner Penny. They are not married, which is probably a good thing: their bitter quarrels provide an incidental soundtrack to the rest of Endicott Terrace. She's thrown his belongings out of the window a time or two (without bothering with the black plastic bin liner) so they scattered all over the lawn and he spent around half an hour sheepishly picking up boxer shorts, odd socks, shirts, ties, jeans, trainers and other paraphernalia. Once a can of aftershave hit him on the head and he did a stagey stagger, watched from the bedroom window by an obviously concerned Penny. Maybe she thought she might be charged with ABH. Hey presto, a few days later, he turns up with a bunch of flowers and they're snogging on the front doorstep and making love before the bedroom curtains even get drawn – again. It's a very hot and cold relationship.

An Indian couple live beyond Darryl and Penny with their four children. The children are amazingly well behaved and smartly dressed, the girls in salwar kameez, their hair in shiny, long black plaits that reach almost to their waists, and the boys with a loose shirt over their trousers. I don't know what Mr and Mrs Kapoor do for a living, but they are out long, long hours, and I see the girls, in particular, peering out of the windows, waiting for them to come home.

And the last house in the cul-de-sac is Marianne Winters, a sixty-something lady whose husband died a few years back. He had a heart attack – she came late on a Tuesday evening, banging on my door till I thought she'd break it. When I opened it she was so distraught she couldn't speak but stood there, chest heaving, gasping out something or other. I saw her front door was open and put my shoes on really quickly, ran over there, and told her to ring for an ambulance straight away. The poor man was suffering, groaning and clutching his chest. His lips were starting to turn blue and I prayed that the ambulance, with oxygen and a defibrillator, would arrive before he went into cardiac arrest. Resuscitation is a very physical affair and though we are updated every year I didn't think I was quite up to managing both chest compressions and the rescue breaths for more than a few minutes on my own, and Marianne looked as though she was about to faint. Luckily the ambulance did arrive in time and bundled him off to Stafford Infirmary where he died three days later, poor man.

You might think that Marianne and I would be good friends after that, but a bottle of wine arrived on my doorstep the following week with a Thank You card sellotaped to it. And that was it.

You see, Marianne has a daughter – Zita, or something like that. And unlike my daughter, Lara, Zita calls every single weekend. Mother and daughter are obviously close. I see them kissing and hugging on the doorstep when she arrives and when she leaves. Sometimes I see them glance across at me and I wonder what they are saying or thinking. Do they believe I did not do enough for him? That husband/father would have survived had I done something different? That is the trouble with being a nurse. Get it right and you are a saint. Get it wrong and they think you are Beverley Allitt.

Or were they wondering, like many, what exactly I had done to drive my own husband into the arms of another woman? That underneath my benevolent exterior lurked a bitter, vindictive, sour old maid who had contributed to Mr Winters' death? Because not only had I been abandoned by my husband but my children weren't much in evidence either. Maybe they believed I'd brought my unhappy fate on myself and that Mark was justified for abandoning me. Thing is I didn't know what they were thinking, and so I shrank back into my own place, ignored their suspicious stares, and closed the door.

Public opinion is fickle.

In my darker moments I imagine that Stuart and Lara both see plenty of their father and 'her'. I picture them sharing Sunday lunches together, sitting around the table, passing the gravy, making polite conversation. Or else going out as a 'family' to a local pub where they have a carvery. I have no evidence that this is a true picture, but it is the one that intrudes into my mind on occasions. Sometimes I rail against this scenario and I'm tempted to confront my son and daughter. 'I bore you,' I want to say to my grown-up children, on the rare occasions when I do see or talk to them. 'But remember, I carried you around for nine long months (I hated being pregnant). I breastfed you as babies, spoon-fed you as toddlers and made sure a "proper" meal was ready for you when you came home from school, all the time working, working, working. I have two spare bedrooms now; you could choose to sleep there. But no. You spend time with a traitorous father and a husband-stealer.'

As I said, I have no basis for any of this. But it still exists in my head.

At times I feel as though I was never married, never gave birth, was never a wife *and* mother. That this too exists only in my head. But the neglect of my two offspring perhaps explains my attachment to some of my patients. They are a substitution.

I don't hate Mark. I hate *her* but on the odd occasions when I do hear from him (usually on mundane matters like checking I've renewed the house insurance), my ex looks increasingly like someone caught up in a 'situation'. Not happy. I've seen him on Facebook, arm around her. (I know I shouldn't. It's painful snooping.) But he doesn't look as though he's found his Shangri La – rather as if he finds himself in an alien hell. He looks . . . trapped. I know that look. I saw it when I first told him *I* was pregnant, when the interest increased on our mortgage, when our car failed the MOT, when we missed the ferry coming back from a holiday in France, when he was in the middle of a major investigation and told all leave was cancelled. You see, Mark panics. He's claustrophobic – not at being locked in a small room, but in seeing no way out of a life situation. That was the look I saw now when I peeped on his social media. That rabbit stare in glaring headlights, eyes wide and bulging with expression, almost fright. Then I found out during one brief phone call with my daughter six months ago that neither she nor Stuart had seen their father for more than a year.

All I can say is thank God I do have my work, my ever-grateful patients and my colleagues and friends. Which brings me to an idea that sparked in my mind on that rainy Saturday morning halfway through the vacuuming. One of my friends was the practice nurse who had once worked alongside me but retired eight years ago. Catherine Zenger was a mine of information past and present, even venturing assertions about the future, though they were usually doom and gloom. ('He's a bad 'un. Will come to no good.' Or, 'She'll get in trouble that girl. Just like 'er mum.' Even, 'If he keeps out of prison it'll be a bloody miracle.') More accurate were her health predictions, also doom and gloom, of heart attacks and cancers lurking beneath the skin, drunken accidents, even unwanted pregnancies.

It crossed my mind that she might have met Ben Evans in her previous role. If she knew something about him perhaps it would strengthen my case for concern. And maybe people would sit up and listen. She would also be familiar with Nora.

A visit to her might prove informative. The drawback was that while she was a mine of information, she could also be a mine of *misinformation*. Because Catherine was a born storyteller who simply loved drama. And if the tale lacked the necessary scandal, she would inject it with spurious details. I needed to stick to facts. They were enough to worry me for the moment. At eleven I rang the cottage hospital and was cheered by their assurances that Sebastian had organized a bed and they were expecting Nora Selleck imminently.

I shelved the idea of contacting Catherine. Nora was safe. She would soon be under the care of nurses and out of danger. And I hoped, in spite of their reluctance, that the Hudsons would see her being taken into the ambulance.

TWELVE

Saturday 19 June, 2 p.m.

But something told me the Hudsons were not simply reluctant to act as my spies; they wanted to remain invisible. Why? Mark might have accused me of being too involved in my patients' lives, but I was determined to discover the Hudsons' secret. Because I knew they were anxious to preserve it.

Rain was still pattering down the window as I drank more coffee and tried to decide what to do with the rest of my day. After ten minutes watching the rain streaming down the glass, I stood up. Bugger the rain, I thought, suddenly restless. I need air.

I'd planned to walk towards Aston along the canal, but it is a linear route and it can seem pointless retracing your steps. The high street and the stalls that braved the squall seemed a much more colourful alternative. Besides, I had an idea. Nora might be safe – for now – but it wasn't enough for me. I wanted to find out who Ben Evans was, delve into his background and, possibly, discover his motives. Was Nora his first victim or was there a track record? What was he up to? As I walked into town I had an idea that I could approach this problem from another direction.

The Saturday market was subdued by the rain, a muted version of the Mediterranean picture it portrayed on a sunny day. The rain bouncing on the plastic or tarpaulin roofs of the open-air stalls constantly drummed like a Chinese torture and muffled the normal sounds of people shopping and enjoying themselves. Footsteps splashed and people shopped, but they were not lingering. And, judging by the almost empty streets, anyone with an excuse had stayed at home. Sociability was muted, hurried, diminished, almost to nothing. But outside The Crown Hotel I saw one solitary loiterer. Ryan Wood was standing beneath the canopy, huddled against the rain, his shoulders hunched, collar raised, shifting from foot to foot, agitated. I could guess what he was up to; waiting for his 'fixer' to happen by or alternatively someone – anyone – he could cadge a spliff or two from. Ryan was so easy to read it made me smile but that day his presence seemed opportune. I strode up to him. The minute he recognized me he looked guilty. As I've said before – people do when they recognize me. 'Ryan,' I said, friendly as an old mate. 'Can I buy you a drink?'

That startled him. 'What?'

'Come on,' I said. 'I don't want to drink alone. It's a miserable day. And we know the beer's good in here.'

I could read his face. After the incredulity, suspicion. *What does she want?* Closely followed by guilt. *What have I done now?* I could see him cast his mind round his most recent adventures and shrug them off. They were nothing to do with me. He narrowed those innocent blue eyes so they looked wary and suspicious. Then he grinned. 'You serious?'

'Yeah.'

We entered the bar together. 'So, what'll you have?'

'Pint of Joules,' he said and sloped off to find a seat. I ordered a large red wine for me (I would need it for my audacious plan) and a pint of Joules' best bitter for him, placed it on the table and sat down while he waited nervously. Almost as nervous as

I was. But it was time for me to begin. If the Hudsons wouldn't act as my spies I would have to recruit elsewhere.

'Do you know a man called Ben Evans?'

He took a sip of the dark brew, wiped the foam from around his mouth and frowned. 'Don't think so.' I caught a whiff of relief. So *that* was the price of the free drink. He looked at me expectantly, waiting for the sequitur.

Which I didn't produce – not straightaway. It took him to prompt me. 'What do you want to know for?'

This was tricky. I couldn't be sure how discreet Ryan would be, but he was waiting expectantly. I had to come up with something.

I chose my words very carefully. 'He seems to have befriended' – I felt pleased with my choice of word – 'an elderly patient of mine who is vulnerable.'

Ryan was no fool. He put his beer down, wiped his mouth and challenged me. 'So?'

This was the tricky bit. 'I worry that he's not a good thing in her life.'

He leaned back, a tiny smile hovering round his mouth. He was starting to get this.

And he wasn't one to waste words. 'Why?'

I looked past him again still picking through words like a dancer on a bed of nails. One wrong move and . . .

'Because,' I said, determination spurring me on, 'since he's come into her life she seems to have got a lot worse.'

He had a response to this. ''Spect she was lonely – what with the Covid and everything. Lots of old people have got on really badly. Maybe that's why she's got worse rather it being . . . something to do with him,' he finished lamely.

'It's not just that,' I said. And now I had to avoid sounding a snob which would have alienated him. I wanted – needed – him on my side. 'He's a roughneck, Ryan.'

He looked offended. I knew he was thinking maybe I bracketed this 'Evans guy' with him. And that was why I'd approached him.

'In what way?' he asked guardedly.

'I worry about his motive.'

Ryan drained his glass, indicated the fact with his long eyelashes sweeping down. I finished my wine and lifted *my* eyebrows to indicate. *Another?* He nodded and I knew I had him on side. Some people sell themselves very cheaply.

When I returned with both drinks he gave me an open smile. 'So what's this got to do with me?'

I tried to sound casual. 'I thought you might . . .' I took a deep drink of my wine and felt it go straight to my head. 'Two things,' I said. 'One – find out something about Evans. Where he comes from, who he is.'

'How?'

'Use your imagination, Ryan. You have contacts.'

That sketched a smirk across his face making it look much less innocent. 'And?'

'Keep an eye out for her? She's safe at the moment. We've tucked her up in the cottage hospital but she can't stay there forever.'

I was watching him intently, perfectly aware he could use this against me, to get more drinks or money out of me. I was gambling on my instinct – that there was no real harm in him. Maybe I should have remembered that judges, the police and JPs had been similarly deceived.

'OK,' he said and finished his drink – again, pushed the glass towards me. 'Where does she hang out?'

I told him. 'You might keep an eye out for her "companion" too. See what he gets up to while Nora's away. And, while you're out there, skulking around Swynnerton, maybe you could extend the surveillance to Nora's neighbours, the ones living right opposite her.'

He opened his eyes wide. 'Why?'

'Just watch them. That's all.'

I'd already decided I was not going to give him money. I was not going to bribe him. This wasn't a job. It was a favour. And somewhere, deep in those innocent blue eyes, I realized he recognized this because he retrieved his glass then stood up and smiled. I handed him one of my practice cards. On the back I'd scribbled my own, personal, mobile number.

And then, through the rain, pitter patter, I walked home.

Two glasses of wine on a rainy Saturday afternoon is a recipe for a binge watch. But the drama wasn't over for the day.

It was around eight p.m. and although *Spooks* was dramatic and exciting, I was half asleep when my landline rang.

I sat up, hopeful that it was one of my offspring, ringing to see how I was. I picked it up, realizing it was a mobile number that my phonebook didn't recognize.

'Flo.' Once I had thrilled to hear this voice. That was then. This was now. 'Mark?'

What was he ringing for? And even in that one uttered syllable I had recognized that familiar panic. As I've said. Mark had a low threshold for it. 'What is it?'

And then it all came tumbling out. 'I've made an awful mistake, Flo. I've cocked up. I feel terrible. I wish these last few years hadn't happened. I wish I could go back in time.'

I wished *I* had had a penny for each time I had formed that exact same thought. My mind was cold and detached as it tossed through a few possibilities.

They'd had a row.

He'd had *another* affair.

She'd had another affair. Somehow I'd skated past the real problem.

'She's pregnant. I don't want another baby. Ours are grown up. What would I do with another baby, Flo? A baby, for goodness' sake.' I could hear mounting hysteria in his voice. 'I can't cope with one. I'm fifty-six; I'll be seventy-six by the time the kid is grown up. I don't want another.'

He sounded like a petulant child who'd been given the wrong Christmas present. As if *I* had any control over this. And, as usual, all his pity, all his thoughts, were focused on him.

To my credit I didn't spit out any of the usual: that's what happens when you score with a younger woman; what did you think would happen; what do you want *me* to do about it; you made your bed . . . And all those apt phrases which could have come in pretty useful. Instead – and to my credit – I said, hearing the practicality in my voice, the prosaic tone, the literal sound, the nurse-voice, 'So what do you intend to do about it?'

'I don't know. Oh God, Flo, I can't cope with it. I can't do this. I don't want a child.'

So run away, hide your face, take cover, my ex. Hope it'll go away.

Instead I said, still hearing that practical tone, 'How does Vivian feel about it?' I hated even saying her name.

'Oh, *she's* absolutely over the moon.' I could hear the bitterness in his voice, the sheer hatred of this woman who had put him in this position. (Mark had always portrayed himself as the innocent party led astray by a siren.)

Again, I returned to basics. 'So, she wants the child?'

'Wants it?' He almost spat the words out. 'She's rung all her relatives, her ghastly mother and stepdad, every single one of her brothers, sisters, ex-sisters-in-law. The bloody lot.'

Hang on a minute, I suddenly thought. 'Where are you now?'

'In the car.'

So that was why he sounded furtive.

'I just had to talk to you. I said I was going to fetch some beers. Wet the baby's head,' he finished bitterly. 'That's all she wants to talk about. Baby, baby, baby.'

I swallowed a smile. But then reverted to nurse mode and the proper line. 'Maybe when it's born you'll grow to love it.'

'I won't be there when the child is born. I'm not staying to go through all that again – broken nights, dirty nappies, the persistent bawling . . .'

Again? I hadn't been aware he'd been anywhere near any of this with our two.

Finally I lost patience. 'Mark. This is the path you chose, and this is where it's led. Your life. Your choice, your decision.' And I ended the call in a sudden flame of fury.

Did I still love him? It was still there. But, like a wax bust placed too near a heat source, it had melted, was now misshapen, distorted, unrecognizable. Yet at its core, beneath the wax drips and leaning figure, it was still that well-loved emotion. I poured myself a third glass of wine, held it in both my hands and pressed play on the remote, glad of the torture scene that played out in front of my eyes.

THIRTEEN

Monday 21 June, 9.30 a.m.

I usually checked my emails before starting surgery. Just in case one of the partners wanted me to see an extra patient, take another blood sample, or there could be some new drug warning or a directive from the government. Warnings came at all times with various levels of urgency. Usually Top Priority. Everything in the Health Service is Top Priority. Sometimes I struggle to keep up with the results of continuous worldwide research, particularly since the Covid pandemic. Yesterday's panacea is tomorrow's thalidomide. There was none of that this morning but there was an email from Jack Selleck, not from the email address I'd used, but another one, and I didn't like the subject.

What's going on?

The contents went straight to the point. I scanned the text quickly, feeling my face warm, partly with anger and partly with embarrassment. It began politely enough.

Thank you for your concern, Nurse Shaw.

But as I read on the tone changed to become defensive and then vaguely hostile, making it clear we were on different sides of the fence now.

> *I speak to my mother every couple of weeks or so and haven't detected any problems. Neither has she mentioned having a 'friend' over to stay, male or female. I am not aware of anyone who fits your description, but if, as you say, the man is helping her out with odd jobs around the house, I don't see the problem. I'm tied up with work at the moment and can't spare the time to travel up to Staffordshire. I'm unclear what you are suggesting but will try and visit sometime in the next month. In the meantime,*

perhaps you would visit her when you can and let me know
if there are further developments.
    Jack Selleck.

It was cold. I read it through again. I know when someone is passing the buck. So now if anything went wrong it would be *my* fault. Not his. I tapped my foot in irritation at relatives who neatly sidestep responsibility for their nearest and dearest. It would be *they* who would benefit from their relative's death and *I* who would be appealing to the Nurses' and Midwives' Council for defence when they sued for neglect if things went tits up. If only *I* could sue *them* for lack of care, for failing in *their* duty, for neglect. I read the email through again, this time noticing that the email address he'd replied from contained the name of a well-known private bank. So that was where clever Jack Selleck had ended up. But his response had left me with a quandary. What *should* I do? What *could* I do? I comforted myself with the belief that Nora was now safely tucked up in a cottage hospital bed, being cared for and guarded against Evans. I felt smug. I was a step ahead of him, finally.

But having dragged in Nora's son I felt I should discuss my misgivings with Dr Gubb – again – and tell him I had tracked down Jack's current email address and contacted him. Possibly Sebastian had already told him his patient had been admitted to the cottage hospital. In his vague, negative way, Morris Gubb had ducked away from the problem and Sebastian had picked it up for him. I felt some irritation at our senior partner's Pollyanna view of the world, that no one was *really* bad. And then I chuckled. I was exactly the same about Ryan, only too ready to be hoodwinked.

I settled down to my morning's work.

It was just after eleven o'clock that my new-found contentment started to dissolve when Sebastian knocked on my door. And he didn't look happy.

'I thought you said Mrs Selleck was frail and vulnerable?' His tone was accusatory.

'Yes.'

'I felt a right fool.' He did look cross.

I waited, heart beginning to sink, as he continued.

'I'd made such a fuss getting her a bed. Discharged an old guy who lives alone. New diabetic who could have done with an extra day or two to stabilize.' He was turning away from me already, tossing his remark back over his shoulder before I could respond. 'We-ell. Crisis over, I'd say.'

'What happened?'

'The ambulance turned up at Nora's address.' His mouth was twitching. 'No flashing blue light, luckily. The lady said she didn't need to go to hospital because she was absolutely fine. Her friend was keeping a close eye on her, making sure she had all her medication, cooking her meals.'

I was shaking. He'd done it again: convinced Nora to reject help. Made her believe that she was safe in his hands.

Sebastian recovered his good humour and grinned at me. 'Crisis over, I'd say.'

I couldn't find the words to respond to this and he took my silence for either embarrassment or confusion. After giving me another of his charming smiles he left me there, quaking. I *knew* Nora was in danger. I *knew* Ben Evans was not to be trusted but I couldn't convince anyone. Even Kelly hadn't seen the situation as a full-blown crisis. Her final judgement had been to keep a watch over the situation. I was trying but it was hard when so far the only people I had keeping an eye on events were Ryan and the dubious Hudsons. Their wish to avoid contact with any authority, either me or the police, was positively patho-logical. And so far the doctors were not seeing things from my point of view.

I stared at the door through which Sebastian had exited. Crisis over? I didn't believe that for a minute. It was just beginning.

For a moment my mind was paralysed with disappointment and a continuing worry. I didn't know what to do. Kelly had arranged for Nora to have an assessment at the memory clinic, but the waiting list was long. She would not be seen for weeks – possibly months. Her need wouldn't be seen as acute. I couldn't come up with anything or anyone else who might see things from my point of view, realize the danger of a vulnerable old lady in the clutches of . . . I needed an ally, someone on my side who would anticipate the danger, understand where this was ultimately leading.

And once again I came up with my erstwhile colleague. Catherine Zenger.

Catherine was now in her seventies but bright and active, particularly in the imagination department. If there was a drama she would catapult it into a crisis. Whatever *I* might think, *she* would interpret as something much darker. She was – or had been – the antidote to Dr Gubb. He saw nothing and no one as all bad; she saw trouble from every direction.

I rang her mobile and left a message. Would she be in if I dropped by after work, somewhere between five and six?

An hour later she texted me back.

> *Florence. How absolutely lovely to hear from you. Would simply adore you to drop by this afternoon. I haven't heard from you for absolutely ages. Do come over, my dear friend. I'll look forward to it and will have the kettle on or the wine glasses out. Can't wait to see you. I'll expect you, as you suggest, sometime between five and six this very afternoon when you've finished work. Love Catherine XXXX PS Quite excited.*

She was verbose even in a text message! Her words and kisses were followed by a widely grinning emoji and, touchingly, a heart.

But as I've said, Catherine loved to spread gossip, and if the story was not quite dramatic enough she would gild and embellish it until she'd bent it out of shape. Plus she was garrulous, and when short of material would spread secrets and her own interpretations of them. Also, she was an inveterate fabricator. Any fears or misgivings I had would soon be town gossip and the story would be distorted, like Chinese whispers, into something grotesque. Which could then trickle back to Evans and spur him on to something even worse. And he might trace the original source back to me.

FOURTEEN

5.15 p.m.

I called in at the off licence and bought a bottle of rosé, already chilled, waiting to be drunk.

Catherine lived in a purpose-built block of flats three storeys high. Each had two bedrooms, two bathrooms, an open-plan kitchen, dining room and lounge, with a Juliet balcony over-looking the canal. It was pleasant, functional, modern and near enough to the town for its inhabitants to wander in without needing a bus or a taxi. Those that were less mobile had mobility scooters to the peril of many strolling along the pavement.

She must have been watching for me because she opened the door of her flat when I was a few steps away. She was animated, excited, her eyes bright. That should have warned me her imagination was ready to take flight.

She gave me a bear hug. 'How I've missed this,' she said. 'The camaraderie. The stories, the friends. As a nurse,' she said, 'I had respect. Status. People knew me. They confided in me, asked for my advice, and when I gave it, they listened.' She gave a mirthless little snigger. 'Now I'm just another old lady with too much time on my hands, no structure to my life.' She held her hands out wide and shrugged. 'Nothing interesting to say.'

'Nonsense.' I tried to pooh poo her statement but inwardly I could see the veracity in it. To be fair to her, Catherine had tried all the usual remedies for retirement boredom: helping in charity shops; joining the WI; elderly visiting; even a stint with the Samaritans; but nothing had replaced her job as practice nurse and for months after her final day she'd hung around the surgery like a stray dog. The pandemic had been good for her. She'd stepped up to the line and helped vaccinate, regaining some of her long-lost role, but the bulk of people had been jabbed now and she was no longer needed. Once again, she'd been dumped.

I took in her appearance. Catherine had been prone to a cuddly plumpness; now she was undeniably fat, flesh over-flowing her jeans and a heavy-looking bust which seemed to tilt her forward in a strange lean. But her smile was as wide as an ocean and her welcome toasty-warm.

'Oh my word, Florence,' she began. 'I can't tell you how good it is to see you.'

I followed her through the sitting room to the miniscule Juliet balcony just big enough for the two rattan chairs she'd somehow squeezed on to it, and a stand for the two glasses and the bottle. She poured the wine, handed me a glass, and we sat together companionably watching narrow boats drift down the canal, bright and colourful, engines sputtering with the unmistakable *phut phut* of a two-stroke engine combining with the scent of diesel puffing into the air. Some of the holidaymakers waved at us and we waved enthusiastically back before settling in our chairs. 'Well,' she said. 'Tell me *all* the gossip.'

I fed her a few minor tidbits, that one of the receptionists had recently divorced, that Mandy, one of the cleaners, was pregnant, even though it was common knowledge that her husband had had a vasectomy years ago. We both exclaimed, round-eyed, 'Explain that one!' then laughed as we often had in the years we had worked together. I told her of babies born and tragic deaths, of altered circumstances and elderly patients whose lives had changed with the years, which brought me round neatly to Nora. I took a hefty slurp of wine. Then I told Catherine about the encounter at the Saturday street market back in May, describing Nora's apparent confusion and bewilderment. 'I'm not sure she even recognized me.'

Catherine frowned at this. 'You think she has Alzheimer's?'

'That's part of my worry. Kelly's referred her for an assess-ment, but she didn't think Nora needed an urgent appointment.'

'Ah, Kelly,' she said knowingly.

I then went on to tell her about Ben Evans. 'Do you know him?'

She was thoughtful for moment. Then she laughed. 'You don't mean Benjamin Evans? He's about eighty if he's a day.'

'No,' I said, irritated. 'This guy's about thirty. A roughneck with tattoos and a stroppy, uncouth manner.'

I could practically see the cogs turn in her brain before, reluctantly, she shook her head. 'No one like that,' she said regretfully.

Catherine liked to be at the hub of any story. I'd detected her note of disappointment. How she would love to have been at the heart of this, inventing juicy tidbits about Evans, which would probably include his entire family.

I half expected her to suddenly 'remember' a family of that name who'd ended up badly, but her imagination couldn't supply anything at such short notice. So she instead changed tack.

'Money?' she asked, puzzled, eyes round but still confused. 'You think he's taking *money* from her?'

I shrugged. 'She doesn't have much,' I said. 'Just her pensions – and I suppose Peter had a pension too. But it won't be much. She's not wealthy.'

'No.'

'I have Ryan keeping an eye out for him.' I didn't need to remind her who Ryan was. Everyone in Stone knew who Ryan Wood was. But her words had set me thinking. What *was* in it for Evans? Was he after her money? My thoughts grew darker.

'What do you think I should do?'

Catherine gave me a strange look before glancing away, across the canal, to the other side, and I had the feeling she was about to spin one of her stories. 'There was something about Mrs Selleck,' she said, frowning. 'Something a bit shocking.'

My ears pricked up. 'Really?'

'Oh,' she said, suddenly confused and patently backtracking. 'I can't really remember.'

I waited but she wasn't going to enlarge and my mind discarded it as dross. But the trouble with Catherine's well-deserved reputation was that it was possible to jettison the truth along with her fantasies because they were so tangled up in each other you could never separate fact from fiction.

Before her 'memory' returned we moved on to other subjects. She asked about Dr Gubb and I shared my misgivings about his inability to see the bad in anyone, and then we talked about the other partners while I shared the fact that Sebastian had been cross with me for pressing to have Nora admitted to the cottage hospital, a bed which she had apparently refused.

Catherine now became sympathetic, understanding my dilemma, and sharing my frustration at having the solution I'd set up thwarted.

'So true,' she said, and reminded me about the case of Mrs Foulger, the woman who had been murdered when Morris Gubb had failed to take her stories of marital abuse seriously. He'd listened to the husband's side and referred them to marriage guidance. 'I'm sure she'd still be alive if he'd looked a bit deeper into her stories about her husband.'

'Yes,' I agreed. 'But the coroner absolved him of any blame – said the husband had been deceitful in his testimony. I know Dr Gubb did blame himself and was a bit more cautious with subsequent domestic situations. But I still think he's naive.'

We both agreed on that.

And then I tried to prompt her memory. 'What was it about Nora Selleck, Catherine?'

'Ummm . . .'

I waited but, for once, Catherine was keeping silent on that matter, changing the subject to other topics in quick succession: the opening of a new dress shop, a nail salon in the square which was employing two Ukrainian sisters, the closure of the one remaining bank. I realized I was not going to coax Nora's story out of her.

I left an hour later with a sense that I'd missed an opportunity and I wouldn't be able to retrieve it.

Wednesday 23 June, 1.20 p.m.

Even though it was still raining – the summer was proving a washout – I had decided to bolt my sandwiches and head up the high street in my lunch break. I was running out of the dye I use to disguise my grey roots and was way overdue with half an inch of grey before 'Moonrise auburn' kicked in. I didn't have an appointment at the hairdressers' for three weeks. Truth is the hairdressers weren't cheap and I wanted a summer break somewhere. Doing my roots myself was a way to save some money towards a singletons holiday I had my eye on in Madeira.

I popped into Superdrug and who should I see, when I emerged on to shiny pavements and puddles of rain, but Ryan. He spotted me at almost the same moment and sidled up to me.

'Nurse,' he said, talking out of the side of his mouth like Humphrey Bogart. Maybe this 'spy' thing was going to his head.

'Ryan?'

'Yeah.' He was even working on the accent. 'I bin watchin' them.'

That got my attention. 'And?'

He twisted his mouth in a sort of lopsided grin. Waiting – and I knew what for.

'Tell me.'

Hoping for some inducement, he waited for a millisecond before giving up. 'I saw him,' he said again.

'You already said that.'

'Takin' money out of the cash machine.' He put his face close to me. 'A bloody big wad of it.'

There's a limit on how much you can draw from an ATM in a day, but I had the feeling one of my theories now had been confirmed. Evans was planning to bleed my patient dry. Ryan's next sentence confirmed it. 'A few days runnin',' he added. 'Outside Morrisons. Same machine.' He flicked his eyes around like a close protection officer checking out the surroundings.

'Same sort of time?'

'Late mornin'.' He hesitated before continuing. 'I followed him,' he said. 'He went into The Crown. Had a couple of pints.' He looked pleased with himself now. 'I sat where I could watch him. Without being seen,' he added hastily. 'He was counting the money. I reckon around three hundred quid.'

I felt bound to put in: 'It could have been his money.'

Ryan looked slightly let down. 'Yeah, but . . .' His scepticism matched my own.

'Have you found anything out about him?'

'That's my next step,' he said proudly, folding his arms. 'I'm on it, Nurse. Don't you worry. I'm right on it.'

I wanted to tell him to get a move on before Evans milked Nora's entire savings or she came to further harm. I had already assumed the account Evans was draining was hers. But Ryan was the sort of guy who responded better to praise than criticism or even firm direction. So I held back.

'I don't suppose you noticed anything else?'

'Old lady, your patient,' he substituted respectfully. 'She just stays at home. Doesn't seem to do much.'

'And the Hudsons?'

He put his face near mine. 'Stick to each other like glue. Apart from when they're hobnobbin' with that Evans chap. There's somethin' else.'

'What?' I was having trouble bridling my curiosity.

'When they spotted me watchin' them they was panicked. Hurried inside, slammed the door behind them. I saw them watchin' me through the window like they was terrified.'

'Really,' I responded. 'I wonder why?'

'Don't know.' Ryan looked pleased at having provoked this response. He shrugged.

'Keep up the surveillance,' I said.

'OK.' He responded with a sly wink, sure I would pay him a retainer. He waited politely, hands down at his sides, lifting them only when I handed him a twenty-pound note.

'Thanks,' I said, still suppressing the urge to instill urgency, to press him to get on with it.

I stood still as Ryan stepped back out into the rain (shoulders hunched, collar turned up, managing the 'secret' agent look in the most public way).

I watched him for a moment, then wandered back down the high street, through the rain and feeling glum. I had some knowledge – or did I? Not really. I needed more than that. I couldn't be positive that the money Evans was withdrawing was Nora's, or that she hadn't authorized it possibly to pay for groceries. But I was very suspicious. The trouble was, without proof, I didn't know what I could do about it.

For almost a week I couldn't see my next step. I drove past The Beehive on a few occasions, saw Evans's green van parked outside some of the time. And no sign of Nora.

FIFTEEN

Monday 28 June, 2.20 p.m.

For once, luck was on my side.

One of the patients booked into my Well Man Clinic was a Steven Dortman, a thin, anxious-looking man in his late forties. The fat, happy, ten-pints-a-night smokers whose idea of exercise was reaching for the remote control tended to avoid the Well Man Clinic – for obvious reasons. The guys who did attend these clinics tended to be just like Mr Dortman, the thin, anxious types who already ticked all the right boxes except stress avoidance. These types were hardwired to anxiety. The Well Man Clinic was almost a clinic of reassurance for these burdened types, but just occasionally you turned up a health anomaly. My patient that afternoon was, apparently, an absolute paragon, who suffered only through his chronic anxiety which I tried to allay. 'You'll live till you're two hundred,' I said, laughing and tucking the sphygmomanometer cuff away. He didn't look absolutely reassured, but a few of his frown lines had melted and he stood up. As he prepared to go, I glanced at the screen and realized he was a bank manager. Opportune. So, as he slipped his jacket back on, I said, 'If you have suspicions that a vulnerable, elderly person is having money taken from her is there anything you can do?'

He looked at me very hard. 'A relative of yours?'

I shook my head. 'Just someone I sort of know.'

'With mental health problems?'

I nodded.

He thought about it for a while then said, 'Do you know which bank?'

Again, I shook my head. He chewed his lip this time, then scratched the bald part of his head (which actually was most of it). 'Local?'

I nodded.

'We-ell,' he said, pinning me with a sharp stare. 'Get a relative to look into it. They should be able to speak to the bank on behalf of the victim. Perhaps even put a stop on the account, take over, get a Lasting Power of Attorney over property, health and financial affairs. That is if it can be proved that this person is exercising undue influence over the account holder and he or she can be proven to be vulnerable.' His frown deepened. 'It isn't that easy or quick to secure.' He then asked, 'A patient?'

I nodded, convinced I was already breaking the professional confidentiality clause in my contract. 'I'll do that,' I said quickly. 'I'll speak to a relative. Thanks for the advice.'

He nodded and left. And I'd gone as far as I dared.

But once he'd gone I knew I didn't really have the right or the ability to go any further with this. And I wasn't sure I could persuade Jack to anticipate the seriousness of the situation without witnessing the change in his mother for himself. From the grounded, sensible and intelligent woman she had been, well able to look after herself in her eighties, to this reliance on a dubious stranger. That was the real mystery here. Even patients with dementia don't so suddenly and completely change.

Maybe, I thought, if I visited her again, I could gather real evidence before going back to Jack. I needed something tangible that would persuade him to take my misgivings seriously and visit his mother. Without much hope, I remembered my second concern. Far from being an aid to me, I wondered about the Hudsons' apparent friendliness with Evans. What exactly were they playing at with him? Or more precisely what were they up to? I had hoped they might notice something that I could present to the police from an independent source, something which would trigger an alarm. Maybe Evans shouting at her, bullying her, keeping her almost a prisoner. Something tangible which would grab even Dr Gubb's attention. Jack would surely take action if his mother's *doctor* deemed it necessary. But that seemed highly unlikely now. Maybe Ryan would produce something. He was about my only hope now. I was drawn back to The Beehive. If Evans' van wasn't outside, I might be able to risk talking to Nora on her own and achieve something, maybe even convince her that this state of affairs was troubling. If he was there and challenged me, I could always use the pretence of giving her the results of her blood test.

SIXTEEN

Friday 2 July, midday

I 'd left it a few days, wanting to chew my plans over, consolidate them, or maybe I was hoping something would happen. I suppose I'd hoped to avoid another confrontation with Evans. Maybe Jack or Dr Gubb would intervene. But nothing happened, and my conscience finally nagged me into action.

I'd had an easy surgery with a few gaps and two DNAs (Did Not Attend), with the result that I finished early. I left my lunch request for Jalissa with one of the receptionists and murmured something about catching up with a couple of visits, which was true. I owed one to a lady with a nasty diabetic ulcer and the other to a child who'd defaulted on his childhood vaccinations – or rather his mother had. I stowed my Gladstone bag on the back seat, loaded with the emergency anaphylaxis tray. (It would be just my luck for the child to have a reaction when I was out of the surgery.) Another bag held dressings and Mepore tape for the diabetic ulcer.

But first, feeling like a surreptitious sleuth myself, I headed out towards Swynnerton.

On another sunny day when my mind was less worried, I would have enjoyed the ride.

Swynnerton is a picturesque village with an ancient and proud past. It has a mention in the Domesday Book of 1086 as well as the charter of Edward I in 1306. A plaque at the entrance to the village announces this. Not mentioned in any plaque in the village is the more scandalous connection to a certain Mrs Fitzherbert who either was or wasn't the wife of Prinny, Prince Regent, later a rather corpulent George IV. But Maria Fitzherbert was a Catholic and George would have lost his place in the succession had he married her. The village held to its Catholic connection; Our Lady of the Assumption church, even today, celebrates its mass in Latin. Like many other places with long connections, it has had its share of troubles too. In 1942 the Royal Ordinance Factory was essential to the war effort, making detonators and filling shells with TNT. Unfortunately the TNT turned the workers' (mainly women, of course) skin and hair – and even in one case, a baby – yellow. It was dangerous work. In an almost predictable explosion five women lost their lives. Incidentally the Germans, desperate to bomb the elusive site, but unable to find it, instead mocked it, Lord Haw Haw calling it Swine-er-ton.

Today it is a sleepy village with a fine eighteenth-century hall, home to Lord and Lady Stafford, an equally fine pub, named The Fitzherbert, and a scatter of houses of various ages and architecture including Nora's pretty thatched cottage, The Beehive.

As I turned the corner I was disappointed to see Evans's van parked outside. So I would not be able to speak to Nora alone. Instead of parking at the front I swerved into a side lane, seeing the Hudsons watching me through the window. Even at a distance I could tell that Tobin was eying me stonily and he didn't raise a hand in greeting.

Behind him I saw the shadow of his wife slot in and sensed their hostility. Then, to my surprise, Tobin turned around to speak to his wife before moving away, opening his front door and beckoning me over. Maybe I'd wronged them, I decided as I approached – warily.

Tobin 'ummed' and 'ahhed' for a while, restlessly shifting his weight from foot to foot and refusing to meet my eyes. I could guess what he was about to say. 'I don't feel comfortable about this,' he muttered finally. 'I know you're concerned and have asked us to keep an eye out, but it feels like spying on a neighbour. We can't do it.'

So the 'hobnobbing' Hudsons had switched sides. I drew in a deep sigh and plastered on my wide, friendly, *innocent* nurse face. 'It's only because I'm really worried about her. She's an elderly lady who's becoming increasingly frail and a bit confused.' Then I stuck the dagger in. 'We don't know anything about this person who appears to be hanging around. And I'm not sure about his motives.'

Now Orpah stood behind her husband, chin jutting out. 'What do you mean? He's helping her. He's a really . . . nice guy.'

Tobin too was stout in Evans's defence. 'He seems a nice enough chap. Helped me get the bins down the step the other day. We had a bit of a chat.'

It doesn't take much to gain trust, does it? One small favour, bumping the bins down a couple of steps. People don't see beneath the surface, do they? They prefer to blithely skate over the top. Drink in superficial charm, take the easy road. What my mother would have called the road to destruction. I heaved out another big, tired sigh. Apart from Ryan I didn't have an eye on Nora. He had been right. These two were on Evans's side.

Tobin cleared his throat and I could sense what was coming next. 'Orpah and I—'

'If you're so worried about her, Nurse' – his wife's voice was shrill behind him – 'why don't you contact her relatives?' Her Lancashire accent was pronounced, something they tried to disguise, but I was too disappointed to pay much attention to that.

'I already have,' I said shortly, and with a dignity I hoped had reasserted my authority and integrity. 'Her son is busy. He lives in London.'

Eyebrows raised, they exchanged glances as articulate as if they had commented to each other, impressed, 'Ah, London,' as though it was another country, a far-off continent where they spoke a different language instead of being a mere ninety minutes away by train.

Whatever, the mention of London had released a gear, maybe dissolved some of their hostility. 'Well, Ben does seem to be there a lot.'

I was taken aback. Ben? Had he persuaded them so completely to join his side with one simple 'neighbourly' act combined with a brief chat which would have taken all of a single minute? So now they were chums? How had that happened? Why were they trusting this Ben Evans rather than me? What was behind their bond? My suspicions were like a slug, ugly and slimy.

I tried to convince them of my motives at least.

'All I care about is that she's all right.'

Again, they looked at each other, sheepish now. Tobin was biting his lip and avoiding my gaze, his face slightly flushed. And in that one swift movement I felt a snatch of concern rising. It was Tobin who finally spoke. 'We haven't actually *seen* her.'

His wife was studying the floor.

'When *did* you last see her?'

'I don't know. Maybe a week ago?' They glanced at each other, searching for clarification and confirmation. I noted that Orpah didn't contradict her husband's words. But she was holding her breath.

I thought quickly. A week? It had been a week of rain. Not surprising if Nora had been the sort to sit by the fire and shelter from the weather. But this was July. The Nora I'd known had been out in all weathers and would have been planting out her annuals. I could see her in my mind's eye. Bending over flower beds, trowel in one hand, a weed bucket at her feet. Digging up weeds, hair dripping, long mac and wellingtons, the outfit completed with chamois gardening gloves. '*Makes it easy to grab the thistles. Saves my hands from rose thorns.*' I could hear her voice so clearly. '*British weather?*' She'd accompanied the words with a happy grin. '*Rain? Doesn't bother me. Keeps the garden watered.*'

I missed her.

I looked behind me. 'Through the window?' I asked.

Orpah nodded. 'She doesn't seem to move much from the chair, but he says she's fine,' she said timidly, perhaps realizing now they had been less than vigilant over their neighbour.

I would learn nothing more by pressurizing these two with their tight lips, evasive eyes and firm, resolute chins, not to mention their loyalty towards 'Ben'. I thanked them and left without asking them to be vigilant any longer. I could only push things so far, and this had been far enough without provoking them into making a complaint of harassment. And then what? That complaint would have been upheld. Even I could see that. The unfairness of it riled me. I had no way of protecting Nora unless I could prove something. Which gave me an idea. There was something I could use as evidence.

It was up to me now, with any help Ryan might give, though I wouldn't hold my breath there. Ryan was not exactly reliable.

But he was smart – when he wanted to be. I reached my car and hovered for a while, indecisive.

I took a photo with my phone of the registration number of the van.

Then I drove off.

SEVENTEEN

1.45 p.m.

I attended to my two calls without any problems. The little boy and his mother accepted the immunisation – even without a jelly baby – and to my delight my patient's diabetic leg ulcer was, somehow, healing. One might know that science and nature actually did the work but it is hard not to feel a swell of pride at a job well done, the sight of shiny new pink skin covering a wound previously brown with slough and dead skin. Maybe my clean dressings, medication and TLC (Tender Loving Care – the nurses' secret weapon) had played their part too. Normally I would have returned to the surgery in a buoyant mood at working with nature towards my patients' health. Job done. Boxes ticked, but I still felt haunted by Nora's vulnerability and my inability to protect her.

My mind was busy as I drove back to the surgery. I was wondering whether Evans was withholding some of her medication, most especially the thyroxin, which could explain why her mental state had deteriorated so fast. Confusion is a side effect of hypothyroidism in the elderly. Maybe Evans had latched on to this and was using it to manipulate her into accepting him. I believed he was leeching money from her and, because of her altered mental state, she was allowing him to, that is, if she realized what was going on. The trouble is that confusion plus someone like Evans lurking around could even result in Nora's premature death. Dementia has its cost. As well as the assessment at the memory clinic which would include further blood tests of her therapeutic levels of thyroxin, I needed Jack on side. As her nearest relative, he was the one who had the power to intervene. If Evans had no access to his victim's money he would, I reasoned, surely move on.

My mind stayed weighted down by worry. As I turned into the surgery car park Jalissa's little white van was emerging. We both slowed down and wound down our windows. She gave me one of her beautiful smiles. (What I wouldn't give for such teeth!) 'Florence,' she said, reaching across to touch my hand. 'I thought I'd missed you today.'

'I was out on visits.' I searched the back of her van, saw it was empty. 'No children today?'

She gave me a bold, cheeky look. 'Petronella is at school, and Charles, he be with his father.'

Which surprised me. Brett was known for his work ethic. 'He's not working?'

Her next sentence was accompanied with a huge chuckle. 'He takin' the day off. It is our wedding anniversary. Eight years, Florence. Eight years.'

What could I say but, 'Congratulations. So long? It seems only yesterday Brett came in for his holiday jabs and hardly any time after that you registered with us.'

'I know and I feeling smug.' She looked it too.

'So you're having a date night, are you?' I teased.

'Not exactly.' She burst into one of her deep, rich chuckles. 'Not unless you count havin' Petronella and Charles come along too.'

'I'd babysit.'

She opened her eyes wide. 'You would?'

I hadn't really thought about it before the words came out of my mouth, but now they had. 'Yes. Yes, of course.'

'Thank you. I will see what Brett says. He thinks our two children made of porcelain, you know. He very protective toward them.'

'He's a good father,' I agreed. 'But maybe he'll trust me.'

'I'll call you this afternoon, Florence. And thank you.'

Her confidence lifted my mood.

Sitting in front of the computer in my clinic room later that afternoon I checked whether Nora – or rather Evans – had picked up her latest prescription. It looked like someone had. I sat back in my chair still dissatisfied. That didn't mean she'd actually swallowed the extra tablet of thyroxin. I could have rung the pharmacist to check he'd filled the day-by-day tray, but that didn't really mean anything either.

I worked my way through my afternoon surgery but I was wondering how to involve Jack in my fears without sounding like a histrionic busybody. Or simply a snob.

He'd said he would be up within a month, but I wanted him to sense the urgency even if I didn't have anything tangible to present him with. Time was running out. If we left Evans leeching away at her finances while destroying her health, I worried that Nora would not recover. But without opening myself up to a charge of slander and libel I couldn't see how to convey this in an email. Emails live forever. I started to reply to his email by asking if he knew exactly when he might visit his mother before deleting it. At which point my mobile buzzed for attention and a very excited Jalissa was on the line.

'Florence. You meant it? About the babysitting?'

'Yes. Of course.'

'Can you come here for eight o'clock? Tonight?'

'Yes.'

I heard her shouting behind her, teasing her husband. 'You're on, Mr O'Sullivan. Florence is coming to mind the precious children. We have a date night.' Her voice was rich as treacle, still bubbling with laughter as she switched back to me. 'See you later, Nurse Florence.'

I echoed her words back. 'See you later.'

That was my evening sorted. Dealing with my grey roots would have to wait. It would be my last evening of tranquillity.

EIGHTEEN

Petronella and Charles behaved like perfect angels as I bathed them, put on their nightclothes (in Charles's case a tiger-striped onesie and in Petronella's a blue nightdress with *Frozen*'s Elsa on the bodice). Then we snuggled up under a fleece blanket with an armful of Jellycat animals and I read them Beatrix Potter's *The Tale of Mrs Tiggy-Winkle* until they had practically fallen asleep. I lifted Charles into his *Star Wars* bed and Petronella into a pink-painted Cinderella's coach, then sat downstairs and read my book. It was a peaceful pleasant evening reminiscent of the nights I had sat in a similarly silent house, my children asleep upstairs, waiting for Mark to come off shift. I missed those days.

When the children were in bed and finally silent, I pulled out a nursing textbook I'd brought with me. I wanted to check the details. I compared the chapter on hypothyroidism with the results of a Google search on my tablet. And there it was, the list of symptoms. Which could almost have been a description of my patient. The cold extremities, the mental confusion, the depression, dry skin, brittle hair and nails and the missing outer third of the eyebrows. In spite of the situation, I couldn't help but smile at some of the other symptoms which would not be a problem to her: irregular periods, loss of libido and so on.

The computer records had shown regular pickups of Nora's medication, but I was sure Evans was withholding her thyroxin – which would explain why her TSH was raised but her T4 remained low, and it provided an explanation for her confusion. 'So now you know, Florence,' I mused, 'what are you going to do about it?'

Nora had refused to be admitted to the cottage hospital, where we could have made sure she had the prescribed dose and hopefully restore her health. But if Nora was adamant she was not going to be admitted, our hands were tied. Unless we sectioned her or could get Jack to persuade his mother to go. More than ever, I needed him on side – and now.

I was toying with this conclusion when I heard the taxi pull up outside, some giggling, and watched Jalissa totter in, the worse for wear, Brett practically holding her up. She had a smear of scarlet lipstick across her cheek and a skin-tight red mini dress that left little to the imagination. She had a strong, voluptuous figure. She'd had a light coat over it when they'd left so I hadn't glimpsed her siren outfit. They were still sharing their joke. Brett was a good-looking, muscular guy in his thirties with a small, neat beard, dark curly hair and brown eyes. They looked such a happy couple that I felt an intruder, stood up awkwardly, told them their children were safely tucked up in bed and hurriedly left.

As I walked down the path to my car I could still hear Jalissa's maniacal laugh.

But when I let myself in my answerphone was blinking a message notification. And when I pressed play, thinking it might be Catherine, finalizing details for our rendezvous, I had a shock.

'You need to back off.' The voice was hoarse, strange, unfamiliar. I couldn't tell if it sounded male or female.

I re-played it three times, still unable to pin it down to him. 'Back off.' The clearest of warnings, even though the voice didn't sound like Evans. Maybe he'd used a voice changer, though even the accent was, somehow, different. But I was clear enough *who* was warning me off and *why*. Control, financial and mental. Maybe he even had something worse planned.

Even now, on the following morning, as I showered and dressed, I still felt the threat. I'd played it a second, third time. But I couldn't pin down the voice.

And now I had a full day ahead of me.

Saturday 3 July

The town was celebrating its annual food fair at Westbridge Park. A virtual gourmet's delight with the field spread full of tents with their locally produced cheeses, pies, ciders and beers. I was going later with Catherine. The weather was perfect for it, hot and sunny and I couldn't wait to lick an ice cream. Such days and the excitement they generate sustain us through the dull cold nights of winter and the disappointing drenchings of wet summer days. They conjure up little memories that flick on and off like fairy lights, lighting up dark, cold nights and dull days. Today was Disney brilliant, each colour bright and clear, the hues heightened by the general excitement furthered by people crowding towards the entrance and the lines of traffic directed in by attendants in Day-Glo tabards as they hunted for a parking space.

I was meeting Catherine at one thirty p.m. at the main entrance and had walked down. There was no way I was going to queue for a space as well as pay the five-pound parking charge. As I made my way towards the park, I recognized the town had been transformed into a noisy, heaving, gourmet's fairground, filled with the scent of frying onions and a backing soundtrack of an ice-cream van's tinkling *Greensleeves*. People milled around the tents, eating, drinking and greeting one another with exclamations. Emotions heightened since the Covid pandemic had robbed them of such social festivities. No one took these encounters for granted any more. Their hugs were warmer, their greetings louder. Everyone was as excitable and jolly as the first day of a holiday. And I admit I was feeling better about Nora. Her clinic appointment had come through. And, surely, now Ben Evans knew we were watching, nothing bad would happen to her? I might not be able to affect a rescue, but I did, at least, know what was happening.

To add to my optimism that morning an email had flashed up on my screen.

Plan to visit Mum this weekend. J

And as an added bonus, Kelly had arranged for Katie Truman, our home help, to start cleaning and tidying The Beehive on Monday. The subtext was that she would keep an eye on Nora and I had asked her to make sure my patient swallowed the pills from the pharmacist's tray. Katie had already left a message on Nora's phone and told her she'd be there, nine a.m. on Monday morning. I felt I had put a ring of safety around my patient. Evans wouldn't dare make a move with another pair of eyes watching him.

So as I waited for Catherine on that Saturday lunchtime, amidst the happy milling crowds, I felt smug.

This would see Evans off, back to whatever worm pit he'd crawled out of. I was going to enjoy myself. I hadn't felt as excited and carefree since I'd staggered into a party many years ago, Mark practically holding me up. I felt good. The food fair had drawn in crowds from miles away and I recognized plenty of faces, for once seeing my patients in happy, healthy moods, not asking them how many units of alcohol they had drunk that week or how many cigarettes they'd had that day. I could even turn a blind eye as they tucked into burgers and slices of pizza. Everyone wanted to share a piece of this festivity and I wasn't going to spoil it. Let loose from the Covid restrictions the atmosphere was wild. Not only were there lots of food stalls but they also liberally handed out free samples of food and drink. I walked past the lines of traffic. Congestion seemed a small price to pay. We were all bursting for exactly this sort of event. There seemed much to celebrate. Sunshine and freedom, a heady mix.

For a moment, as I reached the entrance, I closed my eyes against the heaving crowds and brilliant sunlight and pictured Evans's thwarted furious face, and I smiled. In my mind I was already crowing in Evans's ear, smearing mud across his face, rubbing in the sheer humiliation he'd feel when he realized I'd beaten him. Katie was fearless and smart. She would make sure Nora was OK. Perhaps I could even persuade Jack to look into his mother's financial affairs and if he unearthed irregularities (how I loved that word) he could involve the police and they could press charges. He could certainly put a stop to Evans's nasty little tricks forever. I had the events neatly lined up chronologically in my head. Monday, Katie. And this weekend, Jack. Added to that, I could keep an eye out. I had him, I thought. I'd done what I could. And the main thing was that I'd summoned Jack Selleck to his mother's side, alerted him to his mother's precarious position. With him to back us we would be able to move her to a residential home, if that was necessary, although on the right medication and with Evans's influence kicked into touch, plus Katie Truman's perspicacious help around the house, that might not be necessary. Faced with Jack Selleck, instinct told me Evans would soon disappear. Preferably with a puff of smoke.

I could finally relax.

I opened my eyes, still smiling.

At which point Catherine turned up, in a pair of unflattering khaki shorts, slightly out of breath from the heat and the hurry, but grinning from ear to ear as she linked arms with me. 'You're looking very pleased with yourself.'

'I am,' I responded, and gave her a potted version of the events I had triggered. 'Jack'll soon send Evans scurrying,' I said, full of confidence.

'Well done you,' she said, slapping a high five. We linked arms to join the queue. 'And isn't this fun?'

That was the moment when I forgot all my worries, about Nora and Evans, about the Hudson's reluctance to spy, about asking Ryan to dig into Evans's track record, even about Mark and the hated villainous Vivian.

I treated Catherine to half a pint of Rudyard Ruby, and we spread a picnic blanket on the edge of the site, greeting a few patients who mocked the pair of us for drinking alcohol in public. 'And you, a pair of nurses,' they teased as they passed. We simply raised our plastic glasses in silent, defiant toast. We just didn't care. We were in a festive mood.

By three o'clock we had found our way back into the tents and were heading for the cake stall where we tried a few more samples, then moved on to the cheese stall. I had just helped myself to a cube of Cheddleton Original when my mobile phone rang with a local landline. I swiped it to answer.

What registered first was an angry voice. An angry male voice.

'Is that the nurse from the surgery?'

I didn't like the sound of this aggression, which mixed poorly with the celebratory atmosphere around me. And I resented this puncturing of the festive spirit, so my response was grumpy. 'Yes, it is,' I said as I checked the number.

The next sentence chilled me.

'What have you done with my mother?'

As I say, a nurse is never really off duty.

NINETEEN

I almost choked on my cube of cheese and looked desperately across at Catherine as the voice continued its rant.

'Where is she? What have you done with her? There's no one here. The house is empty.'

I dreaded the answer as I asked the question, 'Who is this please?' I could hear the quiver in my voice.

'You know perfectly well who this is. It's Jack Selleck. You've summoned me up from London to see my mother. I've driven up this morning and she's not here. So where is she?'

My mind whisked through various scenarios. The best one, the nicest one, being that Nora, with or without Evans's help, had decided to join the masses and visit the food fair. It was also the least likely one.

'Maybe she's here,' I started, 'at the food—'

He interrupted furiously. 'That was not the impression you gave me. I understood *from you* that she is frail, vulnerable, incapable of visiting a . . . food fair.' He almost spat the words out.

My next suggestion was even more feeble. 'Have you tried her mob—?'

He cut me off. 'It's switched off. You know she never has it on.'

Cold water was trickling down my spine. 'Are you at—?'

Again, he cut me off. 'Yes, I'm at my mother's house.'

'Is *anyone* there? Is there a van outside?'

'No, there isn't.'

I clutched at straws then. 'Have you tried the duty doctor – just in case she's been admitted to the cottage hospital?'

'I have not. *Yours* is the number that I had. *You're* the one who wanted me up here in such a bloody hurry. I thought . . .' For the first time I heard a catch of emotion as he asked again, 'Nurse Shaw. Where is my mother?'

The cube of free cheese I'd recently enjoyed now made me feel sick. I couldn't even form my fears into rational thought or make a plan. I felt helpless. Paralysed, my brain shut down. Catherine was watching me, her mouth open, her eyes bright with concern but also lit with prurient curiosity. God only knew what she would make of this. For a shameful instant the thought crossed my mind that my friend liked to feed on carrion, dead, rotting flesh, filthy stories, drama. Anything damaging. The human note was less important than The Story.

I forced myself to calm down and steadied my voice. 'Leave it with me, Jack. I'll make a few calls and get back to you. Are you staying there?'

'I might take a look around.'

'Text me your mobile number and I'll get back to you.'

His response was a grunt.

In my mind there was only one place I'd want her to be. I clutched at the straw that, in the past week, Evans had assured the Hudsons that all was well. I might not trust them, but surely they wouldn't have misled me over such an important detail? Could they be covering for him? Without much hope, I tried the cottage hospital and got through to one of the desk clerks. My obvious impatience made her drag her feet in answer to my question.

'Let me see. Sorry . . .' Long pause. Slow words. 'I'll just try the ward, shall I . . .?' Another interminable silence. 'What did you say your patient's name is . . .?' Then: 'Sorry, no one's answering on the ward. Can I call you back?'

I responded with gritted teeth. 'I'll hold if you don't mind.'

Ten minutes later I faced Catherine, feeling the blood drain from my face as I shook my head. 'She's not there.'

I tried the duty doctor next and had Dr Bhatt's calm, but confused, voice on the other end. 'Florence? My dear. I don't understand. No, I have not seen your patient today. She is not here. I have not sent her in to the hospital. I don't know where she is. I am so sorry but I cannot help you.'

I thanked him.

Another blind alley, one I'd entered without much hope anyway. So where was she? I looked around me at the crowds stuffing their faces, drinking cider and beer and generally having a whale of a time. The scene was fading in front of my eyes. However much I was willing her to be here I knew she wasn't. She was with Evans – somewhere. I had to find her. I made my apologies to Catherine, who still looked wide-eyed, both intrigued and disappointed at the premature ending of our jolly, but couldn't quite hide her joy at the potential for a real drama. But for me, the day was ruined.

Catherine gave me a rueful smile. 'Keep me up to date, won't you?' I promised her I would, hugged her and practically ran all the way back to my road and picked up my car, though I didn't have a clear plan.

Ten minutes later I was battling through the crowds and traffic, all heading in the opposite direction.

There was only one place to go.

As soon as I was on the A34 the sounds, smells and crowds

of the food fair were left behind. I drove along roads, empty now, and pulled up in record time outside Nora's front door which stood wide open. A man was standing in the doorway, presumably Jack. Even as I pulled up, I sensed his bewilderment, but also his anger. He was tall, slim with dark hair, and was wearing a pair of khaki chinos and a pale blue short-sleeved shirt. I recognized him from his father's funeral, though I'd seen him only briefly. He didn't move as I locked my car; neither did he speak as I drew nearer, but kept his gaze on me. My mouth was dry and I felt my shoulders tense up. And I worried I smelt of food-fair beer and cheese as I reached him. I guessed he was somewhere in his mid-forties. Nora had had him late. His eyes were brown and his mouth an angry straight line. But there was vulnerability there too, the faintest quiver in his mouth. Behind the nicely dressed banker man there was a frightened boy. I also recognized that he blamed me for this whole sorry scenario. There was no sign of the green van.

He didn't waste much time launching his verbal assault. 'I thought you were keeping an eye on my mother.'

I was forced to defend myself. 'Even *I* have off-duty time. Jack, I presume.'

'Yes.'

'I'd arranged for—'

He cut me off with another angry missile indicating the empty house behind him. 'I hope you have some explanation for this, Nurse Shaw.'

I was quaking now. 'Not so far.'

Then he cut to the chase. 'Have you any idea where my mother is?'

I shook my head. 'I've tried the cottage hospital and spoken to the duty doctor.'

'No luck?'

Again, I shook my head.

He ran his hands through his hair. '*Could* she be at the food fair?'

He obviously hadn't seen his mother over the past few months or fully taken in the contents of my emails. 'I doubt it. But . . . it's possible.'

He stood back then and I walked through into the sitting room

which had a disturbing look, as though someone had left in a
hurry. The chair had been moved; the blanket that had been
draped across her knees was now dropped on to the floor. The
table on which Nora had kept her reading glasses, glass of water,
cup of tea, reading matter and TV remote had also been pushed
out of the way. Even more worryingly, her handbag still lay to
the side of her chair. Nora went nowhere without it. I turned
to face him, concern written all over my face.

As it was on his. 'Could this – Evans person – have driven
her to the hospital at Stoke or Stafford?'

'I can check.' But I knew we were both grasping at straws.
My fingers were shaking as I pressed the number for the Stafford
General Infirmary – and got the answer I'd expected. Jack was
still watching me, so I tried Stoke next. That took a little longer
– the hospital is huge – but the answer was the same. Jack's
features tightened as he dropped into his mother's chair. And
there was no mistaking the accusation as well as the bewilderment in his next question. 'So where is she?'

I didn't even attempt to answer this one but looked carefully
around the room, wondering whether Jack had absorbed the little
details as I had. 'Have you checked upstairs?'

'I took a quick look. Just in case—'

I knew what he had feared as he followed me up the stairs.

It was years since I'd been upstairs in The Beehive – not since
just before Peter had died. It was small. There were only two
bedrooms and a bathroom. One was obviously Nora's, with an
unmade double bed, duvet thrown back, tubs of face and hand
cream set in front of a toilet mirror which stood on a chest of
drawers. There was a faint scent of lavender and the window was
ajar. It was slightly chintzy, an elderly lady's bedroom, pretty,
gentle and fragrant. The other bedroom also contained a double
bed but in all other aspects it couldn't have been more different.
A sleeping bag lay across the bed. The curtains were still drawn.
It smelt of him, fusty and stale. Standing in the doorway, reluctant
to enter, Jack wrinkled up his nose and looked at me, but said
nothing. We peeped inside the bathroom, which needed a good
scrub with bleach, and I backed out. Remembering how house-
proud Nora had been, I felt sad as I descended the staircase, and
knew Jack must be feeling the same. At the bottom he turned to

me, still saying nothing, but I could tell what he was thinking. It was in his face, his body language, the accusation. *Why didn't you tell me things were this bad? How could you have let this happen?*

So it was going to be *my* fault – again. I could have turned the question around, asked him how *he* could have let this happen – to his own mother. But I spared him that because behind the accusation I'd watched his face flush with guilt and, behind that, shame.

We went into the kitchen with its sink full of dirty crockery. I was about to ask him if he wanted a cup of tea when I had another thought. 'Do you think we should call the police?'

He nodded.

I dialled 101 and was put through to a distracted and not particularly sympathetic officer who barked out a few questions, finally saying, sarcastically, 'Well, if she's with her carer, I can't see the problem.' (I'd had difficulty describing Evans as unsuitable. No one was on my side in this.)

To be fair, the officer did listen to my reasoning, although he struggled a bit.

'So what you're saying is that you don't think she *is* safe with her carer?'

'That is exactly what I'm saying, Officer.' I eyed Jack. 'Mrs Selleck likely has mild dementia. I think her judgement is impaired.'

But when he suggested I should have spoken to the patient's GP about my concerns I had to come clean. 'I already have. We're waiting for a formal assessment.' I was desperate now. I could see how weak and prejudiced my story sounded. 'I'm sorry,' I said, 'but I'm her nurse and I am concerned. Her son is here too and—'

'Put him on.' The officer sounded relieved to have someone else to speak to.

Jack's response to the questions didn't exactly spell out a valid reason for contacting the police. I realized, as I listened to his responses, that it was all being laid fairly and squarely back on my shoulders.

'I haven't actually met him.' His voice was clipped and tight. 'I last spoke to my mother a couple of months ago. She seemed a bit vague, maybe, but . . .'

I gestured to him that he should let me speak to the officer when they'd finished and he nodded, his eyes grave and troubled.

'She wants to speak to you again.' He handed me the phone.

'It looks as though they left in a bit of a hurry.'

'How so?'

'Stuff on the floor, all her things on the table. Her handbag is here.' I mouthed to Jack, *Was the door locked when you arrived?*

He nodded. 'She insisted I have my own key even though I rarely visit.' The guilt in his voice made it sound sullen and grumpy.

'No, the door wasn't left open.' I felt I had to underline this. 'I'm telling you, I'm her nurse and I'm worried about her.'

'Did she know her son was visiting?' I sensed the officer was trying his best to get a handle on this.

I mouthed this question too across to Jack and he shook his head.

'No.' And I improvised. 'He thought he'd surprise her.'

'Hmm.' There was a pause as the officer digested all he'd been told and made a decision. 'OK, we'll send someone.'

And I had to be content with that.

TWENTY

The local force was, of course, occupied with policing the food fair. We settled for a long wait, Jack and I sitting outside (I didn't want to sully the 'crime scene'), not even exchanging pleasantries. He blamed me for this as I blamed myself, but I was also reminded of my own two offspring, from whom I had heard almost nothing for nearly a year, apart from that one brief phone call from Lara. Which took me back, in turn, to the relationship between me and my own mother, with whom I had a similarly distant bond. Occasionally Jack or I stepped along the lane to look out for either a police car or in the vain hope that Evans's van would swing round the corner, Nora in the passenger seat, but the lane stayed empty. The noisy atmosphere of the bustling food fair seemed a lifetime away from this silent, abandoned village.

Jack and I studiously avoided looking at each other.

Finally, at almost seven o'clock, when the day was cooling and we had retired into the sitting room, we heard the sound of a car pulling up outside. And in walked Pants.

Who looked from one to the other while we both spoke at the same time.

'My mother appears to be . . .'

'My patient . . .'

'One at a time, please.' Then he gave me a hard stare, frowning, head tilted to one side. 'Mrs Shaw?'

I felt some relief. Particularly when he followed that up with: 'Stuart's mum?'

I exhaled. 'Yes.' I hadn't been convinced he'd recognize me second time around as I hadn't seen him for a few years now, although we both lived in the same town. We'd probably walked past each other on numerous occasions. Maybe he'd been seconded elsewhere. But who remembers their friends' mother? Particularly when she's a stone or two heavier these days and has different coloured hair? I had recognized him but knew it didn't necessarily work both ways.

Pants gave me a watery, not unfriendly smile, and reverted to PC mode. 'So what's happenin' here then?'

It was Jack who answered, tight-lipped and with a black scowl at me. 'My mother appears to be missing.'

True to form, Pants looked confused and glanced at me for enlightenment.

I began at the beginning while Jack huffed and puffed at the delay, periodically glancing out of the window as though he expected his mother to come walking up the path imminently.

I started with the meeting on the high street. 'She seemed confused, bewildered. I was concerned about her, so I invited her into the surgery for a health check.'

Jack was tapping his foot now. *Hurry up. Hurry up. Hurry up.* I got the message.

But what was the hurry? She wouldn't be turning up while I was trying to relate my story, hoping to have at least one police officer on my side.

Pants was taking all this down, word for word, slowly. When he'd finished writing, he looked up. 'So?'

'She didn't come in. I went . . .' I changed that to: 'So I called in to see her.' With a swift glance at Jack, I blundered on, about Evans, about my dislike for him which morphed into suspicion as to his motives for 'befriending' my patient. At the back of my mind was Ryan's involvement but I couldn't see any way to introduce this. Pants would have his own opinion about Ryan Wood. And I wasn't absolutely sure that my part in it would pass the Professional Standards Authority.

Jack was snorting like a horse who has just run the Derby and couldn't resist hurrying me along. 'Get on with it,' he said through tight lips.

I described the consultation and the doctor's involvement but kept the details short, partly because Pants was looking equally bewildered, turning now to Jack for enlightenment. 'And then . . .?' As an afterthought, he added, 'Sir?'

Jack was even more angry. 'She wasn't here,' he practically shouted.

Pants turned hastily back to me. He always had backed away from any form of aggression. Strange to think he had entered the police force.

'Can you think of anywhere she . . .' He changed that to: 'They might be, Mrs Shaw?'

I drew in a deep breath. This was my moment. 'I've checked with the duty doctor. He hasn't seen her. All I do know is that she hasn't been admitted to the cottage hospital or to Stafford or Stoke. Ben Evans's small green van is missing, so I thought he might have . . .' I rejected the word *abducted*, changing it to: '. . . I presume they are together. Mrs Selleck doesn't drive. And . . .' I looked around me, stepping into his train of thought, '. . . considering the fact that the room seems . . . disordered. Her bag is still here. She goes nowhere without it.'

Pants looked around, apparently seeing the state of the room for the first time, and nodded.

'And' – this was more tricky – 'as she appeared confused and vulnerable, she also seemed unable to account for Mr Evans's involvement. I don't know who he is.' Finally I blurted it out. 'I'm worried about her.'

'Right.' Pants looked at me thoughtfully, taking his time to reflect on my statement and its appeal. 'I'll just take a look around.'

I tried to ignore Jack's eye-roll and waited while Pants poked around the ground-floor rooms, before climbing the stairs. He was back minutes later looking as though he was on home ground. 'This Evans person. He's in a green van?'

I nodded and told him the model.

He looked impressed. 'You didn't happen to note the registration number, did you?' Bless him. He was taking this seriously.

I felt hopeful. 'I did, as it happens,' and I produced my mobile phone.

Pants made a note of the registration number. Then he spoke into his radio while giving us both a reassuring smile in turn. He listened, then frowned, and addressed me. 'What sort of vehicle did you say this was?'

I gave him more details. He spoke again into his radio then shook his head, and for a moment looked disappointed as he nodded before sharing what he'd learned with us. 'They're not matching up, Mrs Shaw. That number plate belongs to another vehicle.'

That was when my heart plummeted. I had suspected Evans of being a sort of petty trickster. But this indicated a more serious criminal element.

And Pants' manner changed. 'We're going to need a description. Of both.' His eyes moved to Jack. 'Not to worry, sir. We'll find your mum.'

Oddly enough Jack looked taken aback, almost tearful. I could see right inside him. It had been the phrase 'your mum'. Her title. While his was 'Nora's boy'. It had reduced him from adult banker to Nora's boy. As I had been similarly reduced from Nurse Shaw to Stuart's mum.

Jack's face had softened; he looked sad and a little confused. Unused to such kindness, now he wasn't sure whether to still be angry with me or grateful for alerting people to his mother's situation. I tried out a smile on him which didn't seem to register. He was still adjusting his place in the world to 'Nora's boy'.

Pants took over again, giving an impressive display of professionalism. 'If you wouldn't mind,' he said to both of us, 'we'd better lock this place up, put a watch on, just in case they return.'

It was a vain hope but one both Jack and I appreciated, knowing it lay behind kindness rather than true and futile optimism. Pants followed that up with a more realistic evaluation. 'It may be a . . .' He swallowed the words, *crime scene*, and found instead: 'Important.'

Jack was eager. 'Anything I can do, Officer?'

Pants looked at him. I could tell he was trying to put a positive note on this. 'You can start by giving me a description of your mum,' he said. Then added, 'I'm sure she's OK, sir. She'll turn up, wondering what all the fuss is about.' He even managed a sort of laugh to accompany the false hope.

Jack cleared his throat. 'Short white hair,' he said, looking at me. 'Quite slim. About five foot three.'

Pants took it all down. 'Wear glasses?'

'For reading.' All our eyes turned to the small table on which they stood. 'Oh, and her eyes are blue.'

'Lovely. Do you have somewhere to stay, sir?'

'I'll find somewhere.'

I pitied Jack. He looked distraught and guilty. I knew whatever the outcome he would blame himself, feeling he'd been so focused on his London life and job that he'd neglected his mother. As though he'd picked up on my thoughts he nodded and gave me a ghost of a smile, then looked around him at what had been the family home. 'So what will happen now?'

Pants looked awkward. 'Well, we're a bit busy with the food fair and all,' he finished lamely, 'but as soon as we can we'll have a couple of crime scene guys come and check it over.' He turned his attention on me and managed a smile. 'Shame about the number plate, Stuart's mum.'

So, like Jack, I had been reduced to this relationship. It made me smile.

Unlike Jack I wasn't uncomfortable at the moniker but pleased. But I did wonder, had the discrepancy in the number plate been what had alerted the police?

Jack stepped forward. 'Please find her,' he said to Pants. 'There's no time to waste. My mother's elderly, vulnerable – and missing.'

TWENTY-ONE

P ants' shoulders drooped. 'Quite,' he agreed hastily. 'We'll keep an eye out for people answering the description and look out for the vehicle.' He turned to me, speaking quickly. 'Green, did you say?'

'Yes.'

I felt my load begin to lighten. I'd had my concerns but now I could relax. I'd handed the problem over to the police. They had more powers than I. They could track down villains, stop cars, search CCTV, take samples from Nora's home, subject them to DNA analysis, compare them to evidence on their databases.

And then I sat down with a bump. CCTV? Today of all days when the town was heaving, queues of traffic congesting the town? Search for a vehicle which we already knew had false number plates? I knew I'd got the numberplate right because I had it on my phone. No one could argue with that. It hit me then that today had been no coincidence. Today, when the entire town was in a festive mood, relaxed and happy and off guard, the streets and roads crowded, had been chosen deliberately because there was less chance anything unusual would be spotted. Coincidence? I didn't think so.

I gaped at Pants, wondering whether he had realized all this. But this story was new to him. It would take time for him to absorb. He was doing his best, reading through his notes and frowning. He drew himself up to his full height and squared his shoulders.

'I don't suppose you have any idea what she might have been wearing?' He was addressing us both but looking at me. There was a touching mixture of hope and doubt in his voice.

We both shook our heads. Pants continued, 'Or when she was *actually* last seen?'

'I saw her last Friday, just over a week ago.'

'Or talked to her?'

'The same day.'

Jack was looking at the floor.

Then I had a mini-brainwave. The presence of a policeman would surely loosen the Hudsons' tongues? Maybe I would find out why they'd been so averse to having anything to do with my request to 'watch' over their neighbour. Or why they had taken Evans's side.

'The neighbours,' I proffered, 'in the house opposite.' Pants turned his head towards the window. The difference between the two houses had never appeared more pronounced. The Hudsons' was square, sixties, had plain windows and a concrete slab drive, while The Beehive was a pretty Victorian cottage. For the first time I wondered whether Nora and Peter had resented their ugly outlook, whereas the Hudsons overlooked a chocolate box exterior. Pants saw me looking and surprised me with his next statement.

'Eyesore, isn't it? Ugly old place.'

I wouldn't exactly have put it like that, but he had a point. I nodded.

'I'll just take another look around.' And off he went, accoutrements clanking as he walked. On such a warm day I bet he could have done without the thick uniform and extra weight. But his presence was welcome. He gave me a reassuring smile which was warm and friendly. 'Don't you worry, Stuart's mum,' he said to me. 'We'll find her. I'm sure nothing's happened to your patient.'

By my side Jack was twitching and I knew he was thinking the same as I. Though Pants's words were kindly meant, they were empty words.

'You might have to come down to the station,' he continued, 'and make a statement. Ah.' His eyes had been drawn towards the window where two more officers had pulled up in a squad car. They looked around them first – a middle-aged guy in uniform and a woman in plain clothes. I watched them approach the front door, looking around them, and then they were inside.

They greeted Pants first with a 'How're you doin'?' and a 'What's going on 'ere then?'

It was Jack who answered, lips tight. 'My mother seems to have vanished, along with . . .'

I realized he didn't know how to describe Evans. I had to remind myself. He hadn't met him but was relying solely on my opinion.

All three officers looked at him seriously, waiting. The woman spoke. 'Sorry to hear that.' And then they introduced themselves as PC Tony Dawlish and DC Samantha Eaton. Dawlish, it seemed, recognized me. 'Aren't you Mark Shaw's . . .' His voice dwindled away as his brain caught up belatedly with the facts. He flushed. I wondered if he was a friend of Vivian's and felt myself glower.

The two officers disappeared and when they reappeared from their rummaging around the cottage their faces were grim.

They looked at each other and then had a confab, backs to me and Jack. Then they turned round and faced us.

'I think I'll stay here,' PC Dawlish began, apparently with the approval of his two colleagues. 'PC Pantini will be takin' you both down the station for a formal interview while DC Eaton will be makin' some house-to-house enquiries.' He too focused on the view through the window before beaming at us both. 'That suit you?'

'Perfectly,' Jack said through gritted teeth.

I just nodded.

'Give you a lift, sir?'

Jack accepted, so I followed the squad car down to the station, noting they blasted through the traffic using the blue light only when absolutely essential.

A few officers were drifting around the station which seemed almost deserted, probably due to the food fair. And then followed a sort of hiatus during which time they spent ages on discussion. They allocated us rooms, asked us repeatedly if we wanted a drink or a sandwich and finally I was seated opposite a plain-clothes detective whose name was Summers. He was a good-looking guy with nice teeth, dark curly hair and a mouth that seemed to hover on the edge of a smile, twitching whenever I said anything that particularly interested him. His cheeks were dimpled and I took to him immediately, particularly when he began his interrogation with the words, 'I believe you were married to a DS. I didn't know Mark. Before my time.' That would have sealed the friend-for-life thing even without the dimples.

I gave him a dignified smile and crossed my legs. I liked the way his brown eyes fixed intently on me as I spoke. If he wasn't sure what I'd said or the implications, he asked me, very politely, to repeat. So it was to him that I shared the way I had asked Ryan Wood to keep an eye on my patient.

'Ryan Wood?' His mouth twitched and I could read his mind. *Ask a villain to watch a villain?*

But his face wasn't judgemental. Rather, it was thoughtful, as though he found the prospect interesting. He leaned forward on his elbows. 'That's an interesting choice, Mrs Shaw. So what did your source find out?'

I told him about the ATM withdrawals and he leaned back in his chair, watching the light flicker on the recording machine and frowning before making a note on his iPad in bold capitals.

I knew then. He would explore where I could not.

When he felt he'd squeezed the entire story out of me he sat for a while, frowning. I watched him think and think.

'I don't like the sound of this,' he said finally. Then stood up and checked a few more details with me. 'You say Dr Bhatt had had no contact?'

'No.'

'Dr Gubb is her doctor?'

I nodded.

'And Dr Timor was going to send her in to the cottage hospital but *she* refused?'

'Yes, but she could have been—'

'Coerced. Manipulated. Yes, I see that.' He hesitated before heading for the door, then spoke. 'I'll go and have a chat with her son now. Thank you very much for your help, Mrs Shaw. You've been most informative. I suggest you go home now. It's late enough.' He flushed and held out his hand. 'It's nice to have met you – at last,' he added, embarrassed.

His comment made me wonder what was said about me at the station. I'd never really thought about it, what the gossip was among Mark's fellow officers. I'd not had any contact with them since he'd gone and, if anything, I'd assumed the lads would chortle about swapping the wife for a younger model, while the women might or might not have sympathized. Of course, I'd reminded myself, the female officers would have been Vivian's colleagues, so probably took her side along with their male counterparts.

It was almost ten o'clock by the time I finally left the station – much too late now to return to the food fair. I toyed with the idea of looking out for Ryan but the town was still congested, early revellers morphing into noisy, drunken groups, arms around each other as they staggered around the fairground rides which had opened on the field, all flashing lights and candy floss. The families had all gone home. The town felt edgy and the night was hot.

I battled my way through the traffic and headed for home, seeing that I'd missed a call. Another mobile, but a number I didn't recognize.

When I'd parked up and was sitting in my lounge with a glass of wine, I tried it.

'Nurse Shaw?'

I still didn't recognize the voice so responded gingerly. 'Ye-es?'

'It's Ryan.'

The very person I wanted to speak to. 'Ryan, where are you? The police want to talk to you.'

'They do?' I could hear the alarm in his voice and was quick to reassure him. 'Nora's disappeared.'

Silence at the other end.

I hadn't expected him to seem so crushed. 'Ryan?'

'Nurse.'

I wished he'd call me Florence but I said nothing. I didn't want to rock the boat any further. 'Where are you?'

'I'm at the pub. I need to talk to you.'

'And I need to talk to you.'

TWENTY-TWO

10.20 p.m.

I t was almost closing time when I walked the short distance to the canal lock. Ryan was waiting for me, stepping out of the shadows. He had a hoodie on and gripped my elbow, guiding me towards a disused warehouse that had once unloaded pottery on to narrow boats heading for London down the Trent and Mersey canal but had been derelict for years and years.

Even in the gloom I realized Ryan was pale and nervy with a distinct tremor. But it was I who opened the conversation. 'You already knew?'

He nodded.

'Already?'

He gave a cynical bark then looked back over his shoulder as though he didn't want anyone to see or hear. 'This is a small town,' he said. 'Word rips around the place. I know her son has come up from London and is raisin' hell.'

I nodded. That too.

'But what else do you know?'

'You first.' Ryan was no fool. 'What have the police found out?'

'The number plates on the van are false.'

Ryan nodded. 'No surprise there then.'

'No. What have you found out about him?'

He looked even more frightened and jerked away from me. 'I followed him,' he said, glances still darting around, along the shiny strip of canal, up at the tall walls of the warehouse with its windows all smashed in looking sad and neglected. Finally he looked towards the humpbacked bridge, across the bridge, towards the lights of the town.

'You followed him? How? When?'

'In the week.' He was vague and looked proud of himself. 'I sort of borrowed a scooter.'

I made no comment at that, particularly as I'd sensed a whiff of pride at his audacity. But I was tempted to prompt him.

'Up near Kidsgrove there's a travellin' community.'

'Travellers?' I'd thought Ben Evans was rough, but I hadn't marked him out as a traveller.

Ryan looked worried and quickly backtracked. 'Maybe he isn't one of them,' he protested. 'But he has some friends who are.'

I digested that but it didn't make me feel any better. 'Did you see him today?'

He looked regretful at missing a trick. 'No,' he said. 'I was at the fair. All day.'

I could translate that into Ryan Wood-speak. *Hoping to cadge some money. Failing that, pinch some and help myself to free food.*

He sighed. 'I wish I had. I might have been able to help. Maybe stop him takin' her.' He looked at me. 'Where do you think he's took her?'

'Who knows? I wish I did.'

I tried another angle – without much hope. 'You didn't see her round the town today?' He shook his head quickly.

And then I tried the police's favourite question. 'So when *did* you last see her?'

'Two, three days ago.'

'Where?'

'Sittin' in her chair, like always. I peeped in through the window and there she was.'

I made my decision. 'We need to tell the police about the traveller connection.'

Predictably that raised alarm in Ryan's face. 'But what about the—?'

'Scooter?'

His face twisted.

'They won't be interested in how you got there.'

'Police is interested in anythin' they can get a conviction on.'

'Well, don't tell them about it then.' I was not going to have this investigation stutter for a bit of TWOCing (taking without consent).

DC Summers had given me a card with a mobile number

on it which I tried now – straight to answerphone. But my sense of urgency was acute. I felt every moment lost put Nora in more danger. And the mention of the travelling community had hardly put my mind at rest. I rang the station only to be told by a yawning desk sergeant that the officers dealing with it were now off duty and would speak to me in the morning. It had been a long day and it was way gone ten o'clock now. Ryan was itching for a pint, hopping from foot to foot in anxiety.

The pair of us headed for the pub.

TWENTY-THREE

Sunday 4 July, 6.30 a.m.

T he phone call was early – too early for my mind to have engaged in any forward gear. I'd spent a sleepless night with terrors of Nora, bewildered and confused, surrounded by hostile members of the travelling community. And the ringtone on my phone ('The Flight of the Valkyries') was extremely irritating. Not for the first time I vowed to change it to something a little more gentle. Like Brahms' 'Lullaby'. But that wouldn't have woken me.

I swiped the green icon.

'I'm sorry to ring so early. I feel awful. Responsible somehow. I didn't know who else to ring.'

It took me a moment to string the words together and put a face to them. Jack – of course it was Jack. The second fact to register was how terrible he sounded; his voice cracked with emotion. 'Jack?' I even *sounded* confused and bleary-eyed. 'Hello, Jack. Good morning. How are you?'

'Awful. Florence, I feel awful. I don't suppose . . .'

'Heard anything? No. Sorry.' I didn't want to tell him about the traveller link. Because . . . one: my source was Ryan Wood, who didn't exactly have a reputation for telling the truth in this town; and two: travellers have an edgy reputation. No one would want their vulnerable, elderly mother to have landed there. It would only make his anguish worse.

'Please, can I . . .?'

I anticipated his request. 'You want me to come round?'

'Would you? It seems an imposition.'

I glanced at my alarm clock. Six thirty-seven a.m. 'Now?'

'Please. Look. I'm sorry if I was a bit curt yesterday. To be honest I feel so guilty about Mum and I'm really, really worried about her.'

'Apology accepted,' I said graciously. 'Where are you?'

'At home,' he said. I didn't point out the strangeness of his calling The Beehive home, nor did I complain that the sun had hardly risen, but my pause must have sent a message because his apology came fast if belatedly. 'I'm so sorry. I bet I've woken you.'

I put on my best nurse voice, the one I used when a patient came up with a second health problem in spite of the directive that one appointment meant *one* health problem. 'Not at all. Give me fifteen minutes.'

I swigged down two cups of coffee to restore me to the land of the living, showered, put on clean jeans and a T-shirt, smeared a touch of make-up over my face (not neglecting a couple of swipes of mascara) and sprayed perfume. I was not going to face Nora's son, however distraught he might be, without my usual mask. On the way out I stopped off at Walton Stores, which opened at seven, and bought two pain au chocolats. A bit of sugar wouldn't go amiss either.

Then I drove to Swynnerton.

Truth? Jack did look terrible. Yesterday he'd looked smart, casual, in control, a banker on a day off. Today he was bordering on scruffy. I suspected he'd slept in his clothes and his hair was . . . wild. He must have realized this when I took in his appearance because he made an attempt to flatten his hair with the palm of his hand. Which was shaking. I felt like grabbing hold of it, calming him, telling him (however disingenuous) not to worry. That everything would be all right.

But I didn't. I simply watched as he boiled up the kettle, handed me a mug of coffee (my third of the day) and thanked me politely for the pain au chocolats. Which he held in his hand without taking a single bite.

'I thought PC Dawlish was staying over?'

'He left at the end of his shift. Somewhere around midnight.'

I studied his face, watching thoughts drift across like clouds on a breezy day, sometimes scudding along, at others hovering, almost motionless, and I could nearly anticipate the words he would use next. I wasn't far wrong.

'I've neglected her.'

I had my answer ready because I'd heard this phrase from relatives time and time again. So the wheels were well oiled as I pushed it out now. 'You have your life to live, Jack, your career.' It didn't seem to help him, as it rarely did. A guilty conscience is too powerful a thing.

He looked shame-faced now. 'I know. I have my work and Mum's proud of it, but since Dad died . . . I should have . . .' He let the sentence drift and settle where it would before adding softly, 'Mum didn't really approve of my way of life.'

I kept my face neutral.

'I have a partner,' he said, and I filled in the rest.

He looked like a little boy lost, forlorn and unhappy, nothing like the assured, confident banker who had arrived only yesterday, angry but in control. I was tempted to do what I did to patients who'd miscarried, or been told they had terminal cancer; frightened, vulnerable people at a terrible point in their lives, whom I put my arms around and hugged. My primary instinct was to say to myself, *This poor boy*. I touched his hand, at the very moment he'd decided to take a bite out of his pain au chocolat, scattering flakes of pastry over us both and leaving his mouth chocolate-rimmed, so he now looked like a little boy who'd sneaked his hand into the biscuit tin.

'Regular phone calls.' He was continuing with his guilty diatribe. He looked up. 'The odd visit; maybe spent a few days of my holidays with her. I could have done that.'

True.

I felt awkward then and slightly unsympathetic because of the resonance to my own life. I could imagine Stuart or Lara saying the very same words. Heavy with pointless regret. I stayed silent, fearing my own bitterness would make things worse for Nora's son. And I felt sorry for him.

He finished the pain au chocolat in silence before saying softly, 'Tell me about her.'

Which struck me as strange. How can you do that – ask a stranger to describe your own mother? I did it anyway.

'Intelligent.' I smiled. 'But you know that.'

He blinked so I pressed on. 'Well read. Funny. She always had some interesting facts to produce or a funny quip about something she'd heard on the radio. She loved the garden, of course. And she was on the town council, you know.'

'No, I didn't.'

But looking at Jack, I realized this was not what he'd wanted. He'd wanted something more intimate.

'Does she talk about me?' He hesitated before adding, 'Much?'

And this was where I either had to make something up or tell the truth, which might hurt him. I plumped for the latter. 'Not so much, lately.' The words had the anticipated effect. His eyes now looked haunted – an expression I feared might stick for a while.

I tried to meliorate it. 'She leads an interesting and varied life, gardening, WI, stuff in the community. You know. But she misses your dad terribly.'

Jack looked down at the floor, drank some of his coffee and swallowed it with a gulp. I dredged something else up. Something lighter. 'She loves *The Archers* and *Woman's Hour.* And . . .' I smiled now because this felt like the essence of his mother. 'She's a soft touch for any charity, particularly the ones involving children. She can't bear to see them half-starved because of some political situation in a foreign country. She gets really angry. Shouts at the TV.' We both laughed at that. 'I've even seen her throwing a shoe at it. She gets so angry when those little kids blink away the flies on their faces. Skinny arms, pot bellies, weeping mothers, themselves underfed, exhausted, hopeless.'

Jack was biting his lip now, close to tears. 'She loves children,' he said softly. 'I know that. She would have loved a bigger family but they only had me.' He looked straight at me then, the question ready on his lips. 'Why? I would have loved a brother – or a sister.'

I knew why. When Jack had been born Nora had had a severe post-partum haemorrhage. When they couldn't stop it, they'd been forced to perform a hysterectomy to save her life. If someone is haemorrhaging you can only pump blood in so fast. We use a pressure cuff on the blood bag, but if you've ever seen anyone exsanguinate you'll know it can happen too fast for replacement, however much O-negative blood is coming out of the fridge.

Nora had confided this detail to me, adding for some weird reason that it was her just desserts. I'd queried that but she had tucked the phrase away and I'd not pursued the subject.

Jack would have grown up never knowing this detail about his mother and had judged her for himself. But I could not defend her for keeping this from him. I could have only one response. 'You know I can't share your mother's medical details with you.'

Maybe he guessed then. Anyway, he gave a watery smile and quickly backed off. 'I get that. Patient confidentiality.'

I nodded then we both fell silent, thoughtful as though we'd run out of words and the real horror of the situation closed in on us. Oddly enough, my professional protection of his mum seemed to have drawn us, if not a little closer, at least to a détente. We were no longer on different sides of a fence. He recognized professionally my hands were often tied behind my back by rules and regulations.

I broke the silence. 'Let's focus on finding your mother and getting her back, helping the police in any way we can. And then . . .' I didn't dare put my fears into words but they were there, like a sooty cloud of ash drifting upwards from a chimney. *If she's still alive, you still have a chance of reconciliation. If . . . If . . . If . . .*

Partly to distract him, I shared some of my fears. 'I don't think abduction was in his plan. I just think he wanted to take money from her.'

Jack's eyes flipped up to me. 'So why take her? What could be the possible motive for abducting a woman in her eighties? What's he playing at?'

We looked at each other and couldn't find any rationality behind the act.

Jack was thoughtful so I continued, not knowing why or whether I was making things better or worse – or even having no effect on him at all. 'I had – have – a suspicion that he's tinkered with her medication. I had some blood tests done and it shows she was hypothyroid.'

Now Jack looked puzzled. 'Explain.'

'I think he was withholding her thyroxin.'

'Why would he do that?'

'One of the side effects of a low level is confusion.' I didn't want to go into the details of TSH/T4 levels. That would have to wait for another time.

He gave me a straight look then. 'So are you saying that if my mother has the correct dose of her medication her confusion might reverse?'

And like all scientists my answer was cautious. 'Possibly.'

I still wasn't going to share Ryan's information from last night with him. But I would tell the police. They would have access to the travellers' site. The sooner they followed up this connection the better. I would have told them last night but I hadn't been able to get hold of PC Summers. And then there was the Hudsons' role too that I needed to follow up on. I couldn't rid myself of the instinct that they had something to hide – whether it was to do with Nora's disappearance or not. 'Look,' I said awkwardly, 'I have to go. I'll keep you informed.' He looked distraught, even slightly sulky, as though I was removing a tangible link to his mother. But I had that scary, sketchy picture provided by Ryan. And I wasn't sure how reliable Ryan was. A little like Catherine, he could exaggerate for dramatic effect or even invent a scenario to squeeze an extra ten pounds out of me.

I left Jack still sitting at the kitchen table where he must have eaten breakfast, dinner and tea through his schoolboy years. Nora wasn't one to replace furniture to keep in fashion.

He looked as lost and bereft as a little boy on his first day at school.

TWENTY-FOUR

10 a.m.

'd waited until I was back home before trying DC Summers again. I couldn't bear to put Jack through any more anguish and I suspected no news was exactly that – no news at all. Luckily DC Summers picked up this time and I heard the tone of his voice, worried and at the same time full of energy. I delivered Ryan's information, hoping that perhaps he had got it wrong. DC Summers listened without comment, even when I leaked my source. He was silent for a moment before speaking. 'Ryan Wood followed this Ben Evans to a traveller community in Kidsgrove?'

'Yes.'

'We'll get someone out there,' he said, still sounding unconvinced. 'But in the past the travelling community haven't exactly been anxious to help the police.'

I got it.

'It does rather alter things, but the travelling community . . .' He continued, still thinking aloud, 'This isn't their style. Abducting an elderly lady. But I suppose we'd better send someone out there to find out what the connection is. I have to say this is a very unusual case. None of it makes sense. You say she was a teacher?'

'Yes. Geography.'

He gave a heavy sigh. 'So she wouldn't have had any connections with the travelling community.'

'I wouldn't have thought so.'

He paused before coming to a decision. 'Right,' he said. 'Well, I suppose I'd better organize the forensic team, see what they come up with at Mrs Selleck's home.' There was a faint hint of amusement. 'I have to say, Nurse Shaw, you have some very interesting sources.'

I waited.

'And I'm not sure where all this is leading.'

'Have you spoken to Mr and Mrs Hudson yet? I'm sure they . . .' My voice trailed away as I sensed disapproval.

'Is there anything else you want to add?'

'No.' I couldn't understand why he was making me feel like a naughty schoolgirl. I hadn't done anything wrong except try to help my patient.

I noticed that DC Summers wasn't holding out an olive branch, promising to keep me 'in the loop'. I had no right to expect it but it would have been nice. Instead, I got a rather dismissive final comment: 'OK then, well, thanks for the information,' and the line went dead. Leaving me more frustrated and worried than ever.

I spent the rest of the morning in a fret of pent-up energy, nothing to do except pace the house, check my mobile phone every couple of minutes and for some unknown reason stare out of the window, catching the eye of Mr Ford, who appeared to be spending his Sunday morning reading the paper. At one point he waved at me and I waved back before moving behind the curtain. I recalled his wife's question and felt embarrassed.

I was tempted to drive back out to Swynnerton, to see whether the forensic team had arrived, but I thought I would be labelled a voyeur. So I was alone with my anguish. Where was she? Why had he taken her? What was happening to her? The worries went round and round, gnawing at my brain till I thought I might go mad.

Luckily for me, at two thirty p.m. Jack rang sounding as frustrated as I. 'I can't stand this,' he said. 'Mum hasn't come back. There's no sign of her and now some police guys are going over the place, testing for bloodstains and God knows what else. Do *you* know anything more?'

This was difficult, skipping around the truth. 'One of my patients . . .' And that was where I started to edit. 'One of my patients happened to see Ben Evans's van heading out towards Kidsgrove. I passed that information on to the police.'

'Kidsgrove?'

'Yes.'

'Is that where he lives?'

'I don't think they know where he actually lives.' Surely they'd told him. 'The van's registration number doesn't seem correct, so they haven't yet found out who Ben Evans actually is.'

That resulted in a longer silence before he came back with a small voice. 'Oh no, Florence. This is awful.'

'Jack,' I responded gently, 'it might help if you went to the bank tomorrow, just in case he's still withdrawing—'

He cut me off. 'What good will that do? I don't even know who she banks with.'

'The police will be able to get details of her account.' I hesitated. There was a brief silence while I wondered what he was thinking. Was he suspicious that I knew so much about his mother's financial affairs?

I know I felt I needed to explain. 'I've had my suspicions about Evans for a while. I was gathering any information . . .' I had never been more aware that I hadn't been able to connect my jumbled thoughts with any rational theory.

'Oh.' And Jack had already lost interest.

I tried to retrieve my original plan. 'Find out whether he really was taking substantial amounts of money from your mum. At least it would give us an indicator as to his motive, whether he's been stealing from her.'

'What difference will that make?'

'It's proof of intent, isn't it? It might persuade the police to escalate their search for your mum or give them a . . .' A thought was worming its way through my mind. What if Evans had done this before? It would give the police a link.

Jack, however, was heading along a different route. 'Doesn't the fact that he's abducted my mother against her will . . .'

In spite of my own feelings, I had to point it out. 'We don't know it was against her will.'

His response to this was stubborn. 'She wouldn't have left the house and gone with him voluntarily. Not from your description of him.'

We were both silent until he came back in a small voice. 'I'm dreading they'll find something. They've taken some of Mum's belongings. Her hairbrush . . . and stuff,' he finished lamely. Then he launched into something else, speaking quickly. 'I know it's inappropriate and I know you're probably having a lovely

Sunday lunch with your family' (I wish!) 'but I wondered if
you'd let me take you for a late pub lunch? Please,' he added in
response to my silence, 'a very late pub lunch?'

'OK,' I said, thoughts tumbling out like ABC blocks, one on
top of the other; embarrassment colliding with realism: what else
was I going to do with this desert afternoon? 'The Star does a
nice carvery on a Sunday, all day. We can meet there if you like.
Can you get there?' I didn't want to pick him up.

'I've hired a car.'

'Good. Parking's in the car park by the canal. It's free today.'

'Ten minutes. See you there.'

In spite of the circumstances, I managed a laugh. 'I'm a woman,
Jack. Give me at least thirty.'

3. p.m.

In the end it was a little longer than thirty minutes when we
finally walked into The Star. I'd had a shower, washed my hair,
found a skirt and top that was the least unflattering to my figure,
slipped into sandals and refreshed my make-up. By the looks of
him he'd also had a shower, washed his hair and retrieved some
of his previous neatness in a navy polo shirt and khaki Bermudas.
Added to that he did look slightly more relaxed – and hopeful,
greeting me with a friendly grin. He was a good-looking guy.
We'd met in the car park, waving as I'd slid my Fiesta into an
empty space, one of the many. Today most of the residents of
Stone seemed to be recovering from the food fair. Over the road
I could see vans loading up, tents being dismantled and loaded
into lorries and there was an atmosphere of anti-climax, rubbish
blowing across the field. Jack had greeted me with a hopeful
grin. His smile had melted my heart as he'd thanked me for
coming.

We found a table in the pub garden under a bright pink beach
umbrella and for a moment we sat, slightly awkward now,
reflecting how we'd arrived at this place and time. A few children
were playing some sort of tag while others were stuffing chips,
dripping with tomato sauce, into their mouths. Parents were
chatting with friends and the atmosphere was summer genial; all
was well with the world except – or rather until – just after we'd

sat down and were deciding on our food and drinks. Jack's phone rang, and at almost the same time mine buzzed with a message. We looked at each other with foreboding.

TWENTY-FIVE

3.10 p.m.

Jack had his phone on speaker mode so I could hear all that DC Summers was saying while I scanned the message DC Summers had left me.

Please get in touch asap.

Interestingly he'd signed off as William Summers.

So that was his name. I watched Jack's face blench as we listened to DC Summers' voice, which began with a sort of explanation mixed with an apology in a voice that was less than steady. He couldn't have known that I was actually with Jack so could hear all that was being said.

'Jack.' He sounded nervous. 'I wanted to inform you myself before the story breaks.' He paused.

Neither of us could breathe now. I felt sick. We looked at each other, both of us dreading what was about to be said. Both already knowing it was bad news.

'I'm really sorry to tell you . . .' His hesitance gave us just enough time to work it out.

Her body's been found?

'We've found a vehicle burnt out. On a patch of waste ground in the Potteries. It matches the description and the false number plate you gave us . . .'

I could tell from Jack's face that he was terrified about what was coming next. His face was stone white and he was holding his breath as though if he didn't breathe the detective's news would not break. If it wasn't said it hadn't happened. Couldn't happen.

'It's just the van, Jack. There are no bodies inside.'

At Jack's silence DC William Summers spoke again,

emphasizing his words. 'No bodies, Jack. Your mother is not there. It's just the van. You understand what we're saying?' He ploughed on without waiting for a response. 'We haven't found her . . .' A pause. 'Yet.'

Jack swallowed and looked at me. Neither of us could find any words. Finally he managed, 'Thank you for telling me,' his voice strangled.

DC Summers continued, and I could hear relief in his voice now he'd broken the news. 'I want to emphasize. We *haven't* found her yet. We have a team working twenty-four/seven to find her. Until we do, I will keep you up to date every step of the way.' He paused. 'Every single step of the way,' he repeated. 'I promise.'

Jack managed another weak 'thank you' and the call was ended. My text had simply asked me to contact DC Summers. I could guess what he had to say. It would be an echo of the conversation he'd just had with Jack, who even now was toying with his Sunday roast, appetite gone. I excused myself and moved away from the table, found a quiet corner where I wouldn't be overheard.

As I'd thought. DC Summers gave me more or less the word for word account he'd already given Jack, except there was less reassurance, more straightforward fact. The van had been found on a patch of waste ground near the travellers' site in Kidsgrove. But there was one important detail that he'd left out of Jack's account. 'A forensic investigation hasn't turned up any bloodstains in Mrs Selleck's house. In fact, we haven't found anything of significance there'– he was sounding gloomy – 'so far.'

'What does that mean?'

This resulted in a long sigh. 'The place has been cleaned pretty well. We've got some of Evans's DNA, presumably, but it'll take a couple of weeks to run it through the system.'

'Can't you hurry that up?'

He gave a long sigh. 'I wish. We'll keep looking for her.'

'Right. And the travellers' site?'

'A couple of local officers have been round with an artist's impression of Evans. Their belief is that the link is the van with the false numberplates. They're working on the assumption that Evans bought it from there and that is the connection.'

'Nothing more?'

'Not so far, Florence.'

There was an awkward pause. Knowing it wasn't really part of the remit, I thanked him for keeping me up to date. 'It's OK,' he said awkwardly. 'I know this matters to you. And to be fair, it was you who first alerted us to the' – another pause while he selected the word – 'situation.' I wanted to ask him to keep me informed. I couldn't keep asking Jack for updates. But it would be asking too much. I'd been a policeman's wife and knew how major investigations worked. He would be busy, working almost constantly. He wouldn't have time to keep giving me updates. I let it go, returned his goodbye and threaded past the tables back to Jack.

Who was still sitting where I'd left him, a pint of beer pushed to one side, his hands flat on the surface, as though he was about to get to his feet and run. But run where? Neither of us had anywhere to run to. He watched me sit down, his breathing a slow, mindful breathe in – breathe out – breathe in – breathe out. It made me think he must have been to classes for anxiety. When we meet someone we only scratch the surface of who they are, what they are, why they are.

He paused the breathing exercise long enough to ask me a despairing, 'So what now?' I liked the implication that we were working together, side by side. And I wasn't out of ideas yet. I still had Ryan who, so far, appeared to be telling the truth – about the travellers, anyway. And then there was Catherine, who had hinted at something in Nora's past – unless it was another of her famous fantasies. Jalissa – or rather Charles – might even have seen something which hadn't, so far, come to light, though at four years old, of what value would that be? And now . . . I looked across the table at Jack, who was wrapped up in his own thoughts. I had an unexpected ally in Nora's son. A sort of sidekick. I liked the idea.

But when he asked me if my text message had been from DC Summers, I limited my response to a brief nod and smile and didn't tell him the content of the conversation I'd had or the ideas it had sparked. I pushed any ugly visions I might have about Nora's fate to one side and focused on the positive. One doesn't get to be a nurse unless you focus on healing and hope for better outcomes. Dwelling on the worst scenario tends to be a self-fulfilling prophecy.

We ate our meal; neither of us had much appetite and we both left half the meal to grow cold. I was realizing I could use Jack to persuade the Hudsons to cooperate. Now Nora was missing and the police were involved, surely they would want to help Nora's son?

So. 'Why don't we drive out to Swynnerton?' I suggested casually, so he could back off if he wanted, no hard feelings either way. 'Your mother's neighbours are patients of mine. I asked them to keep an eye on her.' What I didn't add were some key facts: they'd refused to help before; they seemed to have confidence in the unsavoury Evans; and I didn't quite trust them. They were holding something back. But maybe Jack might be able to persuade them to give us any extra details that might help us find Nora.

He looked dubious. 'Won't the police already have spoken to them?'

'Yes,' I said briskly. 'But they might remember something extra. Police tend to stress people out. They might have worried that telling the police something might be too official. You want to come?'

His nod was slow and still unconvinced.

As I headed out again to Swynnerton my mind was trying to knit together the facts as I knew them, fearing where my thoughts would end up. The van being torched was a worrying development. Evans must have known it would draw attention to him and probably double the number of officers assigned to the case. Torching a vehicle is a well-known method of obliterating forensic evidence but I'd been a policeman's wife for long enough to know that a false number plate indicates a stolen vehicle or one that has been previously written off. So the current theory would be that, realizing this, Evans had torched the van because it was worthless rather than to obliterate forensic evidence. If so, the traveller lead might not take us directly to Nora.

My mind wandered.

I pictured her as I'd last seen her, hunched in her chair, swathed in the blanket, empty eyes, passive. She'd looked so vulnerable.

And I had just walked out, left her there to Evans's attention. I didn't want to face the fact that he had intimidated me, not just by his physical presence but also by the menace he emitted. He'd felt threatening. He'd threatened me; I was under no elusion that the strange voice on the phone had been his. I couldn't console myself by saying I'd done what I could and alerted Nora's GP. For the umpteenth time, at the back of my mind lay the question: how had this happened? How had he gained Nora's trust to such an extent? Mark had sometimes described perpetrators he was glad to see locked up as inherently evil. I'd nodded, but until I'd been exposed to Evans I'd never really felt the full force of the phrase. Now, as I pictured Nora, I felt it like a punch in the solar plexus. I felt sick and guilty. I should have fought harder for her. I went through everything I'd tried to do, roping Kelly in, getting Ryan to watch Evans and the neighbours, trying to persuade Dr Gubb that his patient was in danger, making the futile appeal to the Hudsons, even convincing Sebastian that she needed admitting. Not enough, I thought, but what else could I have done? Somehow got Jack up here quicker?

But I sensed that Jack, too, was drowning in guilt, thinking the same thoughts, blaming himself. *If I'd got here quicker . . .*

We'd arrived at The Beehive. Two police cars and a big white forensic van were parked outside. I recognized Pants standing guard, talking to someone in a suit. Another detective? I pulled up outside the Hudsons' neat semi but it looked quiet, deserted.

Jack walked over to my car. 'So what now?'

To my relief the Hudsons' car drew up behind us and they climbed out, arms full of bulging supermarket carrier bags. Still laughing at their afternoon. Then they saw us, stared for a moment without waving or calling, simply staring.

We walked towards them. I took the lead. 'This is Jack, Nora's son.' It felt strange to be introducing them in the road but I sensed neither Orpah nor Tobin were going to invite us in. In fact, Orpah's stare was quite hard, though she made an effort to smile at Jack.

'I'm sure your mum will turn up,' she said without any sense of belief. I could tell Jack didn't believe it either. He grimaced.

'We've already given the police our statement,' was Tobin's contribution, still hostile.

Orpah made a movement towards the house. 'Excuse me. I need to get some stuff in the freezer.' She did manage a polite but meaningless parting comment, 'Nice to have met you,' to Jack which didn't include me, I noticed, wondering why on earth they felt so hostile towards me, so guarded. I'd done nothing to them except ask them if they'd keep an eye on a vulnerable neighbour. Then I remembered: they'd nailed their colours to the mast. Neither of the Hudsons could meet my eyes, which made me not only suspicious but steaming angry. Which was probably why I dropped the brick into the pond, to try and shock them into something.

'They've found Evans's van,' I said, noting the look of alarm they couldn't conceal. 'Burnt out.' I'd felt like adding, *No thanks to you*, but they'd already headed for refuge behind their own front door, leaving me to wonder. Was there any connection between the Hudsons and my patient's abductor? Had their friendship persuaded them to cover for him, or had they kept back from me, and possibly the police, some other vital detail? Was it even pure chance that they had ended up living right opposite her, close enough to peer straight into her living room? As I drove back along the A34 I wondered some more. Had they really come out on Evans's side because of that one neighbourly action? Or had they known him before? Had this all been a set-up? Had they been keeping an eye on Nora not for me but for him? I even wondered whether they were the ones who had alerted Evans to an elderly lady living alone, with no close relative nearby to notify the authorities.

TWENTY-SIX

Inside The Beehive all was busy, busy activity, men in white paper suits discussing samples. They seemed to be everywhere. I couldn't see DC Summers anywhere and they patently didn't want us around. My frustration was compounding. Some member of the team, probably the senior investigating officer, had some idea whether Nora was dead or alive and maybe even where she was. They probably also had some idea just who Evans really was and whether he had a track record with elderly ladies. They would soon be able to add Evans's DNA to their database, but they weren't sharing any details. While Jack was in conversation with one of the white-suited figures I felt in the way. I glanced across at the Hudsons' place and saw them watching through the window. Both of them, I stared right back at them. And then, feeling at a loose end, I left and went in search of Ryan. Jack was staying at the cottage saying he was shattered, which I interpreted as wanting to be left alone. Or maybe he'd worked out that the forensics team would have more sympathy with the missing person's son than the nosey nurse. Mark had often told me that most of the time the investigators resented the input of the general public.

I could remember his words. 'Half the time when they think they're helping they're just getting in the way, telling us stuff that isn't relevant and half the time they get their facts wrong.'

His disdain for these would-be sleuths was only matched by his resentment of the press, who pretty well always sent people scuttling down the wrong path. 'And that's if they don't prejudice the court case,' he'd continued, having given vent to his exasperation. 'No one realizes just how tight a case has to be to secure a guilty verdict, or how long it takes to get the results back from a lab who've had their funding cut by sixty per cent, or how bloody difficult getting all the evidence together is.'

So the last thing I wanted to do was to bother DC William Summers.

And I didn't want to go home. I didn't want to sit in my sitting room, staring at four walls which could tell me nothing. I wondered if Ryan had any more information to give me. After all, he had pointed the way towards the travelling community. Perhaps it was just as well I was searching him out on my own. He might have been suspicious of Jack anyway.

I found him at his usual haunt, hanging around outside The Crown. Ryan was nothing if not predictable. But as I approached him I almost groaned. God only knew what old movies he'd been watching. He was wearing sunglasses, leaning 'nonchalantly' against the front pillar, looking up and down the high street, a cigarette hanging from his lips. He couldn't have looked more incongruous. But I revised my opinion of this hammy James Bond when he spotted me, sidled up to me and delivered me his information. Thank goodness he'd dropped the Yankee twang and was talking normally. Maybe the movies had been British made.

'I've found out a bit more about your man,' he said in a low voice.

I wasn't sure I liked the description of Evans as 'my man', but this wasn't the time for semantics and I didn't want to stop Ryan's flow. Instead, I focused on listening – hard.

'I got a sort of address for him.'

'An address?' I was astonished.

Ryan continued to look super pleased with himself. 'Sort of,' he repeated.

'How?'

He looked even more pleased with himself. 'Dressed myself up real scruffy,' he said, 'this morning, early, and got a mate to take me up to the travellers' site.'

'A bit risky, wasn't it?'

He winked at me. 'Not without its dangers, I agree.'

'They've found the van burnt up.'

'Oh, shit.' He paused, frowning. 'Where?'

'I don't know exactly where but not far from the travellers' site.'

He was thoughtful. 'That makes it a bit more serious, doesn't it?'

I nodded.

He looked away. 'No sign of . . .?'

I shook my head.

'If I'd known I wouldn't have gone.' His eyes were bright. 'I did think there was a few police around but . . .'

Of course Ryan was well used to the police – and dodging them.

He tried to look modest. 'I figured it was worth takin' a risk. I thought I might find her for you.' He grinned. 'Zero to hero?'

I was touched. 'Have you spoken to the police?'

Ryan gave me the full beam of his wide eyes. 'Not yet.'

I got the implication and pulled some cash from my pocket. Not a lot. No one carries cash these days but Ryan was hardly going to accept a card payment. 'Fifteen quid, Ryan. It's all I've got.' He did look disappointed but pocketed the notes.

I sensed the story might be tarted up a bit with detail and so I took him inside and lined up a couple of pints for him and a large glass of wine for me. I could walk back home and pick up the car in the morning before the charges kicked in.

We hunched over a table in the corner. 'So?'

'I pitched up to the traveller site,' he said. 'Couple of guys came over. They looked . . .' He blew out through his lips. 'They looked like they'd quite like to practice their fistwork on me.' He gave a merry smile then. 'So I eyed them up.'

I suspected this story, like one of Catherine's, was suffering from over-embellishment, but hey ho. I had to give Ryan his due. He'd walked right into the lion's den. And he'd probably found out a lot more than any uniformed officer would.

Why had he risked it? I suspected it was that good, inexplicable side of him at work again. He cared about my missing patient as he'd cared about that elderly lady whose shopping bag had split, and the dogs abandoned outside pubs and shops. I even thought he sort of cared about me.

'I acted tough.' He accompanied this with another flash of his eyes and a mischievous grin. I had to remember Ryan had suffered abuse from a young age. Maybe he was inured to drunken threats and physical violence.

'I said the bastard owed me money and if he didn't pay he'd be in trouble.'

'And?'

'They said he already was in big trouble but they knew where he was.'

'Where?'

'Holed up with some old biddy in Bentilee. They didn't know the exact street but said I'd easy track the little shit down.'

I pictured the sheer bulk of Evans. 'Big shit,' I said and grabbed my mobile phone. 'You have to tell the police, Ryan. There's no time to waste . . .'

'Already did,' he admitted. 'Made an anonymous nine-nine-nine from a phone box.'

While realizing he'd been after some money, I was in awe of him. 'You,' I said, 'are brilliant but devious. If that call means they find her and she's all right it'll be down to you and your sleuthing.'

He tried to look modest and failed. 'Yeah,' he said, and I felt mean for having such disparaging thoughts about his undercover work. He was the one who'd found her.

Not yet, Florence, I reminded myself. *Not yet.*

I had one last question. 'So is Ben Evans his real name?'

Ryan shrugged. 'Far as I know,' he said.

We parted a little later when Ryan had downed his pints and I'd drunk a couple of glasses of wine.

Celebratory?

Premature.

I was buzzing too much to simply go home and sleep. And the mention of Bentilee had reminded me. I had another source up my sleeve. It wasn't one I used lightly but this was an emergency. I wouldn't be able to sleep unless I knew she was safe or at least this time I really had done everything I could and should.

Mark was an officer in Stoke-on-Trent. Maybe Bentilee was even on his patch. If I could only speak to him I believed he would be able to feed me some tidbits. I would find out where and when the police intended to close in on Evans and my patient. For sure they would have the exact address.

If I could bypass the Rottweiler.

And there was a risk – to me. Inside me. Any contact with Mark resurrected memories, not all of them bad. Not enough of them bad.

Already I was buried in the past, in our first meeting.

I'd been seconded to A & E from theatres, where I was a staff nurse, when a man had been admitted with a stab wound accompanied by a very good-looking policeman. And that was where and how I met my future husband. The good-looking policeman had obtained my phone number.

The rest is history, though a chequered history. Mark had the sort of bright-eyed smile and cheeky manner which had always attracted a great deal of female attention. Never short of words or charm, women had always warmed to him – as I had. Our marriage had survived almost twenty years and two children, and although he'd sometimes spoken of female colleagues, there had never been anything serious, until . . .

Middle age, like the setting sun dropping below the horizon, can signal to some men – and women – waning sexual prowess. And so it had proved. When ten-years-younger-than-me Vivian had joined the force he had exchanged me for a newer model – though I'd hardly have called Vivian Morris a model. According to Mark's colleagues (afterwards) she had made a beeline for my husband and had snared him as surely as a mantrap set on the ground (illegal since 1827).

When we divorced he had sensibly transferred from Stone to the city of Stoke-on-Trent. Both he and Vivian had previously been stationed on my doorstep and some of his ex-colleagues had had mixed feelings about the relationship. The police can be surprisingly traditional in their views. So the love birds had flown and now (apparently) had a love nest in Newcastle-under-Lyme.

I swallowed my pride, absorbed my resentment, and tried his mobile number, receiving a recorded message. As in most divorces, the situation had become acrimonious with plenty of mudslinging on my behalf and sheepish excuses on his. Somewhere along the line, though, a sort of détente had moved in; though I would never stop blaming her, I had stopped hating my husband. I left a message on his mobile phone, half apologetic, the other half explanatory.

'It's OK, Mark,' I began. 'Nothing to worry about. I don't even know why I'm ringing you – except you're police and might have some knowledge. Or advice,' I added quickly. (Like many men, my ex was susceptible to flattery.) 'You've probably heard about my patient, Nora Selleck, going missing. I think she's somewhere in Bentilee, but never mind how I found out about that. Can you check if the Potteries police are heading out there to look for her? If so, I wondered if you might have an exact address?' I felt I had to justify my ringing him. 'I'm really anxious about Nora and hope you've been called in to follow the lead up? Or know something about it? Maybe you can help? Please? You probably remember Nora. She was a geography teacher at Alleyne's. Her husband died a few years back.' I could have kicked myself. I was rambling into irrelevance. He wouldn't remember that. I tried to find some other way to reach him. 'She has a son, Jack. I think he went to Stafford Grammar.' I mentally kicked myself again. Why on earth would he remember a boy who wasn't even the same generation as Stuart? 'She disappeared a few days ago. She was – is – vulnerable. She sort of struck up a friendship with a pretty unsavoury guy. They've found his van – burnt out – by the traveller site in Kidsgrove. Just wondered if and what you know about it. That's all.' I let my voice trail away, feeling close to an unwelcome rush of resurrected affection towards him. 'Hope all's well.' My voice sounded husky. Once I would have ended with a 'love you', but that habit had died through a lack of nourishment. So I signed off with: 'If you can help, that'd be great.'

Then I settled down to watch a film and afterwards couldn't remember anything about it – not its title, plot or a single actor.

TWENTY-SEVEN

An hour later . . .

'Florence,' she said, obviously having recognized my number. 'How nice to hear from you.' The lie oozed out of her mouth like slug-slime. God, I hated her.

'Hello, Vivian.'

'Was it anything special?' I could hear the edge in *her* voice too and suspected my loathing of her was reciprocated, though why I couldn't imagine. She was the winner here, after all.

'I'm a bit worried about a patient,' I said, swallowing my pride. 'An elderly lady who's gone missing.'

'Oh dear,' she said, insincerity continuing to ooze out of her mouth. 'Well. Mark's in the shower at the moment.'

I wiped away the vision of his plump, pasty body being soaped.

'I'll ask him to ring you back, shall I?'

'Thank you.' I knew she wouldn't.

'Oh – and by the way.' As though it was an afterthought. 'I'm pregnant.'

I could have told her I already knew. That would have given me a chance to even the score. But to my credit I didn't. I was suddenly swamped with pity for her. Because I knew something she didn't. This was not going to end well for either her or the child. Or, for that matter, my ex. And, I guessed, at forty, it was a sort of now or never.

'Congratulations.' Now I had the top score for insincerity.

I don't know why I waited for his call back, half continuing with the film, cradling a glass of white wine but hardly drinking it, so it grew warm until it was undrinkable. I couldn't ring again. It would be too humiliating. And so that opportunity was lost, for now.

Which was a shame. Mark might have some information that the police had and which I didn't. Of course Vivian, also being an officer, would have access to the same information. But pass it on to me? I didn't think so.

TWENTY-EIGHT

Monday 5 July, 8.45 a.m.

DC Summers had gone quiet. Not a text or a missed call appeared on my phone. I felt excluded, outside the loop. I hoped Jack would be looking into his mother's finances and would share any information he handed to the police. But there was no word from him either. I felt overwhelmingly that I had to do something.

Without really thinking it through or planning my approach, I went into Dr Gubb's room. He looked startled, as well he might. He'd been examining a patient behind the curtains, a receptionist acting as chaperone. I apologized and said I needed to speak to him urgently. He nodded but frowned, and I withdrew and waited.

Five or six minutes later he knocked on my door. And in a typically polite, soft manner, he asked gently, 'What is it, Florence?'

The words tumbled out then, helter-skelter, chaotic and muddled, hopping from detail to detail, trying to give them some sort of order. Some of the details he knew about – Nora's rapid deterioration, coinciding with the appearance of Ben Evans; and some he didn't – Nora's disappearance, the torching of the van, my suspicion of theft. 'He's been seen withdrawing large amounts of money.'

His eyes narrowed. 'How do you know all this, Florence?'

I realized his suspicion had turned on me. And I had no answer, no explanation ready. I gaped, opened my mouth, closed it again. A guilty goldfish movement which did nothing to convince him.

'Someone saw him.' It was a lame explanation at best.

He waited for more then frowned and, as usual, followed the path of least resistance. 'I had no concerns about Mr Evans,' he said with dignity. 'He seemed genuine . . . to me.'

When I didn't agree, he added, 'It could be his own money he was withdrawing. Or money Nora asked him to withdraw. She seemed to trust him,' he added, apparently anxious to put the subject behind him.

'And now she's disappeared.' It had come out bluntly, clumsily, accusatory. Dr Gubb put his head on one side. 'The police have been in touch with me,' he said. 'I'm afraid I wasn't able to help them. But if you know anything you should speak to them.'

'I have,' I said shortly, aware it had come out snappily. 'What did you say to them?'

Dr Gubb had picked up on my irritation and frowned. The trouble with life's innocents is that they cannot perceive harm; they always find the good in a person however hard they have to burrow to find it. He lowered his head. 'I told the police that I'd met him and I had no concerns.'

Even now? I was incredulous.

'To me he seemed a perfectly decent sort of guy.'

A decent sort of guy? *Just like Harold Shipman, Dennis Nielsen and for all we know Jack the Ripper? Just like Fred West was considered a man with no real harm in him?*

'So where do you think she is?'

Dr Gubb put a hand on my shoulder. 'I'm sure she'll turn up,' he said in the voice he used when a patient feared they had cancer. I'd heard it so many times before the results of the CTs and scans and biopsies arrived. It was based on hope rather than fact, and it didn't shift my misgivings one single inch. When he added, 'There will be a perfectly logical explanation, I'm sure. Mr Evans is not a bad man,' he accompanied that assurance with one of his gentle, beatific smiles.

'And the low level of thyroxin?'

'As patients grow older they often need a higher and higher dose to maintain their levels.'

It was then I realized this was a waste of time. But I remembered what Catherine had said – or rather hinted at when I'd told her about Nora. 'Did something happen to Nora years ago?'

Dr Gubb frowned. 'What sort of thing?'

And that was the trouble. I didn't know.

He waited before responding. 'Not that I recollect.' Another pause. 'Nothing that could have any bearing on Mrs Selleck's current predicament.'

That was one way of putting it.

He left with a Parthian shot. 'If I were you, I would leave it to the police.'

And that was it. No help there. But there was no way I was going to leave it to the police. Nora might not be highest on their list of priorities. But she was way out on top of mine.

I was not done with my involvement. I hadn't run out of ideas or finished with my sources.

When Jalissa called with the lunch, Charles trotting close behind, Petronella being at school, I closed my door behind them. She looked alarmed. 'Anything wrong, Florence?' She gave her son a questioning look, as though deciding he must be the one to blame.

'No. Absolutely not.'

Her face lightened. 'So what is it?'

'You remember Charles saying something about the man at Nora Selleck's house?'

She was puzzled at this and quick to give me an explanation – of sorts. 'He shouted at him for just walkin' inside. Boy was only tryin' to help but the man obviously don't like him just wanderin' in without knocking.' She blinked. 'But Charles, he like to help.' She rubbed his head. 'Don't you, son?'

That drew a vigorous nod.

'Usually Nora gives him a sweet or a biscuit.' She gave him a fond smile.

'But not that day.'

'No. Not that day. She was sittin' in a chair and didn't say much.'

'When was this?'

'Months ago.' She looked around her as though searching for the calendar. 'Must have been around Easter – March, early April.'

'She rang and left a message sayin' she had a friend doin' the cookin' for her.'

So Nora had been in his thrall even as far back as then. Way before I'd seen her at the street market. I was thoughtful and she touched my arm.

'What is it, Florence?'

But I couldn't voice my worst fears. Instead I shifted around the topic. 'Had you seen that man before?'

She shook her head. 'He was a stranger to me.'

I persisted. 'You hadn't seen him around the town?'

Slowly she shook her head. But Charles was tugging her sleeve. 'She was givin' him a kiss. The man with the . . .' He pushed back the sleeve of his top and rubbed his hand up and down his arm, his eyes still fixed on mine. 'The man with the snake biting his fingers,' he said.

We both voiced our incredulity in a single expletive. Then: '*What?*'

And then we looked at each other. I hunkered down so my face was on a level with the little boy who was nodding, head up and down like a donkey. 'She kissed him there.' He grazed my cheek with his fingers.' He grinned. 'Like this.' And he smacked his lips together in an unmistakable '*Mmmmmsh*'.

Jalissa too bent down, her face furious. 'I told you, Charles, you are not to tell lies.'

The little boy's large brown eyes filled with tears. 'I'm not tellin' you lies. I never tell lies, Ma.'

And Jalissa looked at me. 'That is true, Florence. My son, he never tell lies.'

They both looked at me, and I believed them.

TWENTY-NINE

2 p.m.

I ate my sandwiches in my clinic room – I needed to be alone to think. What did I make of Charles's claim? Nora had kissed the reptile Evans? I couldn't believe it. The only explanation I could dream up, because I didn't for a moment believe that Charles would lie, was that he had misunderstood something. Maybe she had had something in her eye or . . .

I couldn't think of anything else.

To add to my confusion, Jack called in the middle of the afternoon. I was between patients so responded, still puzzling over Charles O'Sullivan's statement.

'I went to the bank,' he said, 'and spoke to one of the senior cashiers. She was really helpful. Florence,' he said, sounding worried, 'Evans wasn't draining her account. He did withdraw sums of money but they were only what would have been spent on normal household bills.'

I was silent, feeling that my instincts were slowly being proven wrong on all counts. I was still puzzling over 'the kiss'. 'So why was he hanging around then? And where is she now? What does he want with her, Jack?'

'I wish I knew,' Jack said. 'But it doesn't look as though he was stealing from her. The bank assured me there were no irregularities in her finances.'

I thanked him and we made a loose arrangement to meet up again. But I sensed being together would only emphasize how little we knew or understood about his mother's disappearance. We would go round and round in circles, doing little more than asking each other questions neither of us had the answers to. Maybe Jack sensed that too and that was why, for now, the arrangements to meet up did not firm into an actual day, time and place.

I was dying to get in touch with DC Summers, partly to check that Ryan really had passed the information on about his trailing Evans to Bentilee. I wanted to know whether they were acting on it, whether they were liaising with the Potteries police. Instead, I spent the next half hour trying to convince two patients, between hacking coughs, that giving up smoking, even at this late stage, was still worth it. I think I got a fifty-fifty result. One, I knew, would try; the other was a lost cause.

So I was diverted from puzzling about Nora and Evans. Or trying to work out little Charles's bald statement.

Maybe, I thought, I was clinging to the fact that Charles, Dr Gubb and possibly Jack all trusted that Evans wasn't a malicious person, so perhaps Nora was still alive – somewhere – when my heart was telling me I was clutching at straws. The likelihood was . . . I couldn't think of any rational explanation. Not in words anyway or in pictures.

I toyed with the idea of calling round to see Catherine again. I even tried her number. But for once she didn't answer. I left her a garbled message, asking her if she could tell me whether that something she knew about Nora's past might have a bearing on her disappearance. While my mind was stuck on Charles's version, I didn't want to be led up the garden path with one of her half true, mostly false, stories. 'Can you ring me. Please?' Even I heard the desperation in my voice.

The rest of my afternoon was taken up with baby jabs again interspersed with triaging of three emergency cases who had arrived at the front hatch insisting they see the doctor – today. Now. Two truly were emergency cases: one a suspected MI; the other had had a gastric bleed. I diverted those straight to the doctor who sent them both into hospital, but the third was a minor ailment, a patient well known for histrionics who had been bitten by a horse fly. I smeared some cream containing a local anaesthetic, gave her an antihistamine and she was happy.

After a two-hour diabetic clinic it was time to log off my computer and head for home, still in that disturbed frame of mind. I was tired as I pulled into Endicott Terrace to see Mark's car in the drive.

I pulled up alongside it, wondering what this meant. He still had a key, though God knew why. But he hadn't used it. He was sitting in the car, apparently either in a trance or asleep, head tilted back, eyes closed. I watched him for a moment, remembering that noisy snore, before knocking on the window. He jumped, then smiled when he realized it was me.

I tugged the door open. 'What are you doing here?'

He gave me one of those grins that used to melt my heart – once – and now had no effect on the organ at all – not even a quickening of the beat or an irregularity. 'You left a message on my phone. You sounded a bit . . . bothered. I thought I'd come over and find out what's going on.'

It was a lie as weak as the tea he used to drink. I didn't even ask, Does she know you're here?

'Come on in, then.'

He followed me through, looking around. 'Place looks nice.'

I turned around to catch his expression which was carefully and politely neutral. I didn't bother responding but I was ridiculously pleased. I am, actually, a dab hand with a paintbrush.

'Drink?'

'Better not.' Another grin. 'Have to drive back.'

'I wasn't offering alcohol,' I said coldly. 'I meant would you like a tea or a coffee?'

He tried to pretend he wasn't checking his watch. 'No.' He recovered his manners. 'No, thanks. I'm fine.'

I sat down and waited, but he seemed in no great hurry, so I prompted him again. 'Mark,' I said. 'Why are you here?'

He looked awkward then and I hoped he wasn't about to launch into another 'I hate babies' rant.

But when his expression softened into sympathy I realized that wasn't the case and I felt a snatch of anxiety, reluctant, suddenly, to prompt him.

'I shouldn't be telling you this,' he began. 'But there's a sort of ongoing case,' he said, 'into the manipulation and exploitation of elderly women. It's been going on for a few years. I'm not involved in the investigation,' he added hastily, picking up on my alarm. 'But it's my understanding that the details the team have is only the tip of the iceberg. It's a bigger case than the few instances which are known about.'

I knew my mouth was gaping but I also felt sick. I'd sensed it, had known it was coming. The fact that Jack hadn't unearthed any appropriation of his mother's money didn't necessarily mean that it hadn't happened – or been planned. Maybe my vigilance had stopped it.

Mark's expression was soft as he looked at me. It was the exact copy of the expression he'd worn when he'd told me my father had died. 'Understandably, some of the ladies have been reluctant to report the felony. They felt stupid for having been duped. There may even be more. A few of them have died so details are patchy. Sometimes relatives haven't realized what's been happening until after the person's died and they've looked into their financial affairs. Some may never have realized what went on.' He was stalling. I knew that way of extending the preamble while looking away. 'A few of the relatives' – he gave a long, slow blink – 'were probably relieved that their elderly' – he gave me a sweet smile – 'and sometimes difficult relative . . . had someone "taking care of them".'

When I didn't respond, he continued, 'Because of the nature of the offences and the patchy reports of concerns it's taken us a long time to realize there was a pattern.' Another tentative smile. 'And probably just one person behind it.' He chewed his cheek as though wondering whether to tell me the next bit. Then he plunged in. 'A year ago a lady called Bryony Hopper was reported missing.'

Something was snatching at my heart, squeezing it so hard each beat hurt.

'She was ninety-one years old, but, according to the nurse' – a quick smile at me – 'who visited her periodically and her daughter who lives in South Africa, she had all her marbles and looked after herself well. But six months before' – he eyed me dubiously – 'a neighbour noticed a man hanging around.' I could see where this was going and I didn't like the direction. I stiffened my shoulders, prepared for the worst, not wanting Mark to reach the inevitable end of the story. 'He was described as an odd-job man. Thick-set, with a beer belly and tattoos of dragons and castles on his arms.'

That was when I first began to wonder.

Mark narrowed his eyes as though picking up on my doubt, but after a pause, giving me a chance to speak, he continued. 'He drove a small green van. A Citroen, I think. Anyway – once he'd got himself involved, according to her daughter, Bryony's mental – and physical – condition deteriorated rapidly. With the lockdowns he registered as her carer and gave the name Tom Jones.'

Tom Jones, Ben Evans. Names so commonplace they hardly narrowed the field.

Mark had probably recognized that. He permitted himself a tiny hint of a smile. 'The van he drove had false number plates. Mrs Hopper, a widow, was not able to use the Internet and the neighbours, because of the pandemic, were understandably reluctant to call on her, sufficing themselves with waving through the window. When this Tom Jones said he was her registered carer they felt she was being looked after, in spite of his rough appearance. They said he seemed kind.'

'What happened to her?'

I'd asked the question so quietly I hadn't even been aware of speaking. But Mark's eyes flickered across to me and he frowned. 'No one really knows when she was last seen. Her daughter spoke to her on the phone last July but, of course, she couldn't visit because of the travel restrictions. She said her mother sounded as though she'd slowed up and was having trouble knowing who she was. But when Mr Jones came on the phone she was reassured that her mother was being looked after.'

I reflected. 'Ben Evans' had convinced Dr Gubb of his integrity. 'Evans/Jones' was a consummate actor able to switch the charm on and off. And what an opportunity – a daughter, lone child presumably, stranded on another continent, who would want to believe her mother was well and being looked after.

'Go on.'

'Mrs Hopper had been a relatively wealthy woman but her current account had been emptied with numerous cash withdrawals. More than eighty thousand pounds.'

He waited, perhaps for me to catch up. 'Mrs Hopper went missing on August the fourteenth last year.'

'She was reported missing?'

Mark looked uncomfortable. 'Florrie,' he said. 'I wasn't on the case. But as I understand it . . .' He stopped and did that thing where he chewed his cheek again. 'That's when the final withdrawal was made from her bank account.' I didn't like that word – final. Neither did he. He couldn't meet my eyes as he spoke his next sentence.

'Her body was discovered eight miles from her home in woodland just outside Macclesfield. The post-mortem was inconclusive. Her death was put down to exposure. It was November. Not incredibly cold but very wet.' He waited for me to absorb all this before saying, 'Florrie, I'm sorry.'

'To be the bearer of bad news?'

'That and . . .' He paused, then changed the conversation back to the subject at hand. 'I do remember Nora Selleck,' he said thoughtfully. 'Teacher, wasn't she?'

'Yes. At Alleyne's. Geography.'

He screwed his face up as he thought. 'Tall and skinny with . . .' He touched his head. 'Salt and pepper hair?'

'Yes.'

'She had a husband.'

'Peter,' I supplied.

'They lived out in Swynnerton, didn't they, in one of those pretty cottages near The Fitzherbert?'

Our favourite pub – once. 'Correct again,' I said before filling in the intervening years. 'Peter died so she was left on her own.' I didn't draw any parallels but, omitting to mention the different tattoos, I reverted to Evans. 'I didn't trust him right from the start.'

Mark was watching me, smiling. Maybe remembering other people I hadn't trusted – one in particular. 'Come on now, Florrie. Not being liked by you is hardly a criminal offence.' There was an undercurrent of something, but I wasn't sure what.

I was irritated, less by his tacit reproof than his charm, the birds-off-the-trees smile. And it wasn't ringing true. 'I know that.' I sounded sharp as glass.

'Go on.' He was definitely prompting me to add detail.

'It was something more. He *deliberately* antagonized *me*. Encouraged her to miss surgery appointments, distanced me. And another thing, Mark – he's clever. Not the thug he appears. He was discouraging her from taking her routine medication and at the same time putting on an act for everyone else so Dr Gubb and Sebastian thought I was prejudiced and took little notice.'

Although, I reflected, he'd taken enough notice to find her a bed at the cottage hospital.

Mark's hands were on his knees now, elbows splayed out. It was his thinking pose while his eyes were trained on my face. 'Dropping her medication would have had the effect of . . .?'

'If it was the thyroxin it could have accounted for the deterioration in her cognitive state.'

I was aware he was watching me with absolute absorption.

'If it's not your case, why are you so interested?'

He didn't speak for a moment, perhaps weighing up how much to tell me. It was left to me to prompt him.

'There were more cases?'

'Not exactly on my patch and they didn't have such tragic results. One was in Macclesfield.'

'What happened?'

'Same MO,' he said quietly, lapsing into his familiar police jargon. 'Elderly lady befriended.'

'What happened to her?' I asked even more softly.

'Drained her bank account.'

'And?' Now it was I who was doing the prompting.

He looked uncomfortable now. 'Put it like this,' he said awkwardly. 'She deteriorated rapidly while he was draining her of all her money on the pretence of helping her with odd jobs. And then he disappeared – vanished off the face of the earth.'

'Did you get a photo kit?'

He nodded and brought up an image on his phone. I could have thrown my hands up in sheer frustration. Not only was it taken from above but the man had a thick, black, almost pantomime beard. Added to that his hair, which practically obscured the rest of his face, might or might not have been a wig. Curly, thick and jet black. 'Where did you get this?'

'ATM,' he said. 'It was the best image we got.' He waited before asking me, 'Is it him?'

'It could be anyone.' I handed the phone back to him. 'Can't see much of his . . . Hang on a minute. Let's have another look.'

This time I focused on the arm extended towards the keypad and focused on the dragon sleeve tattoo. I met Mark's eyes and shook my head. 'I think it might not be.'

'Really? Are you sure?'

'The tattoo's different.'

He looked again. 'But the MO's the same. Don't tell me,' he groaned, 'there's two guys playing the same game?'

I shrugged, feeling hopeless and reverting to my original question while fearing the answer.

'What happened to her? The lady in Macclesfield?'

'I think she ended up going into a home.' He looked apologetic. 'I think the entire episode, the police questioning, and the fact that they hadn't caught him, unnerved her. She couldn't face living alone anymore.'

So her life, too, had changed irrevocably. He continued, 'She felt she couldn't trust anyone. And she'd lost a lot of money. Did Nora have a lot of money?'

I shook my head. 'I don't know. I don't think so. She owns the cottage, I suppose, but he couldn't have touched that. And both she and Peter will have had work pensions. Evans – or whatever his name is – was removing money regularly from a cashpoint but Jack said his mother's finances were in order.'

After a moment's thought, Mark picked up on something. 'How do you know about the withdrawals at the cashpoint? *Who* saw him there? You?'

'No.' This was difficult. 'Ryan Wood. He was keeping an eye out for me.'

My ex-husband gave a blast of laughter. 'Ryan Wood? You're kidding, aren't you? He'd sell his own grandmother for a fiver and a spliff.'

Which was true, but I felt bound to defend my 'spy'. 'He's not that bad. He has a good side.'

Considering the response. I wasn't sure whether to add a further observation of Ryan's but I did anyway. 'He says Evans is connected with the travelling community.'

Mark looked up. 'Really?' And then his focus changed. 'And you're investigating for yourself?' His smile warmed a degree more and he moved closer to me. 'Always the Good Samaritan, Florrie. My little warrior.'

I didn't respond.

'Be careful.' When I still didn't respond he realized he'd overstepped the mark and his expression changed. 'I mean it, Florrie. Be very careful. OK?'

I'd been tempted to tease him with a comment about protecting his ex but when I saw his expression I held back. There was no doubt. My ex was deadly serious.

'So the current investigation?'

'Is centred round Bentilee. That's all I know. It's top secret – otherwise they'll lose the surprise element. They're planning a raid sometime in the next couple of days.'

I know about police raids. Usually happened at dawn. Nora would be terrified.

Mark made a feeble attempt at regaining my good books. 'I'll keep an eye out for you. Maybe I can let you know when it's likely to be. But promise me you won't try anything.'

'Like what?' I made an attempt at levity. 'My own dawn raid, armed with a baseball bat?'

He managed a smile.

'Let me know if there are any developments.' I'd picked up that he was shifting around in his seat, preparing to leave. Always an awkward moment these days.

'Better go. If Vivian finds out I've been here . . .' He drew a slash across his throat and added, 'She has a bit of a jealous streak. Can get quite . . .' He couldn't seem to find the word.

He was at the front door when he turned and looked even more awkward. 'The investigating team might want to talk to you. Florrie. You can't tell them what I've just told you.'

I nodded.

'And Florrie . . .'

I could anticipate what was coming.

'I'm sorry,' he said. 'I'm really sorry how things have turned out.'

I acknowledged the inadequacy of the words with a tightening of my mouth and a shrug, a sort of 'whatever'. But he still didn't move. With a sick feeling in the pit of my stomach, I had an idea I knew what it was. I searched those honest hazel eyes and found my answer. But I wanted him to mention it. Not me.

'I don't know what to do' – he wafted his hands around – 'about this baby business.'

'There isn't a lot you can do, Mark,' I responded, and then felt the words squeeze out of me like toothpaste from an almost empty tube. 'She really wants it.'

He couldn't find any words and neither could I, but I read his shamed apology as he must have read the still-raw hurt that I'd buried so deep and so successfully inside me. I broke the spell with a blink and opened the front door. Closed it behind him, waited to hear his engine start up, move away and accelerate down the main road. Then I took the cork out of a bottle of wine going cheap because no one buys wine with a cork in it these days.

THIRTY

Tuesday 6 July, 10.30 a.m.

I'd almost forgotten about Jack.

But I picked up a text from him at around half ten the following morning asking me to ring him. I was in the middle of a very nasty-looking ECG at the time so it had to wait while I sorted out the patient, involved Dr Bhatt and waited for an ambulance before I could focus on whatever Jack had to say. On reading it again I worried about the tone of the text; the please at the end sounding desperate. I finally rang him back at twelve and he picked up straight away, sounding agitated and humble.

'Thanks for ringing back.' He sounded a hundred miles away from the confident young banker I'd witnessed only days ago.

'The police have told me they're linking Mum's abduction with a couple of other cases.' There was a catch in his voice as he added, 'And one of them's dead.'

I didn't know what to say, particularly when he added, 'I'm going mad here. I'm heading back to London, Florence. My partner, Gerald, is missing me. I have to get back. I'm doing no good here. Just hanging around, too much time to think. Work will keep me occupied. And the bank need me back. They won't keep my job open for ever.' He hurried on as though worried I'd think he was being a neglectful son. But I wasn't. I was reflecting how life goes on for some at the same speed, the same events occurring, while for others the wheel has shifted; their lives will never be the same again. And for still others life has stopped abruptly. We both knew that there was a possibility this was what had happened to his mother. And I, for one, was facing the terrible fact that we might never even know.

I couldn't mention the Bentilee raid because Mark had given me the information in secret. Leaking an undercover operation could cost him his job. I had to let the police do this their way and trust Nora would stay safe.

Jack was still talking. Quickly, as though to get it over with. 'If she hadn't disapproved of my lifestyle I'd have seen more of her. But . . . the police have my contact details. They've promised to keep me up to date. And I can get back here in less than a couple of hours.' He stopped, maybe already anticipating my doubt in his next sentence. 'When they find Mum they'll get back to me.' There was a catch in his throat as he repeated, 'I can't do any good here, Florence. Too much time to think. But thanks for . . .' He cleared his throat with a loud harrumph. 'Thanks for your . . .' Another pause while his voice finally broke, 'Help.'

There is nothing that makes you feel more of a failure than someone thanking you for help you've never provided.

I made a neutral bleat of a noise meant to respond to this. 'That's OK. I haven't done—'

He cut me off mid-flow. 'You've *been* here.'

And that was about it. Little more than a presence.

We both paused before saying almost simultaneously, 'Keep in touch.' I'd wanted to add that I hoped we found her soon but was afraid he would pick up on the false and hearty missing words – the *when* or *if*, that I couldn't even utter.

We disconnected.

Saying goodbye to Jack rubbed in how we were stagnating, no nearer finding Nora. I didn't have a clue where the police were on this. I assumed Ryan had been telling the truth when he said he'd pointed them in the direction of Bentilee, but every day seemed like a week, each hour a lifetime. And every day, every minute that passed, made it less and less likely that we would find her alive. I'd tried to block out the image of her body lying somewhere, undiscovered, like Bryony Hopper's, but it kept pushing into my mind in various stages of decomposition. Nora's skinny body in those old clothes she wore that she could so easily be mistaken for an empty pile of rags. I saw her soaking wet, covered in earth, in leaves, hidden. I wanted it to be found and at the same time I didn't. Because it would manifest the measures I hadn't taken. My guilt would have physical form; the part I had failed to play splayed out for everyone to see. And now my roping in of Ryan Wood, a well-known petty criminal, seemed pathetic. After the exposure would come the judgements. I hadn't done enough. I could have prevented it if I had spoken to the right people, said the right words, done the right thing, in the right way. Social media would pick me to pieces like a piece of carrion pegged out in the open.

The nurse who knew but failed to protect her patient.

I wished I couldn't see the future with such clarity. But I had to face it. If I had made my case clearer in the first place, stated my reasons for being alarmed at Ben Evans's interest in my vulnerable patient rather than making my intervention personal and prejudiced, I might have succeeded in convincing the right people. Perhaps if I had appealed to them in the right way I *could* have prevented this. Maybe involved Kelly more. I should have overridden the practice rule that we had to discuss our patients with their registered doctor, though I had tried that. Maybe if her doctor had been any one of the others who did not have Dr Gubb's Pollyanna view on life. Any of the other doctors would have been more perceptive and less likely to be hoodwinked by Ben Evans's acting. If only I'd spoken to them. This is one of the worst aspects of being a nurse. The guilt. You blame yourself, always feeling you didn't do enough. You should have done more. And then some. I had to remind myself, Sebastian had arranged her admission to the cottage hospital and she had sent the ambulance away. I couldn't lay the blame entirely at my door. Nora had played her part too.

But then it was obvious from the detail Mark had leaked to me that 'Ben Evans' or whatever his real name was had been practised at his role, that of concerned and caring bystander. Had he been less convincing even Dr Gubb might have realized his true intentions. That was when I stopped. If Evans really hadn't blindly robbed Nora, what had his intention been? What was he doing there? And then why run? That only drew attention to him. Had he run because I'd told him Jack was coming up and he'd realized he couldn't pull the wool over Nora's son's eyes? I sat in my clinic room feeling forlorn. For all the good it might have done I could have put my head in my hands and cried. But self-pity isn't really in my repertoire. A minute later I picked myself up and found DC Summers' number instead. I hoped I might learn something positive. And what was the worst that could happen? He'd tick me off or ghost me. In my mind the worst had already happened.

Of course, I reminded myself as I listened to the ringtone, I must skip skilfully around the details Mark had leaked to me. That wouldn't do his career any good.

But when DC Summers picked up I didn't know where to start and fumbled my way clumsily. 'I wondered if you've found her?'

There was a surprised and awkward silence, during which I read his mind. He didn't recognize my number.

'It's Florence Shaw,' I said, 'the nurse from the surgery.'

He recovered quickly. 'Yes, of course. Sorry.' There was a brief silence, during which I read his mind. *Found her? What planet is she on? Nora Selleck is as unlikely to be found alive as Elvis Presley or Princess Di.* 'Umm,' he began before surprising me. 'Do you have a lunch break?'

'Yes.'

'What time?'

'Around twelve thirty to one thirty.' I couldn't see where this was going.

'It's a lovely day,' he said gently and politely. 'Why don't I meet you outside the surgery with some sandwiches and we can eat them on the towpath seat?'

The 'thank you' came automatically followed closely by aston-ishment. Where had that come from?

Whatever, half an hour later found me parked on the bench at the side of the towpath watching a group of mallards squabbling and paddling around. It was a pleasant, peaceful sight. I closed my eyes to the sunshine and absorbed the warmth.

He arrived a few minutes later, in casual wear, jeans and a T-shirt, which belied the serious expression he tried to hide with a smile the moment he spotted me, and which made my chest

tighten with panic. Surely only really bad news would be delivered face-to-face – and with sandwiches? He lifted a hand as a
greeting before sitting down and passing me a brown paper
package which smelled of onions. He looked around at the picture
postcard canal scene, boats drifting past in the bright colours of
the water gypsies. Roses and castles. We ate our lunch in sync
while he filled me in, beginning with a warning.

'You realize I am sharing this in confidence because I know
just how closely you've been . . . involved.'

'Yes.'

'And you probably know,' he said awkwardly, but very gently,
the way one does when breaking bad news, 'that when a person
goes missing the first twenty-four hours are critical.'

I nodded and chewed my sandwich trying to distract myself
with eating.

'I know you were married to a cop so "get" the way things
work.' He was watching me carefully. 'I think the chances of
finding Mrs Selleck . . .' (I was glad he'd given her the dignity
of her name and title), '. . . are not good.'

I stared into the water. 'I realize that.'

'You're not to blame,' he said, reading my thoughts.

I shook my head. 'If I'd—'

He forestalled me. 'You were just her nurse,' he said, without
it sounding like an insult.

I faced him then. 'I was in a position of awareness.'

'But your role isn't to—'

'I did try to involve her doctor but . . .'

'Look.' His voice was firm now. 'This is an ongoing investigation. And not just our force. I can't tell you more, except the
guy is a professional. He's done it before and if we don't catch
him he will do it again. He's a con artist, Florence. Someone
who preys on vulnerable elderly women, inveigling himself into
their confidence, emptying their bank accounts and then dis-
appearing into the fog. You weren't to know that.' He paused.
'Neither did she. How could she? His sort of person is outside
her experience. That's why he's so successful. He chooses his
victims with care. And it's why and how he's got away with it
before. It's an easy crime, a soft target, and the assumption has
been that somehow' – he looked ashamed – 'these old ladies

were muddled about their finances when they complained to relatives or carers. Some of this is down to us,' he added quickly, maybe anticipating my response, that Nora Selleck had been anything but muddled. At least until recently.

I still felt I'd let my patient down, but I knew that DC Summers was here out of kindness, not to make a judgement.

'If it hadn't been for you he'd have completely robbed her of all her savings.'

Then, perhaps sensing something, he looked at me sharply.

'Jack said her bank account was still healthy.'

He nodded. 'So far. We think that due to your focus he ended this sooner than he'd meant to.'

I didn't mention the different tattoos but diverted.

'You mentioned other women?' I was having trouble keeping back the fact that this wasn't news to me. Mark had already told me about Bryony Hopper and I'd suspected then that there might be more victims.

DC Summers looked at me sharply, wondering how much detail to give me. 'So far,' he said carefully, 'we know of five women who've been targeted.'

'Did any of those just disappear, like Nora?'

He was watching the mallards and didn't respond except for a small nod.

'And when they were found?'

DC Summers frowned and his answer evaded my direct question. 'He seems to have become more adept at what he's done.' He looked at me. 'And more ambitious. At first it was simply pinching stuff from the house and when the old lady mentioned it he'd say she was mistaken or muddled and then he'd move on, go missing.'

'But . . .'

He was looking at me sharply now, sensing my mind was elsewhere and trying to follow my train of thought. 'Did you say you thought he'd fiddled with her medication?'

It put me on the spot. 'I couldn't prove it,' I said. 'But I suspected it.'

'As I thought.' His voice was quiet, reflective. 'He's become more successful at his work. More subtle. Every time going to a different level.'

'How come he's got away with so much?'

DC Summers drew in another long breath. 'The first two cases were in Birmingham. It took the local force a while to realize there actually had been a crime committed. And a long way down the line to realize the two cases were connected. The two ladies lived in different areas of the city, they were elderly and somewhat muddled, and the investigations cursory at best. It was only when there was a third case in Lichfield that the forces started stringing them together, realizing it was the same perpetrator.'

'What happened to these three elderly ladies?'

'One had a stroke – which, of course, involved relatives' interventions as she had to be admitted to a nursing home where . . .'

I could guess the rest of the sentence.

'Eighteen months later,' he said, 'another was admitted to hospital, where she remained for a couple of months, then was discharged back home with intervention from Social Services.'

'The lady in Lichfield?'

'Went to live with her daughter in Leamington Spa.'

I nodded.

'The third victim was a Bryony Hopper from Congleton. She, umm . . .'

I looked at him and couldn't hide the fact that I already knew.

'Mark,' he asked, cottoning on very quickly. 'Your ex?'

I nodded, frowned and moved the conversation forward. 'How did he identify his victims?'

'That was another point that delayed us. There was no obvious link between the victims. It seems he sort of hung around various town centres and supermarkets. In the Lichfield case we think he identified her from having a stall at the street market, helping a friend out. We think that's where the traveller connection comes in. A few of the travelling community have stalls and go around the Midlands.'

'And that's where and how he met Nora.'

'That's right.' We'd finished our sandwiches but DC Summers showed no inclination to move. 'The guy is no slouch. He's clever and cunning.'

'You mean about reducing Nora's thyroxin?'

'Yeah. We wonder if he has possibly worked in a hospital or—'

I blew that one out of the water. 'Anyone can find that out on the Internet.'

'DNA analysis is ongoing but the links seem incontrovertible.'

I drew the obvious conclusion. 'Are you saying you still don't know who he is? Whether he's an ex-con?'

He shook his head. 'He's probably somewhere on the database but we can't connect him to the case – yet.'

I was silent for a moment. DC Summers might not realize it but I knew more about the case than he might guess. 'I heard mention of Bentilee.'

He looked at me sharply. 'Where?'

'Someone I know – a patient – said he'd heard there was some connection. Maybe . . .' I grasped at any available straw. 'He has a relative there – or a friend,' I finished limply.

DC Summers looked stern. 'As I said. This is an ongoing investigation.'

'What about the traveller lead?'

His mouth twisted. 'They closed ranks. Denied knowing the guy. Said he wasn't one of them. Accused us of picking on them, going for a soft target. They probably think we're going after them for the false number plate which is almost certainly part of a racket "recycling" written-off cars.' He gave me an amused smile. 'Death traps on wheels. We're watching the site but . . .' He let the sentence drift where it would.

Then he looked hard at me. 'You've been our best witness so far, Florence.'

I felt a twitch of disappointment. So that was what was behind all this – the contact, the sandwiches, the pseudo friendship. Of course. What else?

I tried to retrieve some dignity, stood up and held out my hand. 'Thank you for the sandwiches.'

His response was equally polite and formal. 'My pleasure.'

I wanted to make some quip about putting them on expenses but didn't think I could pull it off. 'Detective Summers,' I said, 'what's happened to my patient?'

He looked at me and made no attempt to answer. Except in those soft brown eyes I'd read pity.

It was only as I walked away that I acknowledged something.

And I knew why. I hadn't told him that the tattoo they had captured on the ATM was different to Evans's distinctive snake tattoo gnawing towards his knuckles. The reason? I hadn't wanted to risk Mark getting into trouble. Because, a little like a nurse never really being off duty, there are times when the same is true of an ex-wife.

THIRTY-ONE

Wednesday 7 July

Normally Wednesday night is my favourite night of the week. Argentine Tango night, held at the church hall and schooled by a wrinkled septuagenarian who had once, long, long, long ago, been a professional dancer. His name was Randolph, although I very much doubted this was the name he had been given at birth. He had a distinctly Liverpudlian accent. He was always dressed in true dapper fashion – patent shoes, flared trousers worn tight over the hips and a waistcoat over a red shirt (stained underarm). It could have done with being washed more frequently or else replaced. Oddly enough, I didn't, in spite of digging around, know anything about his personal life except that he lived in Newport – the Shropshire one rather than Newport, Gwent.

I actually had a male partner, a shy young man named Chris, probably half my age, who managed the steps well but never actually met my eyes or made any attempt at conversation. I'd judged him 'on the spectrum' as well as being pathologically shy. But on the plus side he turned up regularly, washed and brushed up in scrupulously clean clothes, and since 'losing' my husband I was glad of the male input. Chris knew the steps and kept in time, though the sparks created between myself and my partner were hardly up to the torrid, sexy dance we acted out. I'd danced with him every Wednesday evening for nearly two years, during which I don't think we'd exchanged more than a dozen words and nods of acknowledgement.

Chemistry between us was, and was likely to remain, dormant. I wore my usual outfit, suitable, in my opinion, for the dance, a calf-length lacy black skirt and scarlet T-shirt teamed with my pride and joy – black leather cowboy boots with a two-inch Cuban heel. I'd bought them over the Internet keeping my fingers crossed they'd be a good fit. And they were. I'd stamp my feet, smack my hands together and arch my back, glaring (as is expected) at Chris, who skilfully avoided my stare.

I hadn't really been in the mood for a dance class and was distracted, frequently leading with the wrong foot or misreading Chris's cues, but it was a welcome break from my anguish. Halfway through, Chris, still staring in my opposite direction, muttered, 'I have a brother.'

I was so startled I nearly fell over. Two years and he came out with *this*?

'What did you say?'

He smiled. 'I have a brother.'

Now what do you say to that? I managed, 'That's nice,' before the music started up again and we were making an attempt at *ganchos*.

Twenty minutes later we'd stopped for a drink of water when Chris spoke again, his hand on my arm now. 'My brother,' he said before losing confidence and staring at the floor, 'is a clairvoyant.'

Now why didn't that surprise me? That my tacit partner of two years had a brother who was a clairvoyant?

Maybe he was just trying to help in his clumsy, gauche way. 'She's all right,' he said, 'but a bit frightened.'

I stared at him for a moment, then remembered my manners and thanked him.

The class lasted two exhausting hours with a soundtrack of Argentine music. For those two hours I'd stopped worrying about Nora and feeling responsible. But the minute I'd changed out of my dance shoes it all came flooding back and I felt sick. The visions of her lying somewhere, slowly dying from starvation, dehydration, exposure – whatever – I could see it as clearly as if I stood there, right by her side. I'd like to say that somewhere in my dreams, I found the location, brushed the leaves from her face and picked her up in my arms, delivered her to the care of the hospital. But whatever my dance partner's brother said, all I felt was her terror and confusion, sharing her plight helplessly without finding any way to help my missing patient. I'd heard nothing more from DC Summers so assumed the case was stagnating. I'd been planning to head home to a couple of glasses of wine and the TV but when I reached into the glove compartment and switched my phone back on there was a text from Mark and a missed call. I opened up the text first. No emojis this time, just a rather sad, *I can't do this.*

Tempted as I was to send back an emoji of a crying baby, a dummy and a cot with: *You don't have a choice*, I simply deleted it. I didn't want to get involved. It was too messy, too sticky. And in a way too sad. I didn't know why Mark was involving me in his domestic quandary. For the second time I even felt a touch of sympathy for PC Vivian Morris. She was about to face one hell of a storm.

And then I rang the number of the missed call which I hadn't recognized and was answered immediately. I heard a background of sounds: people talking, laughing, the clink of glasses, children shouting, laughing, general bonhomie and a voice I recognized. Ryan, and he sounded drunk.

'Florence. I rang you *a-a-a-ge-s* ago. Where've you bin?'

I didn't answer that one.

'I got some news for you.'

I felt the twitch of interest and glanced at my watch. It wasn't that late. 'Where are you?'

'Where d'ya think?

The Star.'

Laughs, hiccups. 'Why don' cha join us?'

It wasn't on my list of desired ends to a strange evening with my brush with the supernatural and my back was aching from the banana stance of the tango, but after my lunch with DC Summers I'd realized I had to leave it to the police. Any help I could give would be minimal, if at all. I was losing hope that Nora was even still alive, let alone that I would see her again. But maybe I could approach this from another angle. Maybe Ryan could help.

The Star was lively with drinkers, mainly outside watching

the narrow boats manoeuvre through the lock. As I'd suspected, Ryan was sitting with a table full of cronies who were laughing as a boat manned by amateurs bumped against the slimy sides of the lock, the holiday makers looking panicked and out of control. While the spectators jeered and cheered a woman in tiny denim shorts stuck two fingers up at them which made their response even louder. The lock filled, the holiday makers opened the gates and the boat slid out and headed downstream.

Ryan greeted me like an old pal. Effusively waving his arms around the way alcohol-fused people do. 'Florence. Come and join us. We need some female company.' Looking me up and down, his cronies didn't look quite so convinced. They were an assorted lot, beards or unshaven, a couple in jeans, the others in shorts and T-shirts, one wearing wraparound shades which reflected a distorted me as I sat opposite him and treated them all to another pint when the barmaid appeared in the doorway. I had a medium glass of white wine. It was a fine evening; I had company. I'd enjoyed my tango class with the zombie partner who had momentarily awakened to alert me to a statement via the supernatural. Somehow the world didn't look too bad.

Ryan slid next to me. 'Van still not turned up then?' Thank goodness he'd dropped the 007 act and was speaking normally. 'No. Mate of mine' – he indicated a portly fellow wearing jogging shorts and a black T-shirt sporting an obscene message – 'thinks he saw him in the Potteries.'

The guy was nodding.

My response was predictable. 'Have you told the police?'

'Yeah.' It was a stroppy response to a polite question. Maybe it was the mention of the word police. 'They didn't seem that interested.'

But I was. 'Whereabouts in the Potteries?'

'Bentilee.' Ryan was looking smug, the I-told-you-so face.

He leered at me. 'I got a girl there, see. Hot stuff an' all.'

I felt like saying good for you, but didn't want to antagonize this source.

'And you told the police?'

He nodded again, slowly. 'They already knew.' Then he leaned in. 'The house I saw him come out of'– he leered again, giving me a good view of a missing incisor – 'belongs to a guy who was in prison.'

I didn't like the sound of this. 'For what?'

'Killed a man.' He said it as casually as if he was telling me the guy had failed to buy his TV licence. 'Got into a fight. He was carryin' a knife. Got away with manslaughter. Couple of years and he was out.'

And Nora was in the power of these people? My hand, wrapped around the stem of the wine glass, had developed a tremor as I tried to block out the vision of her cowering in a corner, terrified. Or worse, as I remembered Bryony's fate and Nora's complete bewilderment in the high street, a familiar setting. How much worse would she be in a place that was unfamiliar? It wasn't that it surprised me that Ben Evans was associating with a killer from a notorious area in the Potteries. It was having it confirmed. 'And you told the police all this?'

He looked shifty. 'Some of it.' He looked around his mates and protested. ''Course I did. What do you take me for? Old lady gone missing? I 'ave a gran myself.' He stuck his chin out, making him look like a parody of Desperate Dan. 'Anyone touched *her* and they'd 'ave me to deal with.' He grinned again, met my eyes. 'See?'

Ryan was practically hopping with excitement. 'Told you I'd be able to help. I knew I could. I knew one of my mates would know something.' He puffed his chest out. 'We're like the Baker Street Irregulars finding stuff out without anyone knowing what we're *really* up to.' His mates nodded their agreement enthusiastically.

But I'd been sidetracked. 'You read Sherlock Holmes, Ryan?'

'Saw the film, didn't I?'

Of course he did. I slapped a twenty-pound note on the table. They could fight it out for themselves.

Midnight.

I didn't know what had wakened me, but I sat up feeling a night terror. I'd had these frequently when Mark had first left, terrible nightmares where he slid away from me into boiling seas, into peat bogs, fiery forests or trying to cross a motorway to reach him. Or the other one where I was sitting alone in a restaurant when he walked in, his arm around his new love, and was unable to move, glued to my seat. The nightmares had been terrible and vivid but they'd largely subsided now. And yet something *had* wakened me. Not the memory of a nightmare, although I had the usual manifestations: my heart was pounding and I had the familiar sick taste of panic in my mouth, akin to bile mixed with sulphurous fear. But this time I didn't know what had caused it. I climbed out of bed and then I heard it, my car alarm shattering the night. I stepped towards the window. The headlights were flashing; my security lights had come on as well as bedroom lights in another house in the cul-de-sac. Mr Ford's. I could see him peering out of the window. I put my dressing gown and slippers on and hurried downstairs. The alarm had stopped for now but as I stepped outside it was on to broken glass. Thank God I had put my slippers on, was my first thought before it registered that my windscreen had been shattered. For a moment I stood, too shocked to move. Then I pressed the release button on my car keys and the alarm subsided leaving a thick, threatening silence. I went inside and rang the police.

THIRTY-TWO

Thursday 8 July, 2 a.m.

As luck would have it, the responding officer who arrived in an impressive fifteen minutes was Police Constable Robert Pantini, who must have been working nights.

I hadn't gone back to bed but had made myself a cup of tea and sat on the sofa waiting for the promised response to my panicky call. It was only when I tried to lift the cup to my lips that I realized I was shaking.

I heard the sound of a car outside, saw the flash of a blue light through my blinds. No siren. Moments later Pants and I were surveying the damage side by side. 'Bit of a mess,' he said. I didn't voice the thought that had taken root in my mind. Was this something to do with Evans? Pants gave me a very straight look. 'Got any enemies, Mrs Shaw?'

'Looks like at least one.'

He took a look inside the car using a powerful flashlight. 'Nothing in there,' he said. 'Must have used a baseball bat or something.'

I nodded. I didn't care how it was done. I only knew it had been meant to intimidate me. And it had succeeded. There is something about the manifestation of hatred in a scatter of shards of glass on your own front drive, an unmistakable, obvious and visible sign of hatred and fury that is quite terrifying when you know it was directed purely at you. I felt queasy and frightened, glad of Pants's solid presence as I looked down the street. No one there. Even Mr Ford had abandoned his window and probably gone back to bed; his house was dark again. The street was hollow, with small and empty puddles of light from the lampposts. Pants followed me inside, thanked me when I made him a cup of tea and took a statement, which was pretty sparse as I didn't really know anything. I'd just woken up, I told him, probably when the glass had been smashed and the car alarm set off. I passed on the information that I'd seen my neighbour looking out of the window. 'Maybe he can give you more detail,' I said without much hope. Half an hour later Pants got another call about a burglar alarm going off in another part of town. He gave me a crime number, 'for the insurance', promised they would investigate, left and that was it. There was no point in my even trying to go back to sleep. I sat up in bed, my arms wrapped around my knees, shivering, even though it was a warm night. Evans, I thought. He wanted me to know he knew where I lived. He would have left some signature mark. I only had to find it.

As soon as it was light, around six o'clock, I showered, dressed, searched again around and inside the car, swept up the glass. And found nothing.

I took a taxi into work and rang the windscreen replacement firm from there.

What I couldn't work out was why now? What was the point of intimidating me now? The police were involved in Nora's disappearance. I had done the best I could, alerted doctors, other health professionals and the psychiatric nurse. I was sidelined.

It wasn't solely up to me anymore. But then I had a chilling thought. Evans wanted me to know that my interfering was what had tipped him into abducting my patient. It was my fault and he wanted to throw it back in my face. Had I left well alone he would have drained her bank account, then melted back into anonymity until his skills were needed again. In other words when he'd run out of money. Then he'd prey on some other poor woman. It was I who had focused on the relationship and flushed him out. So he'd had to run. What I couldn't understand was why had he taken Nora with him? Surely he'd realized that would involve a major police investigation?

And then there was the irrefutable evidence of the tattoo which I'd so far kept to myself. Maybe I should have shared it with the police, but I hadn't. I'd kept it to myself because I wanted to understand it before sharing it. An idea was stirring, but I knew I was missing something.

I yawned my way through my surgeries. Once I would have coped with a broken night's sleep. On call for theatres, covering nights for the district nurses, my midwifery course (babies invariably arrive at night). When people blithely say the NHS is twenty-four seven they don't see the utter exhaustion that trails in the wake of providing such a service.

Dr Gillian Angelo gave me a lift home. My car would be ready sometime tomorrow. Gillian was the empathetic one. Her car smelt of lavender and peppermints, a scent I would always link with her. As she dropped me off, she switched the engine off and turned to me. 'You don't seem yourself lately, Florence.'

I shrugged, pretending to shake the comment off, but she pursued the point with sharp perception. 'You're not blaming yourself about Nora Selleck, are you?'

I couldn't even answer that one and shrugged again, feeling close to tears when I saw the empty space where my car should have been and felt Evans's presence, the malevolence and hatred of those serpent arms reaching out to taunt and terrify me. Gillian stretched out with one of her hands. Long, elegant fingers, shaped nails, large diamond solitaire ring. 'It isn't your fault,' she said. 'It's his. People do this – the decent ones blame themselves instead of the criminal. It's not your fault,' she repeated. 'You did your best so don't shoulder any of the blame. You tried to alert Morris and Sebastian. You did your best.'

I mumbled something about it not having been enough and she tightened her grip. 'You did your best,' she repeated for the third time, then looked around her. 'And now this.'

Last night's drama had, of course, whipped around the surgery like a forest fire.

I climbed out, bent in to thank her for the lift and closed the door behind me, glad to see her reverse, then turn around and head off. I felt even better when I was inside my own house, safe behind the front door.

But the fear had followed me in. When, a few minutes later, a knock landed on my door, I almost dialled 999 before I opened it. Thank goodness I did not.

My neighbour, Mr Ford, dressed in baggy jeans and a check shirt, was standing there, his forehead wrinkled in concern.

'I thought I'd come over, Florence,' he said. 'I saw what happened last night. I'm so sorry.'

My amazement must have leaked through because after he'd said this neither of us spoke for a moment but stared at each other, our thoughts probably tracking in tandem. We'd lived in the same cul-de-sac for years. And in that time I doubt we'd exchanged more than fifty words. Up until now all we'd had was a waving and smiling acquaintance. We'd wished each other a Happy Christmas and followed this up with a card through the letterbox, using our house numbers as identification. We'd clapped on our doorsteps for the NHS and so on. We had a nodding acquaintance, but we'd never really spoken. And he had never been inside my house, as I had never been inside his. He was an inch or two taller than me with thinning blonde hair, a pale, rather unhealthy-looking complexion, watery blue eyes and a thin, anxious, questioning mouth with moist pink lips. In fact, I quickly realized, I didn't even know his Christian name.

'Mr F—'

'Robert,' he inserted quickly, looking behind him as though he didn't want anyone to see him enter. 'My name is Robert.'

His voice was slightly high-pitched but there was no affectation about him. Nothing camp. He looked me in the eye, gave a ghost of a smile. 'And I know your name.' He gave a little hint at a giggle next. 'I should think everyone in Stone knows *your* name, Florence.'

I nodded, deciding to take this as a compliment rather than an insult or a reminder that someone really didn't like my name. I was about to ask him what he'd seen last night but I didn't get the chance. He filled the gap in quickly and neatly. 'You must be wondering what—'

I nodded.

His smile widened by a few more millimetres. 'Can I come in?'

I stood back.

Once inside I offered him a glass of wine. Somehow I sensed this might be an extended conversation. He perched on the edge of my sofa not quite looking at his ease. 'The police have taken a statement from me. They called in today.'

I nodded, pleased that Pants had followed up on his promise.

But his next statement was not so welcome. 'I didn't really see anything except . . . The alarm woke me. I heard glass smashing. I wasn't asleep anyway. I was . . .'

Mark had always told me that witnesses muddled everything up. I prompted him, trying to encourage him to put his jumbled thoughts in some sort of chronological order by combining a sympathetic look with an encouraging smile. 'So you weren't asleep.'

Again, he foiled me. 'No.' His eyes darted around the room as he blinked rapidly. I got the impression this part of his story was upsetting him. 'I was worried about . . .' He changed this to: 'Was thinking about . . . a situation.'

I got it. He gave me a watery, apologetic smile. 'I was trying to work things out.'

He collected himself with a deep, brave breath in. 'I heard the glass shatter.' He followed this up with a smile. 'At least windscreen glass is strengthened, isn't it, so it doesn't really shatter. It sort of crackles, doesn't it?'

I nodded.

'By the time I actually got out of the window she was walking away quickly.'

'*She?*' I held my breath. She? Had I been wrong – it wasn't Evans?

'Yes. Didn't I say? It looked like a woman. You know, the general shape, the way she walked. Plump hips.' He looked at me anxiously. 'You do believe me, don't you?'

I nodded. 'It's just not what I'd expected. That's all.'

'She was wearing a hoodie and tracksuit bottoms, trainers.'

She would. I knew exactly who it was now and why the warning to back off. Vivian, pregnant, vulnerable, maybe sensing Mark hadn't quite left his past behind. I'd met her at various dinners. I knew the way she walked. I could picture the plump hips with their exaggerated sway from side to side. Vivian. Who else?

'I hope I've helped.'

I nodded, wanting to say I wasn't sure, that maybe he had helped. 'I hope your . . . situation resolves.'

This time it was he who shrugged, his expression pessimistic, mouth turned down, and he gave a great big sigh. Then another watery smile. 'I wish I could have given a better description.'

'Thanks,' I said.

And I meant it. Robert Ford took a long sip of wine and I thought he'd be leaving soon, but he set the glass down on the coffee table with a firmness that told me he had more to say.

THIRTY-THREE

He scooped in a breath deep enough to sustain him in a dive from an Olympic high board before asking me if I could be discreet.

I tried to laugh it off as part of the job but inwardly I was concerned. Particularly when he half whispered, 'It's really private,' and moved in closer to me. My heart sank. Oh no, I thought. He's got piles or an STD.

'It's important you keep it to yourself.' His hand was on my arm now, grasping it in drowning-man desperation.

I used my tried and tested advice, saying gently, 'Robert, if it's personal shouldn't you be booking in to see your doctor?'

He looked a bit bemused at this then shook his head vigorously as he followed my train of thought. 'Oh no, it's nothing like that.' His face went a bit pink. 'It's not about *me.*'

Now it was *I* who was embarrassed. 'Sorry,' I said quickly. 'Sorry.'

'It's about Nora.'

Now it was I who was all ears.

I couldn't work out what was coming next. Was this going to be a confession – or what? He sat on the edge of the chair, leaning forward, his hands on his knees and speaking earnestly but avoiding looking at me. 'I know I can trust you, Florence. I suppose you have to make a confidentiality promise, like doctors?'

'Sort of,' I said with a reluctant nod while feeling my shoulders stiffen in preparation for whatever was coming.

'I have a friend,' he began.

And this has what to do with Nora Selleck?

But this information had thrown me into a dilemma. Was he expecting me to congratulate him? Make him realize I understood his secret meaning, like the thumb press of a Mason's handshake? I simply gave a bland smile and said . . . nothing.

His eyes flickered over me, checking I'd deciphered his tacit meaning. I gave him an encouraging smile and waited for his full confession, unable yet to fit Nora into the narrative.

Robert Ford was sending me secret messages with his eyebrows, checking I'd understood his coded information. 'He hasn't come out. He's still in the closet.' And all I thought was why? Same sex couples are as accepted as mixed sex couples these days. No one cares or judges anymore. It's not even a talking point. I shrugged, a sort of bodily, So what?

'He's married.'

I frowned at that, still not understanding his meaning until he spelt it out.

'He's in a hetero marriage.'

Now I understood.

Robert looked at the floor and muttered. 'He has children.' His face was sullen with resentment.

Again, I nodded, trusting this would lead back to Nora somehow. Again, he drew in a deep breath, right to the bottom of his lungs like my COPD patients trying to impress me with their lung function test results.

'He's a solicitor,' Robert said carefully, while now my mind was skittering through any solicitors I knew. *Which one?* A question I did not ask but kept my eye on him.

'He's been worried about a client of his . . .' And with his next words I felt myself tumble backwards into the abyss I had recently climbed out of.

'Mrs Selleck.'

And now it was I who was scooping in long breaths, desperate for more oxygen. I felt dizzy as I tried to guess the rest.

'It was about her will,' Robert said. 'I said I'd have a word with you, find out if she was mentally sound.' He stopped himself. 'You see, my friend was concerned she was being coerced and said he wasn't sure about changing the text of her will. But now she's . . .' He didn't have to finish the sentence.

'When was this?'

'A month or two ago.'

I understood something now. And it explained why Jack had found his mother's current account in order. Evans hadn't just planned to drain her bank account. *This* had been the plan, to persuade her into leaving everything to him. He was upping his game, but it was a clumsy move. It wouldn't have worked. Had Nora been declared 'not in her right mind' or else having been 'coerced' into changing her will, Jack could easily have contested it – and won. Worth a try? I doubted it and I'd flushed him out with the suspicions I'd shared liberally around the surgery. I would even have Kelly Spears' professional opinion. I sat back, feeling my face warm. Wishing more than ever that we could have admitted Nora to the hospital and kept her safe. Instead of which . . . that vision, cold, wet and frightened, drifted across my mind like the moving picture outside a car window.

'Was anyone with her when she altered her will?'

Robert shook his head regretfully.

Oh, clever, clever. Ben Evans to sit outside and wait while she did his bidding.

'Did . . . your friend . . .' I used the phrase eggshell delicately. 'Did he query the change with her?'

'Oh, yes.' Robert's face changed, became animated. 'He was

reluctant to sign it off and suggested a cooling-off period. But, of course, now . . .'

And I felt some sympathy for this couple who could not be open with the world about their relationship. Like, initially, Mark and Vivian, I added sourly to myself. 'He wondered if he could have a word with you? Give him an idea of her mental state.'

'Too late,' I said.

He acknowledged that with a nod. 'I should have spoken to you earlier. Before . . .' He looked crestfallen and I had some sympathy with him. He'd 'come out'. Only to me, it was true, but it had been an act of bravery, considering the circumstances. He couldn't have known how I would react.

People can be unpredictable and it wasn't only his secret. It was someone else's, someone who would risk losing all if this leaked out.

Robert Ford had taken me into his confidence because he'd known Nora was my patient. I felt I owed him something back. Maybe professional advice? 'Your friend,' I said. 'Maybe his family will understand better than you – or he – think. Sometimes families have an inkling . . .' I was tempted to say, 'like your wife'. Except my hands were tied by another pair of handcuffs: professional integrity. But from the way he looked at me I wondered if his wife had shared the contents of our consultation. And so I left it at that. Robert Ford had nothing more to give me. We both rose, knowing the conversation was at an end. We had said what we'd needed to say.

When he'd left I had a few things to mull over. I hadn't recognized how powerful Evans's hold had been over my patient. But I should have. Something else nibbled at my mind. Charles's bald statement that he'd seen Nora kiss Ben Evans. Had it been any other four-year-old I would not have believed the statement. But his mother was right. He did not lie; neither, I felt now, had he been mistaken. Frustratingly I felt I now held all the facts in my hand. But I wasn't able to thread them together.

Worse, I saw my role in subsequent events only too clearly. By my clumsy attempts at intervention I'd succeeded in alerting Evans, forcing him into a corner. I had another hard fact now and was tempted to speak to Jack about it. I should alert him. But I didn't know how to supply him with all these facts without distressing him further. He might find all out. But later when, perhaps, his mother might be able to explain? Fine hope. He was the one who would be affected. So now I had another unpalatable fact to throw into the mix. Robert Ford had left me with a dilemma. But once again I couldn't reveal my source, and if I shared this with DC Summers it wouldn't take much longer than the blink of an eye for him to find the solicitor, who would just as quickly trace the source back to his friend and thence to me. Robert had trusted me. He wanted this 'friendship' to remain under the radar, The will hadn't been signed off, and even if it had, Jack could and would have successfully contested it. If that was Evans's plan it was certain it would fail.

I had another little point to think about. There was only one woman who could possibly hate me enough to smash my car windscreen which takes a great deal of force. Should I point the police in the right direction? And then where would her career go? Right down the chute. Yet again, I felt a waft of pity for her.

On the plus side my car had been returned and sat proudly on the drive, its windscreen pristine, polished and ready to go. A note inside informed me that my insurance had covered the cost. Yay. Even better. Of course there was a tiny warning tucked in. That if it happened a second time within a year the company would not be so generous.

Maybe it was time I cleared out the garage and found some space to keep my vehicle and insurance premium safe. Just until things quietened down a bit.

THIRTY-FOUR

Friday 9 July, 8.15 a.m.

The morning began with a shock.

It was my habit to switch the radio on to Radio Stoke in the morning, get up to speed with the local news as I drank my coffee, showered and had breakfast. I listened with half an ear while I carried out my morning ablutions and tucked into muesli. There were the usual road closures, problems with the M6 and then the headlines, national before local, of which I only heard the first one. I heard it as though it was written in bold type, drawing my attention.

'Police looking for missing pensioner Nora Selleck have found a body.'

I stared at the radio, willing the words to be swallowed back into the device. Then I listened hard.

'No details have yet been released.'

My finger was shaking as I pressed DC Summers' number on my phone. It went straight through to answerphone. No surprise there. He'd be busy. I left a shaky, confused message asking him to ring me, hearing fear in my voice. I kept the radio on during the drive to work, craning for more details, one question banging away in my skull.

Is it Nora? Is it Nora? Is it Nora? I blinked away picture after picture of her body naked, clothed, covered, buried, drowned, strangled, starved to death, exposed, dying by omission, the cruellest death of all. Neglect. My patient. My responsibility dying of neglect. There was no more detail on the radio and DC Summers hadn't called back by the time I started my surgery and struggled to focus on the morning patients' seemingly endless, minor problems. Out of desperation I even tried Jack's number, thinking that surely he would have been the first one to be informed if his mother's body had been found? I would be very much an afterthought, somewhere caught in the slipstream of phone calls, radio interviews and formal statements. But my call to Jack also went straight through to answerphone. Boiling up the kettle for my morning coffee I ran the gauntlet of looks of sympathy and knew the news had spread, that their thoughts were probably tracking along the same cinder path as mine, that I was, to some extent, not only involved, but tortuously to blame. We all waited for news.

Coffee in hand, I headed back to the sanctuary of my clinic room, closed the door behind me, logged back into my computer and slumped into my chair without summoning my next patient or checking my emails. I hardly needed confirmation but waited for details feeling sick at the thought of what she might have suffered, alone, unloved, neglected, believing all of us had failed her. What might her last thoughts have been? I must have sat for ten, fifteen minutes like that, paralysed by the images passing through my mind. I could hardly lift my finger to press the buzzer for my first patient. Another one I might fail.

But as luck would have it my first and second patients were a couple in their sixties who had attended for holiday vaccination advice. They were bouncy, happy and terribly excited. They were heading for Australia to see their son and daughter-in-law and meet their new grandchild for the first time. They slid photo after photo across the screen of their mobile phones and yes, the tiny baby looked a dear little thing. I checked their tetanus status and gave them each a Hepatitis A jab. Their excitement and happiness was infectious. And so life goes on, I reflected, as I filled in the computer records of the injections I'd just given and then tidied up ready for the next patient.

But hesitated.

The pictures of the newborn had naturally turned my thoughts back to Mark and Vivian, who had demonstrated her insecurity and fear by the pathetic phone call, which I now attributed to her, and the windscreen smashing incident. I wondered how *they* would feel when they looked at *their* baby for the first time. Surely Mark would soften? But he was in his mid-fifties and prone to selfishness. I'd always felt that Vivian's attention had been more of a coup than true love. But then what did I know? His version had put the blame fairly and squarely on her shoulders.

Before I pressed my buzzer for the next patient my phone rang, and when I responded DC Summers' calm voice was on the other end. He listened to my rantings of guilt and anguish and then I realized he'd actually said nothing, so I went quiet and listened instead.

'The body we've found isn't that of your patient, Florence. It's a man.' I felt relief and consternation at the same time so didn't respond but took some deep, thankful breaths, while staying quiet.

'Did you hear me?'

'Sorry. Yes. So who is it?'

'We don't know for definite but suspect it's a suicide, someone who was under the auspices of the Mental Health Team. It's a tragedy, Florence, but it's not *your* tragedy.'

I didn't know whether I was relieved or my anxiety had compounded. The truth? I felt numb and was still digesting the fact that we still didn't know what had happened to my patient. I thanked DC Summers and was just about to end the call when he said, very gently, very kindly, 'We think we're getting somewhere, Florence, but I can't tell you any more than that. I'm sorry.'

'I understand.'

But really inside I was teeming with questions. In what direction were their enquiries heading? Into Evans, his true identity, his past? The doppelganger with different tattoos but the same crime? Had they tracked him down? Found him? Did they have any idea what had happened to Nora? Where she was?

'Good.' I sensed he was smiling. I could hear it in his voice even now. 'I know it's pointless repeating the fact that you are not responsible and reassuring you that we will find your patient, but take it as said.' There was a brief pause which he followed speaking quietly, as though he didn't want anyone to hear. 'We have an address. It is being watched. You need to let us do our job now.'

I couldn't stop the acerbic comment. 'You seem to be dragging your feet.'

'It might seem like that, but I can promise we are working as quickly and as safely as possible. There's more than your patient at stake here.'

So I thanked him again, though for what I couldn't imagine. Like me he was just doing his job though I hoped he was making a better job of it than I.

I finished my morning's work, still in a state of anxiety and agitation, and at twelve o'clock in walked Jalissa, Charles trailing behind her. He strutted into the room and fixed on me, chin up, his posture, as always, erect and fearless. I sensed he had something to say. But it was his mother who spoke initially. 'You wantin' sandwiches today or that detective man goin' to bring them for you?' Her eyes were sparkling with mischief. Nothing escaped the numerous eyes which would have watched

my lunchtime 'tryst' with DC Summers. And since my divorce
many of my colleagues had been dying to fix me up with a
romance.

'Cheese and pickle, I think, Jalissa,' I said, with a shred of
dignity.

She put them down on my desk. 'And you wantin' a cake?'

'I don't think so.'

'Very wise.' And now she was laughing. 'Men like a little bit
of flesh but not too much, my Florence.'

Charles's eyes flicked from me to his mother. 'That man that
kissed the lady . . . I saw him in the ice-cream van too.'

Another bombshell. 'What?' It had come out sharper than
I'd meant.

Charles's face crumpled and Jalissa took over. 'When was
that, little fella? Was it before or after you had that' – her eyes
were gleaming and her tongue licked right around her lips –
'delicious strawberry ice cream?'

He nodded.

'May Bank Holiday,' she translated.

Charles smiled. A little boy's self-satisfied smile at being
listened to and believed. 'I was licking it when I saw him.'

'In the van?'

'Yes.'

Jalissa turned back to me. 'In the park,' she said.

A thought entered my mind.

I hunkered back down again. 'Was *he* selling ice cream?'

I couldn't work out why Charles seemed unable to respond to
this. He was frowning, trying to work it out. Then he licked his
lips, perhaps recalling the taste of a strawberry ice cream on
a hot day. He shook his head slowly. 'No, but he was in the
van. I saw the snake when he passed the chocolate flake to
the ice-cream man.'

I felt suddenly anxious for the little boy. 'Did he see you
look?'

Charles shook his head decisively.

I met his mother's eyes. She had her hand on the little boy's
shoulders. 'Why you did not tell me before?'

'Because I forgot.'

At which point Charles reverted to the little boy he really

was and tugged her arm. 'When can we have another strawberry ice cream?'

'Maybe this very weekend,' Jalissa said. 'Because you, boy, have just earned yourself a giant cone of strawberry ice cream with two flakes.'

Charles's eyes were big and round at the thought. And his smile stretched from ear to ear.

THIRTY-FIVE

I knew this would lead somewhere. I rang DC Summers, who listened very attentively to my words before asking questions which checked on time, date and anything else. As I'd anticipated he took Jalissa's number and promised to call her. I felt optimistic. The net around Ben Evans was slowly closing. I whispered to myself and beyond, to her, *We will find you, Nora. Soon we will find you.*

But as I related my information, I realized he'd gone quiet and waited.

'Are you at the surgery?'

'Yes.'

'Can I call round?'

'Of course.' I felt a snatch of worry. 'Detective Summers,' I said. 'What is it?'

'I'd rather tell you face-to-face. I'll be with you in under ten minutes.'

I felt sick as I waited for him. Jalissa's sandwiches sat on my desk but I couldn't face them.

He was with me in a little more than ten minutes and I could tell when I opened my door to him that whatever he had to say it wasn't good news.

He closed the door behind him and sat in the chair to the side of my desk.

'I don't want you to read too much into this,' he began.

My mouth was too dry to ask what 'this' was.

'We haven't worked out the significance of it.'

'What?'

'The DNA recovered from The Beehive doesn't match with the DNA recovered from any of the other properties connected with this scam.'

I jumped to the obvious conclusion I'd been struggling with. 'There are two of them.'

DC Summers had very nice soft brown eyes. Perhaps in another story they might have been described as cow-brown eyes. They held kindness and honesty as he smiled at me. 'We're not concluding anything particular about this,' he said. 'All we know is that the DNA left behind by the man calling himself "Evans" is not a match to the DNA recovered from the scenes at any of the other elderly ladies' houses.'

'The man in the ice-cream van?'

'We'll look into that,' he said. 'We have a register of ice-cream vendors so can hopefully track down the one who supplied' – his face warmed as he laughed – 'your little boy's strawberry cone complete with Cadbury's flake.'

In spite of the circumstances I smiled too. 'What I don't understand, DC Summers . . .'

'My friends call me Will,' he put in gently, his eyes asking the question. *Are you a friend?*

I smiled, not quite sure myself, and continued with my narrative. 'The fact that Charles saw her kiss him . . . That doesn't make any sense at all.' And nothing else did. The link between the coercion of the other women had seemed so certain. And the role of the Hudsons? I couldn't work that out either.

'Not so far,' he said. 'I assure you we will find the answers to all the questions but, as you probably realize, it takes time.'

'Time she might not have,' I urged. Then: 'Have you shared this with Jack?'

'I've spoken to him.'

'What does *he* make of it all?'

'Puzzled, like everyone else. Florence, we're working as quickly as we can. We will find these guys and put a stop to them. But every time we think we have an answer we're proved wrong.'

'I get that.'

We both stood up and again Will smiled at me. 'We're doing our best. The net is closing around them. We have an address but we don't yet have all the facts. And we need hard evidence that will stand up in court. For that we need to wait. We want a conviction. You have no idea how many officers are employed in this horrible case, so you can trust us.'

I put a hand on his arm. 'Just find her,' I urged. 'Bring her home.' I felt tears fill my eyes and turned away. He waited for a moment then left.

When my phone rang at one thirty it was Jack sounding calmer than when I'd last seen him. 'Did you ring this morning?'

'I did.'

'DC Summers has been on the line too.'

'So you know.'

'Not that it makes any sense.'

I tried to cheer him up. 'I think they have a few leads. They'll soon find your mum, Jack.'

'You think?'

I was glad he'd used the word, 'think'.

'What do you make of this latest development?'

'Two of them in cahoots, surely?'

'Looks like it.'

'Not bringing my mum back though.'

I wasn't sure whether to share Charles's observation, but he needed some good news, so when I told him about the will, I emphasized that it hadn't been signed off.

His response was much as I'd anticipated. Initially confused. 'I just don't get that at all.' And then angry. 'Is that a measure of how much he'd duped her?'

I made my response cautious. 'Possibly.'

Scenarios swirled around in my mind, like oil paints neither blending nor mixing nor even forming a discernible pattern. Not yet. As we drew closer to finding Nora, we were at the same time confounded with yet another fact that did not seem to fit any narrative.

Jack was still absorbed in his anger. 'As a con artist he just about takes the bloody biscuit,' Jack spluttered. But now his anger was joined with sourness against both Evans and his mother. 'What's going on, Florence? What the hell . . .? What was she playing at? Can this all be put down to dementia or missing her medication?'

My response was cautious.

I couldn't bear to fall back on the police versions or hide behind clichés to 'let the police do their best', that they would 'find their way through this tangle and soon locate his mother'. I realized now, with a shock, I wasn't convinced the police would find the answers – not all of them. Because there was an element only I had access to: my erstwhile colleague, Catherine Zenger and Dr Gubb. They knew something that would, perhaps, unlock a vital part of this investigation.

I reverted to nurse mode. 'How *are* you, Jack?'

'Conflicted,' he admitted. 'I'm trying to be two people at once. Grieving son, wanting to know . . .' His voice trailed away to nothing before coming back stronger with more than a hint of cynicism. 'And responsible banker making decisions that affect people's money. Money,' he added bitterly. 'All they care about, and it is the last thing on my mind right now.'

Which made me realize that both of us had had our priorities and preconceptions shifted. I wanted to change them back, to say something to the effect that he needed his job, the career he'd worked so hard for, as I did mine, but the words desiccated in my throat. I couldn't say them. I couldn't comfort either of us and take us back to the place where we had valued our careers and felt proud at our qualifications and achievements.

There was a dark, brooding silence which I broke. 'Well, I'd better get back to my patients.' It was only when we'd both ended the call that I realized how crass and stupidly cheery I must have sounded.

But my mind was also burrowing back into the past, remembering something Catherine had said, or rather hinted at.

As always any of her stories could be just that, the result of long, empty days after a challenging and rewarding career where she had felt valued and listened to. But buried deep in the centre could always be a nugget of gold, a truth.

THIRTY-SIX

6 p.m.

hadn't warned her I was coming but had decided to surprise her. There was no rationale behind this except that I didn't want to give her a chance to dream up a new story or embellish an old one.

She did look surprised to see me but pleased as well. 'Florence,' she exclaimed when she opened the door. 'Why didn't you tell me you were coming?'

I lied. 'Spur of the moment thing.'

She hugged me. 'Well, it was an excellent idea. Quite inspired.' But as I followed her into her flat, I got the distinct impression that she wasn't fooled by my weak explanation and knew exactly why I was here.

'You're lucky,' she said. 'I've baked a cake.'

'Mmm.' I smacked my lips as she produced a rich looking chocolate cake and filled the kettle. 'Cup of tea?'

'Lovely.'

'This is delicious.' In truth the cake was so rich it was almost sickly. I needed the tea to wash it down.

Catherine watched me. 'A bar and a half of cooking chocolate, darling. And that's just in the icing.'

I managed another 'Mmm' before I realized she was watching me, waiting for me to speak. She knew I hadn't come on spec but had an agenda.

Time for me to come clean.

'Catherine, you hinted at something about Nora.'

Now she was watchful.

'What was it?'

She was biting her lip as I told her the latest development in Nora's disappearance.

'Little Charles,' she said speculatively. 'That's interesting.'

'It indicates affection between this Evans guy and Nora. And that I can't explain.'

Then I waited.

Catherine loved to be the centre of gossip. I was sure she would spill the beans if I waited. So I did until she did that thing that gossips do: eyes bright, shoulders tensed, she leaned forward.

'I did her cervical smear,' she said. 'Years ago.'

That puzzled me.

'As you well know, Florrie, you have to take an obstetric history.'

And then I did see it – the last piece fitting into a jigsaw puzzle, completing the picture.

'She'd had two pregnancies.'

'A miscarriage?'

'Two children.'

'But there was only Jack.'

'She'd had a child before she was married. She'd had it adopted. A little girl.'

I still couldn't stitch this together. I had asked Dr Gubb about this very question, whether there had been something in Nora's distant medical history. And now I remembered his response. *Nothing that could have any bearing on Mrs Selleck's current predicament.* Now I reflected on that statement and the way his gaze had flickered away from mine. Evasion.

But now Catherine had leaked this story, she pressed on. 'She was adamant that I told no one. She was terribly ashamed, you see.'

'It was in her notes,' I objected.

'Which remain confidential. She was desperate that Peter never found out.'

'And Jack,' I mused.

Catherine nodded.

I was puzzled. 'How old was Nora when this happened?'

Catherine shrugged. 'I don't know. Maybe a teenager?'

I was working it out. She would have been a teenager in the fifties. If Evans was, in some way, related to this child, he must be a grandson or even a great-grandson. What had Ryan said, something about Evans living with an old lady?

Catherine was still watching me, and I summoned up

appropriate responses. '*We-ell*,' I said, injecting shock and horror into my voice. 'I'd never have guessed.'

'So do you think this has any bearing on . . .?'

'I don't know. Maybe.' We looked at each other, trying to work it out but failing.

We chatted for a while, gossiping through more of our patients' secrets, and then she hinted at something that really did intrigue me.

'I always wondered,' she said, 'about Dr Gubb's father.'

I leaned in. 'Really?'

'He always seemed a bit . . . awkward around Nora.'

'Awkward?'

She shrugged. 'It was probably nothing.'

Possibly it was, but . . . Could there be more to Gubb's reluctance to see Nora, to brush my concerns under the carpet? My mind was racing overtime, but as I couldn't yet fit him into the current narrative I pushed it to the back of my mind.

She saw me to the door. 'Come again, Florrie,' she said. 'Please?'

I promised her I would.

But now I had a quandary. The rules of professional integrity rely on nurses (and doctors, et cetera) keeping secrets that they have purely because of their position. A little like the priest's confessional. But there are exceptions when either the person or the general public are at risk. In this case the professional is released from their obligation. I could have discussed this with the Royal College of Nurses but I worried that this would simply delay matters. And I felt that delay, in this case, could be fatal for my patient, if she was still alive. Therefore, I decided, I would take matters into my own hands, rely on my own judgement and speak to DC Will Summers.

I rang him and he picked up straight away.

'I need to speak to you.' Quite unfairly, I added, 'In confidence.'

Many men or officers would have turned this into a joke, teased me about trusting them or rather not trusting them. Not DC Summers. 'OK,' he said in his steady, balanced voice. 'Where do you want to meet?'

I had to think about this and trust him. 'Can you come to my house? In about half an hour?'

That would give me time to tidy the house and myself up.
'Sure.'

I gave him my address and headed for home.

He turned up in a squad car. That would set tongues wagging
around the cul-de-sac but I did have a fallback story. I could
pretend to eyes that might be watching that the visit was
connected with the vandalism on my car. He walked in tentatively, looking around at the room. 'Heard about your trouble
the other night,' he said. Maybe he'd noted that there was no
car in the drive.

'I use the garage now,' I said. 'And that's alarmed.'

'Very wise. Any idea who decided to test your windscreen
insurance policy?' His face was light and bright and friendly.
Maybe he realized I pretty well knew who had bashed my car in.

'I have an idea,' I said, 'but that isn't why I asked you to
come round.'

'OK.'

He waited.

I told him the story Catherine Zenger had given me, adding
a caveat. 'She often exaggerates stories,' I said, 'and is an
inveterate gossip.'

He looked a little troubled at this. 'But she wouldn't have
made the whole thing up, would she?'

'I don't think so.' I felt bound to add, 'Not in this instance
anyway.'

'Should be easy enough to check up on it.'

I let my face relax. 'I hoped you'd say that. But . . .' I hesitated. 'You realize this child would be in her fifties or sixties
now, possibly even her seventies, maybe a grandparent herself.'

'Yes.'

'So what's the connection with Mr "Ben Evans"?'

He hesitated. 'I have news for you. And it fits in with what
you've just told me.'

I shifted forward on the sofa. 'You remember I mentioned that
we had the DNA of the person who had committed the previous
crimes against elderly women?'

I nodded.

'And that it wasn't matching Evans's DNA?'

I nodded again.

'Well, it appears that there is some consanguinity.'

'You mean . . .?'

'I'm no expert.' DC William Summers was smiling, almost merry as he confessed. 'I had to get one of the junior biologists to spell it out for me. It's possible that the man calling himself Evans and our perpetrator of the other crimes are half-brothers, or maybe stepbrothers.'

He waited for me to digest this information before his smile vanished and he looked deadly serious. 'I've told you this is an ongoing police investigation.'

I nodded, tensed up.

'We have a date for the raid.'

'About bloody time. I can't think why the delay.'

'We had our reasons. This was part of a bigger picture.'

'And in the meantime, Nora was at risk.'

DC Summers was instantly on his guard. 'You're not to . . .'

'Let me come along?' I pleaded. 'She'll be frightened. Maybe ill. A familiar face might be critical.'

'No, Florence. Absolutely not. This drugs raid has been months in the planning. We had to cooperate with the Potteries police. We couldn't risk anything that might endanger its success.'

'But . . .' I was trying my best. 'A familiar face.'

'No.'

I didn't seem to be convincing DC Summers, so I switched emphasis. 'Does Jack know?'

He shook his head, then followed that up with: 'And he mustn't know. I've only told you because you've been closely connected from the start and because' – the smile was back – 'you've done your best firstly to try and prevent this sort of scenario and then to protect Mrs Selleck as best you could.' It seemed strange to hear Nora described as Mrs Selleck. But, of course, to the police, that was who she was – an anonymous widow in her eighties. Just a name. It was I who had a fuller picture, of a married woman with a professional career, a husband and a son, as well as possessing energy, aspirations, imagination. Something else struck me.

'You say there's consanguinity between the two men,' I said slowly, not even sure I wanted to hear the truth. 'What about Nora? Is there a link there?'

'We don't have that result yet,' he said. 'In fact, it's pretty amazing the lab have got where they are. It's the equivalent of wearing roller skates.'

I smiled and waited for a direct response to my appeal.

'Florence.' He met my eyes and responded. 'You can't possibly be part of a police raid.'

I was silent. Because I knew that nothing was going to stop me. I knew the address from Ryan and his mates, and I had plans. I would be there. If my patient was going to be part of a dawn raid, which Mark had described to me in the past in graphic detail – shouting, weapons, face masks, noise and bewilderment – I was going to be there to put my arms around her and reassure her. I might have failed her in the past, but I was not ever going to fail her again.

DC Summers was watching me suspiciously but neither of us said anything more.

I sidled past the subject, returning to safer angles. 'If Ben Evans . . . By the way, is that his real name?'

DC Summers relaxed. 'His name is Scott. But his surname really is Evans.'

I continued along the same vein. 'If Scott Evans is a blood relative down the generations, would he want to harm her?'

DC Summers shrugged. 'Who knows,' he said. 'Probably whether Mrs Selleck is a blood relation or not, the main object was to drain away her money and even, rather audaciously, try and persuade her, through conscience, to leave her property to her "rightful" heir. It was a high-risk strategy,' he added quickly, before I could point out my objections.

But I was past that. I was thinking about the apparent anomalies and realizing now that some of them fitted.

Will Summers gave me that honest, steadying look. Then he stood up. 'I should go,' he said. 'There's a lot to be done.'

I was dying to ask him if he'd like a drink or . . .

Don't be pathetic, I lectured myself and forced a smile.

As he reached my front door he hesitated and held out his hand. 'I hope we have a happy outcome,' he said, smiling now. 'And whatever happens, don't feel any of this is your fault.' Unconsciously he echoed Gillian Angelo's sentiments if not the words. '*None* of this is your fault,' he said. 'But then the more decent a person is the more they blame themselves for other people's crimes. You did your best. You tried to alert two doctors to the precariousness of your patient's position. You tried.'

'And it wasn't enough.'

He didn't say anything more but shook his head firmly.

Then he left.

THIRTY-SEVEN

After the windscreen episode I'd worried for a while that Vivian would return with heightened vengeance and watchfulness. I'd been putting my car in the garage, which was alarmed, locking my doors at night as well as bolting them and getting up a couple of times through the night to check I really had locked them. I'd been putting my house alarm on to cover the downstairs and taking my mobile phone to bed with me – fully charged. I'd gradually relaxed.

But that Friday night I knew that the police would soon be raiding the house in Bentilee and I intended being there. The question was when should I head for the Potteries? I couldn't live in my car for days on end, but no one was going to tell me exactly when the raid was planned for. So all I could do was sit and wait and maybe make some forays into Bentilee's housing estate. Surely, I'd reasoned, there would be some way of anticipating when the attack was likely to happen? Until then I had to play the waiting game.

It was almost midnight and I felt wakeful and anxious. I was in my bedroom, cleaning and repainting my toenails, when something triggered a memory. I sat quite still, trying to identify the source. For a moment I was flummoxed. I closed my eyes and tried to think. Which was when I realized. Almost without it registering, my hand had reached out to pick up the bottle of nail varnish remover. Acetone. I sniffed it. And then it came flooding back to me. It was as I'd squeezed past him, the time when he'd almost blocked the doorway so I'd been inches from him. I'd tried to hold my breath against the inevitable beer, sweat and cigarettes that was his signature scent. But I'd been forced to breathe in and had caught a whiff of another scent. I sniffed the bottle again. The acetone was very faint and overlaid by the stronger one of beer and cigarettes as well as a T-shirt sticky with sweat, but it was one I recognized. Rare, it was true. But as I put together known facts about him I made a link too. Diabetes is not exactly hereditary but the tendency does run in families. While Nora had not been a diabetic, I had warned her that she was in a pre-diabetic state and should moderate her diet to foods with a low glycaemic index. If Ben/Scott Evans really was Nora's great-grandson, it fitted together like a perfectly made musical instrument, singing out to me. Fact one: he was in his late thirties or early forties. Fact two: he was overweight if not morbidly obese. The obesity was central. Ben/Scott Evans was a diabetic type 2. Possibly even on insulin. It was unusual to have keto acidosis in type 2 diabetes but fact three slotted in, again, perfectly. Alcohol. Which destabilizes the blood sugar and can cause spikes, leading to events of keto acidosis which causes the body to burn fats instead of glucose. And when this metabolic state happens the breath smells like acetone, the same substance that is found in nail varnish. Nora never wore nail varnish. 'Too busy wrecking my nails with the gardening to draw attention to their ragged state by painting them.' I could hear her saying the words and felt a wave of grief, remembering the exact circumstances. She'd made this comment on my fingernails which I'd had manicured and painted scarlet ready for a party. And we'd chuckled together, sharing the fun. I could see her hands too, in front of me, long-fingered and beautiful in my eyes, with a small lump of a ganglion on her right wrist. 'It needs smashing with the Holy Bible,' she'd said, and I'd joked back that doing that would probably get a doctor struck off these days. It was typical of the sort of banter we'd shared and which I'd not really had with any other patient.

And now I saw, or thought I saw, a link between her, her conscience, her anxiety to keep secrets and Evans. I revisited that moment as I'd passed him in the hallway which now was burning in my memory, beacon-like, pointing the way forward. But how could I use it to my advantage? I sat and plotted. The police might have manpower and many disciplines at their finger-tips, but I was the one with medical knowledge plus an intimate understanding of my patient. Nora was, or rather had been, a robust personality. I knew now how and why Evans had gained such a fishhook of a hold over her. There was even an explanation of Charles witnessing that kiss. So another part of the puzzle was solved. Nora hadn't been brainwashed. Her actions were completely in line with her character – deeply moral, with a strong sense of justice.

I forced myself to squeeze out every single little thing I knew about Evans. Searched for any similarity between Nora and the man who was probably claiming to be her great-grandson. And found nothing. No resemblance at all.

Evans had a strong Potteries accent. So, if he was Nora's great grandson, the fledgling had not fallen far from the nest. Which was the root of the trouble. He had tracked Nora down. Possibly through curiosity, probably with little difficulty. And if this person who shared 'some consanguinity' was having success in his venture, maybe Evans had been persuaded to join the family business – with an added dimension.

THIRTY-EIGHT

Saturday 10 July, 8 a.m.

I'd thought I might have heard something from DC Summers but my phone remained stubbornly quiet. In an effort to tire myself out I went for a walk along the canal, north towards the Potteries, but the towpath was crowded with adults, children and dogs, and there was something about the family units that made me sad – particularly when I passed a couple, the man with a baby strapped to his front. For a split second I could have believed it was Mark with Lara strapped to his chest. The sight reminded me painfully of days gone by. Days that would never be again. Not for me. But Mark would walk that walk again, with another baby strapped to his chest. And that hurt. As I reached home I still felt agitated, an overspill of energy and regret trying to direct me, but where? I was like a rat in a cage.

And part of this agitation spilled and combined with guilt about Nora which was compounding with every hour. I was convinced Nora was still alive and that each hour we failed to find her, her health was deteriorating.

I wondered if the police shared my feeling of impatience.

Then on Sunday evening, early, my phone rang. I recognized the number. I believed this call was momentous. It would be the one which would change everything. And it did.

He didn't introduce himself as if he was worried about being identified. He didn't even say hello, just simply: 'We're almost ready to move.'

And my response was relief mixed with anxiety. 'And Nora? Have you seen her?'

He didn't give me a direct answer, but continued as though someone was listening. 'We're moving ahead cautiously.'

'Do you know how she is?'

'No details – as yet.' He could have been talking to anyone.

'So when, exactly?'

'Uumm . . .' He was sounding really awkward now. 'I think tomorrow is a possibility.'

But as luck would have it my Monday morning was full and I'd arranged to attend a lunchtime meeting on a new form of injectable birth control that day (free lunch) so I couldn't do anything until after five when I'd finally seen my last patient. My anxiety was reaching its pitch by the end of the day.

He was waiting outside the surgery in a car I guessed was his own. It was a Ford Focus estate, slate grey. A quick scan revealed that it was very clean inside, no child seats or any other clues as to his personal life. Which was nothing to do with me anyway.

He didn't speak as I climbed in but gave me a very straight, scrutinizing look as though to gauge my response before he delivered his news. This was followed by a surprisingly tentative smile which I returned – with interest.

I actually had to prompt him. 'Well?'

'How about we head for a quick drink?'

'OK.' I knew he was delaying the moment when he had to break the news to me.

He had his hands on the steering wheel as he leaned back into his seat and hit the accelerator and headed up the A34 and out of Stone towards Swynnerton.

That was a surprise. I glanced across at him, wondering why there.

He parked outside The Fitzherbert and waited until we were both seated, a drink in front of us, before he spoke. 'It might be best if *you* break the more sensitive parts of the news to Jack.'

'You mean the fact that he has or had an older half-sister somewhere?'

He nodded. But I shook my head. 'I can't do that, Detective Summers. It would be breaking the—'

'Rules of confidentiality,' he chimed in, finishing with a half-smile.

Then he paused before continuing. 'We know a little more about Mr Evans,' he said. 'He's divorced and lived most of his life in Tunstall where he has an ex-partner and two small daughters.'

'And now?'

'Now he lives with his grandmother in Bentilee, a few doors away, almost opposite, in fact, to his half-brother.' He looked at me. 'Same mother – different fathers.'

'So when do you go in?'

DC Summers took a long swig of his beer before opening his mouth and then shutting it again.

Then he picked up on another strand, but not before he'd scanned the entire pub lounge to make sure no one was listening.

He leaned in. I sensed he was about to warn me off. While also realizing it was probably pointless.

'Nora . . .' His voice was gentle, almost apologetic. 'There's no sign of an elderly woman fitting Nora's description with any of them.'

'You mean you haven't actually seen her?'

He shook his head and looked away from my accusation.

'So you don't actually know she's there?'

Again, he shook his head.

'And you don't know she's actually still alive – let alone what shape she's in.'

He tried to defend himself. 'We're having to work with the

local police force. They've been setting up Scott and Kai Evans for months. I can't risk jeopardizing the operation. We don't believe Nora is in danger.'

I opened my mouth to make some sharp comment, but again he stopped me, with a hand on my arm this time. 'Listen,' he said. 'Evans – Scott Evans – is not a killer.'

'So why did they abduct her?'

He started to answer. 'We don't—'

But I cut him off. 'You can't possibly know she isn't in danger. She's vulnerable.'

'But safe.'

I was tempted to quote the 'more than one way to skin a cat' line, but the images it conjured up were too graphic, so I contented myself with a blander comment. 'Not directly.'

DC Summers dropped his gaze then.

'I just worry . . .' He was finding this difficult. 'I just think—'

And then I guessed it. 'That I flushed him out.'

DC Summers drew in a very deep breath and nodded.

'And what about the will business?'

'That,' he admitted, 'was out of character. Kai, the person who was involved in the other extortion from elderly women, had his own style. He drained their bank accounts quickly and moved on to his next victim just as quickly.'

We were both silent then, tossing around uncomfortable scenarios.

'So both brothers are involved.'

Summers nodded and seemed on firmer ground. 'We think so. We think someone else gave him that idea. Scott – or Ben – Evans is, at best, a blunt instrument. Brawn not brains. No . . .' He was shaking his head. 'Someone else put this idea into his head. Considering the attempt at getting Nora to change her will, it was probably Kai. He's the one with the financial interest. We'll soon have an idea how this whole scenario came about.'

My silent response must have registered.

'And then we'll know where Nora is.'

'Alive?' I hadn't been able to stop myself, but it resulted in a look of pain in DC Summers' soft brown eyes. Neither of us needed to say anything more.

We drained our glasses quickly and DC Summers drove me home just as quickly. I knew he was anxious for the evening to end. It was only when I put my key in the door and heard him drive off that I realized I hadn't asked the question, just as he hadn't volunteered it.

When?

THIRTY-NINE

I passed a sleepless night but for once it wasn't anything to do with Nora. Sometimes I cursed my shared wall. If I could afford it I would *not* buy a semi. Amelia (number nineteen) was wailing all through the night. I heard Eve try to soothe her, Johnny, angry. Shouting about work in the morning. Me too, I thought sourly. You're not the only one. But once a child has decided it's crying, it doesn't stop. Doors slammed. Lights flicked on and off. Our shared wall wasn't soundproofed. And as I lay there, listening to the child howling, I felt myself smile as I wondered whether Mark in his fifties would cope better with fatherhood than he had in his twenties. I suspected not. It would, at the very least, be a trying time for him – and maybe a period of revelation to Vivian. Unpleasant, I sincerely hoped, feeling sour and spiteful. But I would give her this. I'd keep schtum about the windscreen incident. When the baby came she would need her job – and my ex-husband.

Finally, at around two a.m., an uneasy silence had dropped like a velvet curtain into the night. I waited, tensely, for Amelia to start up again. Maybe she did, maybe she didn't. I don't know because I dropped off into wisps of dreams which dissolved leaving behind only their effects – agitation, happiness, grief and a feeling of dread. I felt today would be a day of revelation.

Tuesday 13 July, 6 p.m.

Without any rational sense behind my decision, when I finished work I decided to drive out to Swynnerton and parked up outside

The Beehive, which today looked abandoned, quiet, normal and a bit sad. Lonely in the bright sunshine under blue skies.

There was no sign of a forensic team anymore, or of anyone else for that matter. They must have felt they'd extracted all the evidence the cottage held. I took it all in, spending some time studying the house I'd visited on so many occasions and making a silent prayer that its owner would soon be back, hoeing the garden, baking scones for the church, listening to Radio 4, head on one side as she absorbed the news and current discussions. I'd spent many hours here, visiting frequently when Peter had been ill and just after his death; less frequently in recent years, though I'd dropped in whenever I'd been passing. It had always had an atmosphere of happiness and peace. As my eyes roved, I noticed the place looked tidier and in order. The curtains were pulled back now, laced into tiebacks. I left the car to approach the yellow front door, breathing in the scent of lavender as I brushed against the hedge. I peered in through the front window into the lounge and found everything tidy. The upset chair and little table had been righted and returned to their normal positions; the blanket had been folded and placed on the seat. I walked around the back and peered in through the kitchen window. The dishes in the rack had all been put away. And, most telling of all, a pair of pink Marigold gloves hung over the sink. I tried the door, which was locked, and when I opened the letterbox I breathed in the scent of polish, detergents and disinfectant. Though her client was absent, Katie Truman must have had clearance from the police and had come in and done her work. As a home help she was conscientious.

Without expecting any response – in fact, I would have jumped out of my skin had there been one – I called out, 'Anyone at home?'

My voice bounced back from an empty house.

I stood for a while, thinking, trying to work out the facts which seemed to contradict one another. My shadow fell across the paintwork of the front door as I analysed all that DC Summers had said. I probably didn't move for some minutes but stood still, ignoring the birds splashing around in the stone birdbath that stood in the centre of the front lawn. DC Summers was right. Evans hadn't worked this out for himself. He was a thug with little to no intelligence but he did possess a degree of cunning. I knew this because if he'd had any sense at all he wouldn't have antagonized me. He would have played the game with me too, aired the 'charm' he'd displayed to Dr Gubb. And he wouldn't have made those statements about Nora's medication either. Even the attempt at getting a will changed had been clumsy and unlikely to stand up in a court of law if challenged, which Jack was pretty well bound to do. But attempts of fraud like this sometimes took years to move through the courts and be resolved. Surely even Evans must have known this, unless . . . I shoved the thought aside. How could he possibly have thought he had a valid claim?

Was that too a sign of his stupidity or was he being clever? I couldn't work it out.

Then I realized. Someone was watching me. From across the lane Tobin Hudson was standing in his doorway, staring at me. I could feel not only their desperation for privacy but a certain vulnerability too. They wanted to stay out of this. More than that, they were frightened about being dragged into it. But living across the street had given them a ringside seat right into Nora's sitting room. They must have seen something. So what were they holding back? Why the secrecy?

I stared back.

The Hudsons were a couple with a secret, I felt. I recalled their secrecy about their antecedents when I had performed their new patient screen, their obsessive privacy, their reluctance to share their history, the fact that they had moved here, somewhere where they seemed to know nobody and nobody knew them, which I felt, instinctively, had been the real reason behind their move. They hadn't wanted to keep an eye on their elderly neighbour but had used the word 'spy', making my request sound ugly. Why? That reason surrounding Evans's help with the bins and a few neighbourly chats buying their friendship and loyalty seemed flimsy now. The answer lay somewhere else. Had they known Evans previously?

I looked harder at Tobin's face and imagined I saw him plead with me not to search too hard or play detective. His hands gave a feeble flap in mute appeal. As hard as I stared across the road, he beamed that appeal right back. But I didn't feel scared, frightened or at all threatened by his unwavering stare, but simply curious. Maybe Tobin, with his sparse hair and bent back, poor eyesight and general demeanour, was wondering about me too, seeing a nurse too nosey for her own good, who had caused a patient and her carer to go underground. I sensed that was their take on events, that some of this situation possibly was my fault, the blame partly at my door. I was tempted to cross the road and challenge him but that would do no good. Instinctively I felt I would squeeze nothing from either of the Hudsons. They were a closed book, tightly preserving their secrets.

Neither of us was smiling now, and after a moment or two more Tobin vanished inside his house and I returned to my car, still wondering. As I drove back along the A34 I wondered some more. I acknowledged I was working blind, fumbling with odd-shaped details which did not appear to lock together into any sort of picture. But in the centre was a great, big, black, empty hole. My fear was that black hole concealed a death.

I felt awful driving home. I was doing nothing except ruminating pointlessly. And then, halfway home, my mobile phone buzzed in a text.

I slowed and pulled into a layby to read it.

It consisted of one word. *Tonight*. And an address.

Instead of going straight over the roundabout I went right round it, heading north for the Potteries. I had the address in Bentilee that Ryan had given me. I needed to be there.

For those who don't know the area, stuck between two of Arnold Bennett's five towns (Hanley and Longton), Bentilee boasts the largest council estate in Europe, built in the 1950s on the fields of two farms: Bentilee Farm and Ubberley Farm. The land was acquired by the council where they built their new town, with 2,586 houses and a population of over 7,000. The Bentilee estate is a maze. Like the game where you have to try and direct a ball bearing into the centre along plastic tracks, many of which have blind endings. So finding the road made even my satnav confused. It kept telling me to 'turn around where possible'. But finally, having gone round and round, I found number thirty-seven Eton Way, the name presumably a bit of a joke on behalf of the council as many of the streets, depressing in their uniformity, were named after public schools. There was an Eton Way, a Harrow Boulevard, a Gordonstoun Crescent, Charterhouse Road and so on.

I drove along slowly, taking in all the details. Many of the houses had been bought by their tenants under Maggie Thatcher's Right to Buy Scheme and had been prettied up and individual-ized. There were cars parked tightly along the road, both sides, effectively making it a single-track highway, but I couldn't see any sign of a police presence. So they weren't watching. They weren't doing anything. I felt cheated, by DC Summers in particular. I pulled in just beyond number thirty-seven, which was the house that Ryan had thought he'd seen Evans disappear into. It looked deserted. So I shifted my attention to a house further down and noted the front door – steel. A giveaway for a house where drug dealing goes on. I smiled inwardly. Now I had an idea what Ryan Wood and his mate had been doing lurking around this area. Not sleuthing for me or pursuing romance, but on a little mission of their own. It shouldn't have surprised me that I'd paid Ryan's petrol money for a provident trip. Steel doors? Almost impossible for the police to stove in even with their famous battering ram which cost the Staffordshire Police a significant bill at the end of every year. I remembered Mark chuckling about it – police gallows humour. It reached tens of thousands of pounds and wasn't really funny, but somehow we hadn't been able to stop giggling about it. The memory was a small prick with a stiletto. Ah well, those were the days.

I pulled up a little further along and sat for a while, with my windows open, watching up and down the street, but it remained ominously still, as though waiting for something. I couldn't even detect the sound of TVs or stereos. No children playing, no barbeques in the garden, no music leaking through bedroom windows. Open to the summer evening. No movement at all. The entire street was holding its breath, watching me watching them, waiting for something to happen. I felt a prickling around my neck as I sat there. It was creepy. Like one of those disaster movies where residents have all been abducted by aliens. There were lots of houses along this road. Plenty of people lived here. Or no one at all. My eyes were drawn back to the steel door. Was Nora behind that? I looked up and down the street, searching the upstairs windows this time. One or two of them still had their curtains drawn. What or who was behind them? I wondered. Teenagers playing on their game consoles? Shift workers? Someone watching TV, working on a computer late into the night? Or was Nora somewhere inside? Frightened, bewildered and lost?

I looked for a face, house by house, window by window and still saw nothing and nobody.

Then a young man sauntered out of one of the houses and, without looking around, opened a car door and drove off, burning rubber as he accelerated. Further along the street, an elderly man was helping his partner who had a Zimmer frame on wheels. They moved at snails' paces, taking an age to reach the car, open the door, climb in, stow the walking frame, creep forward. They had emerged from the house opposite number thirty-seven. Number sixty-three.

I sat and thought, stitching together all the facts I had learned. I was unaware of anyone approaching until there was a knock at my window.

FORTY

'Florence, what on earth are you doing here?'

At first, I'd thought he was angry. Then I realized he was smiling.

'Couldn't keep away, could you?'

I felt bound to defend myself. 'I just thought I'd take a look,' I explained lamely. I felt sheepish and exposed. Then I remembered. *He* had let me know. It had seemed almost an invite.

He climbed in beside me and his face was tense. 'We're nearly there,' he said, 'but you're going to have to take a back seat. The last thing we want is for you to come barging in and expose us.'

I felt even worse. 'I hope I haven't . . . I don't want to—' I was about to say 'jeopardize', but I didn't get the chance.

'You need to leave it to us.'

'I just want to be here for her.'

He nodded and I felt compelled to press my case. 'Just tell me . . .' I looked around at the empty street. 'Have you seen her yet?'

'No.'

'So what are you waiting for?'

'Leave it to us. Please. It's our best chance.' He couldn't prevent his gaze from drifting towards the house with the steel door.

I waited for an answer to my question. He sighed. 'The local policing team,' he said and didn't need to fill in the details.

I felt beaten. Held back but I had one more card up my sleeve. 'Detective Summers,' I said tentatively, unsure whether this would work. 'Will, if Nora is in one of these houses, she's been there for almost three weeks. She'll be confused and frightened. Possibly ill. And that's if . . .' I couldn't complete the sentence, but I knew from the warmth in the detective's brown eyes that he followed my reasoning and could anticipate my request.

He nodded and for a few moments neither of us spoke. Then he nodded again. 'OK,' he said. 'But you need to move your car. These people are watchful and will have noticed a strange vehicle. And you *have* to keep out of sight. This is risky and quite against the rulebook, but you do have a point.'

I started to thank him, but he put a finger up to his lips. 'Don't thank me,' he said. 'The best you can do is not let me down. Just be there and keep quiet.'

I nodded but had to ask, 'Is Evans in there?'

'We believe Kai Evans is.'

'What about *him*?'

'You mean Scott or rather Ben?'

I nodded.

He indicated number sixty-three, the house opposite, the one where the elderly couple had emerged from. 'Let us do our job unimpeded.' He was smiling now and put a hand on my arm. 'Trust me,' he said.

He waited for me to respond but I didn't need to. I knew what was about to happen and I was here. For now, that was enough.

His hand was on the car door when he made a face.

'If I can't dissuade you,' he said, 'then I can at least advise you.'

I waited.

'Go home,' he said, 'for now. Nothing will happen until at least two a.m. Park around the corner. Don't even think of driving up this street. Wear dark clothes and do absolutely nothing. You don't interfere, you don't say anything. You don't call out. If . . .' He must have seen my face as he corrected himself. '*When* we find her you can stay with her, travel in the car with her, and if there's any medical intervention needed we may need to call the police doctor. Get it?'

I nodded and he continued.

'Otherwise, Florence, your role must be passive. Simply to stay with her. A familiar face may help.'

I felt I'd achieved something. His trust at least.

I nodded and he climbed out of the car.

FORTY-ONE

12.30 a.m.

I'd driven home, my mind a jumble of thoughts while I focused on my role. I would do my best for my patient. I ran a bath and lay back, thinking.

As nurses we like to think we heal with our soft hands, kind words, TLC and all the skills and knowledge that nursing entails. But a week into our training we are forced to recognize the truth. We have no magical powers. Nature wins every time. If Nora was critically ill there might be little I would realistically be able to do for her. She might not even recognize me. Rather than being a solution I might become part of the problem. But I would, at least, be there.

I'd lain on the sofa, dressed in jogging bottoms and a hoodie, set my alarm and tried to sleep while working out a timetable. If I set out at one a.m. I could find a place to park

around the corner and walk. In my dark clothes I would merge
into the background, avoiding lamp post lights and attention. I
could slide against walls, merge into the background. I admit
I felt a frisson of excitement. I would be in at a police raid. I
tried not to picture Nora cowering in a corner – or worse, that
we would find nothing but empty rooms and be left still with
questions and no answers to fill the void.

We might not find Nora at all – ever.

1 a.m.

The Potteries, even at one o'clock in the morning on a weeknight,
still held plenty of revellers as I drove through, skirting round
Hanley to reach the Bentilce estate. Here the atmosphere was
instantly more subdued until I noted two police vans parked at
the entrance and a few people moving 'casually' along its streets.
I did as DC Summers had suggested and parked two streets away,
locked my car and walked around the corner, keeping to the side,
clinging to hedges and walls and, wherever possible, behind cars,
so shielded from the orange glow of the street lamps. I couldn't
see DC Summers but a few people were clustered near a lamp-
post at the entrance to Eton Way. As I watched, they inched
closer and I thought they were discussing how to storm the house.
I waited too, fifty or so yards off.

The group split into two, one heading for number sixty-three
and the other moving towards number thirty-seven. I tried to take
heart from the fact that the officers heading towards number
thirty-seven were wearing protective gear, while the officers
heading in the direction of number sixty-three were more
casually dressed.

The light from the streetlamps was speckled with moths,
making the shadows dance along the road. For a moment the
scene reminded me of an Edward Hopper painting, the figures,
moving now, illuminated silhouettes. Everyone waiting.

I looked along the road and remembered that elderly couple
who had struggled to climb in the car and drive off. I pulled my
hoodie up further, put my hands in my pockets and sauntered to
the end of the street. I watched the dark figures, keeping close
to the hedges, using cars as shields, as I was, crouching down,

low as tigers stalking prey. I too bent down as I watched. It was a surreal, creepy scene straight out of a movie, officers – I counted ten – stealing towards the house where the old couple had emerged from, where I was convinced Nora was. I tried to listen, to hear some sound, but it was as though their boots had morphed into cat pads and they were completely silent, communicating only with hand gestures.

Stop.

Down.

Quiet.

Move on.

They inched past number thirty-seven, moving towards the house with the steel door. And then it was all movement and shocking noise as they shouted, screamed, battered the door down and charged in. The steel had held longer than a UPVC or wooden one might, but finally it too had given way.

But I was looking somewhere else. In the house opposite, as the other team had crept towards it, I had seen a flicker of backlight in an upstairs window as though a lamp had been switched on, perhaps in the hallway behind. It had lit up the silhouette of a person standing, perhaps watching the drama from the window. A hand swept the curtain back further. And I recognized her. That angle of her head to a bony neck, that sweep of curling grey hair, slightly messy, the shape of her thin shoulders. It was her. I'd found her. I knew it and stared, frightened to move, in case it drew attention to my presence. But she was the woman in the window. She raised her hand, pressed it flat against the glass, and stared out into the night. I didn't know whether to startle her by coming out of the shadow and crying out. I was mesmerized and undecided. And then I felt the slightest vibrations of footsteps behind me, that rhythmic sound that tells you someone wearing heavy boots is coming your way. I picked up his scent next and thought he must have seen me. Maybe not recognized me out of uniform, but my presence had surely been noted. And he too had witnessed the team who had just entered the house opposite and three doors down.

I didn't know what to do. In spite of the heavy police presence that practically surrounded me I felt paralysed and vulnerable.

But I *had* seen her. She *was* here, alive, probably a prisoner in that upstairs room.

He was near enough for me to smell him strongly now and hear his breaths as he watched the drama playing out on the other side of the road. I had what I wanted. I just needed to attract the attention of just one of the officers. I melted into a garden hedge and Evans passed me, then turned around as though checking behind him. I carried on staring at the pavement and he grunted. For a second there was total silence and I realized then his attention hadn't been on me – or on Nora in the bedroom window. He was watching the police drama surrounding number sixty-three. What puzzled me was that he seemed unconcerned, sauntering towards it quite casually. I risked another glance up at the window, worried that Evans would see her. I felt she was not supposed to be drawing attention to herself. Maybe her carer or minder had been distracted by the noisy raid opposite. She was still there, peering out into the night, both hands on the glass now. And judging by the sudden turn of his head Evans had seen her too. He was standing still, looking up, apparently undecided whether to move forwards or stay where he was, which was only inches away from me. For that split second we three were a tableaux, frozen statues. Then I felt the heat of Evans's scrutiny as he noticed me and I felt very frightened.

'What are you doin' here?'

I had no answer. I was still aware of activity across the road but no one had noticed us. I bent my head lower and muttered something deliberately unintelligible. I had a real fear now. And not just for me. He would move her, hide her again, until he had what he wanted. Which was . . .? I couldn't even answer my own question.

I knew what *I* wanted to do – sidle over to one of the police team and alert them. I wanted to get Nora out of there. After all, I was the only one who knew her by sight. They wouldn't recognize her from a silhouette, or know her mannerisms well enough to identify her from a backlit window, the shape of her head and neck. No one else would be able to reassure her, as I would. Evans had stopped scrutinizing me now and was looking back up at the window. I thought he was about to move. I was ready to bolt.

I glanced up at the window again. Someone was standing by Nora's side now. And that was what frightened me. She wasn't alone. She was being guarded. A hand on her shoulder pulled her back.

Evans gave a soft curse and shifted in the direction of the house, moving swiftly now.

I made it to the waiting team. One of the characters crouching in black stiffened as I approached. He had a baton drawn and what I assumed was a Taser tucked in his belt. He started to tell me to back off, but I forestalled him. 'I'm the nurse from the surgery,' I managed breathlessly.

'Get down,' he ordered. He was focused forward, tensed, ready to spring in case someone emerged from the house. It seemed that I was the only one concerned about Nora. They were looking along the road. Only I saw she was being bundled into a car. I was about to shout out but that was the moment the officers chose to move. There was shouting. There were warnings.

Behind the car holding Nora two other cars had slid into place, blocking its exit.

I saw her being bundled into one of the police cars and Evans being cuffed.

But the cars didn't move away. DC Summers was at my side. 'You'd better come with her,' he said. 'In the squad car.'

'Is she . . .?'

His face was tense. 'If you give me your keys I'll get one of the officers to drive your car.'

FORTY-TWO

S ometimes you meet up with someone you haven't seen for a while and you don't recognize them. They have become, even in a short time, a stranger. As I climbed into the squad car I sat beside my patient, who was a crumpled shell of the woman I had last seen only a few weeks ago.

'Nora?' I said, but her face was blank. She was shaking her head. 'I need to be with my family,' she said.

Initially I interpreted this as shock. 'Jack,' I said gently. 'Don't worry, Nora. I expect the police will soon be telling him you're safe.'

She dug her fingers into me. I thought she was suffering from shock. But her nails were long and I pulled away.

Nora was muttering something to herself. 'Be sure thy sins,' she said, as though quoting from the Bible. 'Sins. Long shadows. Short lives.' Now I decided she was rambling. The sooner we got her to the station and had a doctor and myself to assess her the better, I decided.

All the way back she was doing this, speaking to herself, admonishing herself. Shoulders tense, rocking to and fro.

I leaned forward to speak to DC Summers. 'I need to do some blood sugars and assess her,' I said. 'What happened to the others in the house?'

'We'll have them all,' he said grimly. 'Don't you worry. We'll get to the bottom of this.'

Forty minutes later we pulled up outside Stone police station and I climbed out of the car. Nora did not move but stayed staring ahead of her as though unaware of her surroundings.

The officer opened the door and I took her hand. It felt bony and cold and she was still making no attempt to move.

'Come on, Nora,' I said. 'Let's go into the station.'

'Into the station,' she muttered. 'Into the station.'

'I expect you can have a cup of tea there.' It didn't seem to persuade her. And I noticed she didn't appear to recognize me but was staring ahead, frowning and looking troubled.

'It's all right, Nora,' I said. 'You're safe now.'

She still wasn't making eye contact but was shaking her head. 'I'll never be safe,' she said. 'Everyone will know now.'

My heart was sinking. When I had seen her back in May, at the street market, I had wondered if she had a degree of early dementia. Later I'd blamed Ben/Scott Evans on her deteriorating mental state. I wasn't wondering any more. Her abduction had accelerated the process, her confusion now profound. I led her into the police station. DC Summers was walking towards us. I shook my head.

Unlike me he had had no previous connection with Mrs Selleck. She had been a missing person and he had found her.

Job done; likewise the corroborative drugs raid between Stone and the Potteries were successful. But my role was just beginning.

She was muttering now. 'Be sure . . .' And then to my distress she started weeping.

Emotional fragility can often be a symptom of dementia and I, wrongly as it turned out, put her upset down to confusion and bewilderment. I was almost certain that she didn't know me.

I turned to DC Summers and spoke in a low voice. 'Have you spoken to Jack?'

He nodded. 'He'll be here before long.'

Just then I caught sight of Evans. Uncuffed now and watching me with unmistakable malice in his eyes. 'You just had to keep coming, didn't you? Poking your nose in. Well, you'll be eating humble pie soon.'

I turned to DC Summers. 'And the guy in the house with the steel door?'

'Stoke police got him. And they have Kai Evans as well. They'll deal with that along with the Birmingham police. We have our own problem here.'

We both then looked back at Nora.

'She needs a doctor,' I said. 'She's in no fit state to be questioned. In fact, the sooner we have her in the cottage hospital the better.'

He nodded in agreement.

'Apart from Evans, have you got the others from the house? The ones who were watching Nora?'

He nodded. 'We have them all.'

I only had one more word. 'Why?'

DC Summers looked weary. 'He's been giving us some cock and bull story,' he said in a quiet voice. 'And your patient isn't in any state to either confirm or deny it.'

I recalled Catherine's hints at a story. The secret that she'd kept for so many years which was probably true. Maybe I'd misjudged her too. DC Summers was watching me.

'I think I know the story,' I said. 'What I'm not so sure of is Evans's spurious claim on Nora's estate. But there's no doubt at all that his input has shamed her and accelerated her decline.'

DC Summers was watching me. 'Anything you can share?'

I shook my head.

'The police surgeon will be here soon,' he said. 'Maybe you'd like to be present? That is if she agrees to it.'

'I don't know that she's in a fit state to either agree or not.' I felt helpless. 'And I'm not sure we'll get anything much out of her.'

I jerked my head in the direction I'd seen Evans go. 'What's his story?'

'He says he's her great-grandson.'

'And the lady with the Zimmer frame?'

'Maybe you should read her statement.'

I waited and fretted and watched in the reception area while Nora was led away through some double doors, the female officer trying her best to calm her charge down and reassure her. Nora stumbled along with her, fearful and frightened. I would have been with her but she didn't know me any more than she knew the female officer. I felt for her as I watched the police move around, gathering in groups to chat or exchange information, all under the bright, unforgiving lights of the police station.

Nothing ever happens quickly enough when you're in a blind panic.

It was almost dawn when I saw Dr Cartwright, a doctor from a neighbouring practice who acted as a police surgeon, walk inside. He saw me and looked taken aback but didn't cross over to me or make a comment. He simply sent an abstract smile vaguely in my direction and disappeared through the double key-padded doors. I watched them close behind him.

Half an hour later he emerged and this time he did come over to speak to me. 'Florence,' he said. 'It's good you're here. Maybe you can . . .' He dropped the sentence before sighing. 'She's disturbed, confused and wandering. Not surprising considering . . .'

It was what I'd dreaded. 'I'm going to try and arrange a psychiatric assessment,' he said, looking around him before speaking in a low voice. 'I don't think they'll get much out of her. I've done a blood sugar which is fine as are her vital signs. Nothing troubling there. She can have a Diazepam if she becomes agitated. I've left some with the officer in charge.' That was when he frowned and stood erect. 'What on earth happened here?'

I'm not sure any of us had the answers.

He waited for a response, and when I didn't offer one he simply said, 'Stay with her, Florence.' He glanced in the direction of the interview room and added, 'Poor woman.'

I thanked him politely and waited to be escorted back to the interview room.

She was inside, slumped at a table, DC Summers opposite her. He looked up and gave me the smallest of smiles which I returned before sitting down beside my patient.

'Nora,' I said. The look she gave me as she lifted her head was one of puzzlement.

I shook my head at DC Summers, knowing our thoughts were tracking in the same direction. We would get nothing out of her.

Outside I heard a commotion. At a guess either Evans was kicking up or Jack had arrived. The knock on the door told me the latter.

FORTY-THREE

The door opened. My first thought was that Jack Selleck looked absolutely knackered, the distress etched on his face, hands running through his hair.

'Mum? Mum?'

She didn't even look round. It was as though she hadn't heard him, or she didn't recognize the voice or the mode of address. I met his eyes. They were despairing, while I knew mine expressed sadness mixed with an apology. I still felt I'd let my patient – and her son – down.

Jack knelt down and took her hands in his own. 'Mum?'

She didn't acknowledge him but stared straight ahead, frowning as though trying to puzzle something out. Maybe who he was? Jack looked beyond his mother to me for some explanation. Then across at DC Summers. Neither of us could find the words.

'Mum,' he appealed again.

She was shaking her head. 'Family,' she said, but not to him.

I tried then. 'Yes, your family, Nora. Jack's here. Your son. Doesn't he look well?'

A lie if ever I'd uttered one. He must have driven through the night and looked it.

She was still shaking her head, puzzling over something neither of us could comprehend. Maybe she too just needed a good night's sleep.

'Be sure thy sins,' she said at no one in particular.

I stood up and spoke to DC Summers. 'I think the best place for her now is the cottage hospital – if they've a bed. And we can get a psychiatrist to see her there. Don't you agree, Jack?'

He too was shaking his head and looking bewildered. 'What's going on? What's happened to her?'

I glanced again at DC Summers and spoke for both of us. 'We don't know, Jack.'

'I had to do it.' Again, she was speaking to no one in particular. 'Something I had to do. Put something right that's been wrong.'

When that was greeted with silence she continued speaking to herself. 'Many years. Too many years. I'm tired now.'

Jack looked alarmed at this but I met his gaze and shook my head. 'Let's get her in a warm bed, safe, and we can assess her when she's had a good night's sleep. OK?'

Both Jack and DC Summers nodded and I used my phone to ring the cottage hospital while they watched Nora, who was in a world of her own, muttering, folding and refolding the skirt she was wearing which looked a couple of sizes too big.

As I arranged her admission I was watching her, searching for clues.

Then I addressed DC Summers. 'You have Evans?'

He nodded. I glanced from Nora back to him. 'What does he say?'

He blew out a tired sigh. 'It's a long and complicated story.'

Nora was still talking to herself. 'People must have wondered.'

I knelt down. 'Wondered what, Nora?'

She put her finger to her lips. 'Ssssh. Whisper who dares.'

She looked around her the way paranoid patients do, glancing back, right shoulder, left shoulder. Bent in closer. 'Someone might hear.'

'There's only me.' I took a leap into the dark. 'And I already know.'

She almost screamed like a banshee then. 'You know?'

'Yes, and no one is judging you.'

She drew in closer, still with that same paranoid gesture. 'But they will. They do.'

I sensed that Jack and DC Summers were behind me. I glanced at them and gave a tiny shake of my head while touching my lips with a forefinger. *Don't interrupt.*

Nora was clutching at my hand now as though it was a lifeline. And then her eyes narrowed. 'How do you know?' she demanded. 'Who told you?'

I tried to soothe her. 'That doesn't matter.'

But her nails were digging into my hand. 'Peter mustn't know. Not ever. He must not know.'

'Peter never will know,' I said. Behind me I could read Jack's mind. *What the . . .?*

I met his eyes and gave him my own message. *Not now.*

While I knew it would all come out, I followed that with a movement in his mother's direction. *It was her secret.*

That was when DC Summers gestured me outside.

FORTY-FOUR

Outside he didn't mince his words. 'Are you going to tell me what's going on?'

I didn't answer straight away. 'You brought in an elderly couple?'

'Yes,' he said, maybe understanding, maybe not. 'Scott Evans's grandmother.'

'Nora's daughter,' I said.

William Summers was silent.

'Years ago, before she was married, when she was a teenager, probably in the fifties, Nora had an illegitimate baby, a little girl. That baby was adopted. I believe that Evans posed as her great-grandson. He might be. He might not be. I guess the DNA might prove it. He put emotional pressure on her, possibly threatened to expose her both to friends in the town and also to Jack, her son. The blackmail was cruel and she was terrified. And so she came under his spell. She went along with it. When he tinkered with her medication she felt she had no choice but to recognize him as her heir. Hence the will, though whether that would have stood up in court is anybody's guess. I very much think not. Anyway, it was never signed off.'

'Why abduct her?'

'Because her mind was slowly going and he was worrying that he'd left it too late. And, I think, he wanted to use his grand-mother – her daughter – as leverage.'

DC Summers was looking bemused. 'I knew none of this.'

'Neither did I, at the beginning. But various people have dropped various hints and I've wondered how on earth Nora came under Evans's spell. Two halves of a puzzle,' I said. 'Have you interrogated Evans?'

'Not yet. I thought we should talk to Nora first.' He looked past her. 'But we're not going to get much sense out of her, are we?'

'No. She's been sort of brainwashed by him. And the burden of her guilt was the final straw. I think even if we regulate her medication and look after her she won't recover. I understand the new will has never been signed. Maybe she hadn't quite let go of reality.'

'Or maybe . . .' Another thought was flitting through my mind. 'Maybe he was angry. Nora was leading a pleasant life, relatively comfortably off. And there was her daughter . . .' I broke off to think. 'I take it the lady on the Zimmer frame is . . .'

Summers was being cautious. 'Who says she's Evans's grandma.'

'Yet Nora's eighteen years older. And before this she was in very good, sprightly health.'

'Sobering. Health inequalities?'

'Yeah. Well, all the paperwork and tying up of loose ends is with you now.'

I was still puzzling. 'I still don't understand why he abducted her?'

'Maybe to get her to sign the will.'

'But she'd have needed that to be done in front of witnesses. And if Jack contested it . . .?'

'Remove her from eyes that were too watchful. Not just you, Florence. There was her son too. I think you were getting close to the truth. And Jack was coming up, summoned by you. From what I've seen of him he'd have soon seen Evans off or maybe had his mother admitted to a nursing home where she'd be out of reach. It was imperative Nora was out of Evans' way.'

'So it *was* my interference. I made my suspicions plain and summoned her son. And that was why he had to hide her.'

DC Summers didn't attempt to respond.

'I wonder how he found her?'

'It's not hard. There are plenty of ancestry websites. Maybe his grandmother talked about having been adopted as a baby and he decided to look her up. Maybe his half-brother gave him the initial idea. Kai seemed to be doing OK out of conning old ladies. Florence,' he said, 'we have months of questions, plenty with no answers, ahead of us.'

'So what will you charge him with?'

'I don't know. Maybe we'll try kidnapping.'

'Not sure you'll get that to stick.'

'Me neither.' He looked gloomy. 'Maybe extortion?'

'Manipulation?'

'Florence, I'll come clean with you now. If Evans has a good lawyer we'll get nothing to stick.'

'His name isn't even . . .?'

'It *is* actually. Ben is his middle name. Scott Benjamin Evans.'

'What about the other guy? Will you be able to charge him?'

'Oh yeah.' DC Summers was more confident about this one. 'The Birmingham police have enough evidence to charge him. If Nora was able to give a statement,' he added, 'we might be able to file a charge against Scott. But with her in the state she's in I'm very dubious.'

'So all for nothing?'

'Not quite. We've put a stop to the other trickster. He won't be befriending any old ladies any time soon. We have our eye on him.'

'That's something.'

'And maybe next time a muddled elderly person makes a claim we might look at it a little bit harder.'

There was an awkward silence between us. 'I should go back in. I should be with her.'

Summers nodded. 'And you need to have a word with Jack.' He looked towards the door. 'The poor guy is in a bad way.'

Jack was pacing the room while his mother sat, looking around her, periodically meeting his eye and shaking her head with total confusion.

'She says that . . .' He came towards me. 'I give up,' he said. 'I just give up.' He looked down at his mother whose lips were moving, possibly in supplication. Possibly incantation. 'I don't feel I know her any more. Keeping that secret – for all those years – keeping it from me. I can't believe it. Why not say?'

'Things were different then, Jack. People were more judgemental. Maybe your dad wouldn't even have married her.'

'He adored her.'

'Go back to The Beehive, Jack,' I advised. 'Get some sleep. I'll stay with her. She'll be in the cottage hospital. Sleep on it. Think before you say something you regret.'

But I noticed he didn't bid his mother goodbye. He didn't bend and kiss her. Just marched out, anger in every brisk step.

I took Nora to the cottage hospital, stayed with her while they offered tea and sympathy, gave her a bath and tucked her up. As she lay there, she had a moment of something, perhaps bordering on lucidity. She grabbed my arm. 'Keeping secrets, Florence,' she said, 'is exhausting.'

I nodded, understanding it now and I stayed with her until she slept.

And then I went home. My mind was scrambled egg.

It wasn't until late the next morning that my questions started stacking up. I'd rung the surgery and told them I wouldn't be in today. I felt a momentary guilt while I considered the fallout.

Patients diverted, appointments cancelled, my colleagues having to double up on their appointments. With an effort I shoved them all aside and went to sleep.

Hours later as I was brewing myself a coffee, there was a knock on the door. DC Summers was standing there and he looked as though he hadn't slept a wink.

So there were two for coffee.

As we sat in the kitchen I finally started asking questions that had jumbled up in my mind during the night. 'How did you actually find him?'

He gave a rueful smile. 'We have you to thank for that. We suspected that your' – his eyes brightened – 'mole really had found the right area if not the exact right address. When his mate had the exact address we liaised with the local force who had the entire area under surveillance anyway. We just had to work together.'

'The drug dealers.'

'You noticed the steel door.'

I nodded. 'I do have some experience of the rougher end of the Potteries.'

'Yeah. Well, they knew an elderly couple was living in number sixty-three Eton Way and they'd noticed the curtains remained shut practically all of the time.'

'Which wouldn't have done much for Nora's mental health, not knowing night from day.'

'Yeah. So we decided to mount a joint operation. While they were dealing with the guys over the road we would slip in and recover Nora. Except . . .'

I finished the sentence for him. 'Except Evans was out.'

'Yeah. The other point that helped was the fact that you suspected Evans was probably a diabetic. We used that possibility to interview various GPs in the area. That narrowed the field.'

He drank from the coffee mug. 'How's she doing?'

I shook my head. 'She's not great.'

'But if you reinstate . . .'

'The thyroxin? We have to wait for the blood levels to come back from the lab. Even if we adjust that it would take weeks until her levels are rectified, and even then there's no guarantee her mental state will return. For myself I doubt it.'

'So this will be permanent?'

'I think so.'

DC Summers looked gloomy. 'Without a witness statement we're going to have trouble making anything stick.'

'Yes.' I said, before remembering something I had said to Mark once years ago when he had fretted about failing to bring a perpetrator to a guilty verdict. I said the same thing to DC Summers now. 'Not all situations respond to even the best nursing or policing. Sometimes we just have to acknowledge that we can't heal everybody, just as *you* can't put every guilty person behind bars.'

DC Summers gave me a long hard look then. 'Wise words,' he said. 'There's something else.'

'I'm listening.'

'We owe some thanks to your little boy, to his observations.'

'Really? He'll be delighted.'

DC Summers nodded. 'The ice-cream van helped us close in on Evans. And what does an ice-cream vendor do through the winter? Street markets and scouting around for business. And there was the fact that, according to his testimony, Nora Selleck kissed him. It set us off on a track.' He was smiling as he added, 'Let me know when he wants a job.'

Neither could I hide the smile that was spreading across my face. 'He's four years old, Will.'

'Ah yes. I forgot.'

'So there we are. Mystery solved.'

'And an old wound re-opened.'

'Yep.'

FORTY-FIVE

Thursday 15 July, 10.30 a.m.

I t was halfway through the morning when my car arrived, delivered by Pants who seemed to have taken a back seat during the investigation and subsequent drama. He'd been tailed by a squad car, its door held open to return him to the station. He dangled my keys in front of me. 'Thought you'd want your wheels back,' he said jauntily. 'I'm sorry I missed all the excitement in the night, but I expect you're glad to have your patient returned safe and sound.'

My yes was unenthusiastic and flat. Safe and sound? Got my patient back? I shook my head. I wasn't sure I would ever have my patient back. Somehow Nora Selleck had drifted downstream.

I was planning on going to see Nora in the cottage hospital so I could spend some time with her – and Jack. I showered and tidied myself up ready for visiting time.

It was two o'clock in the afternoon but something was still bugging me. I didn't quite have all the answers. I hadn't been able to squeeze the details out of DC Summers, who would have deemed them irrelevant anyway, but my mind had diverted back to the Hudsons. In desperation, and aware that I would be running the gauntlet of *her*, I tried Mark, who picked up straightaway.

'Hello?' He sounded surprised and a little nervous, probably wondering why I was ringing him and what would be the repercussions. At a guess Vivian was in the room, eavesdropping, and curious why I was calling after she'd tried to warn me off – incognito, of course.

Knowing Mark would have put the phone on speaker phone, to allay his wife's suspicions as well as avoid any hostilities later, I was quick to reassure them both. 'I just wondered. How easy is it to track someone down?'

'Is this to do with your patient?'

'Not any more. We've found her.'

'That's good news, isn't it?'

I couldn't answer that. There was a yes but there was also a no. And I didn't want to tell him any of it or that my mind had veered off piste. He'd often accused me of having a short attention span, of skittering from one subject to another. Butterfly on a bush, he used to call it, and I didn't want to give him another excuse. 'It's more to do with some patients who've joined our list. They live opposite The Beehive. I just wondered about them.'

'Why? Do they have anything to do with it?'

'I don't know. They seem secretive. That's all. As though they have something to hide, keeping their heads down. And I wondered what it was.'

'Where did they move from?'

'Blackpool, or so they said. But although they've been here around eighteen months, we haven't got their old paper notes yet.'

'Is that usual?'

'Well, it isn't *that* unusual for the Lloyd George envelopes to go missing sometimes for months, at other times for ever.'

'So what about their computer files?'

'Their computer files only have the barest details. Diagnoses, medication, significant family history. Maybe Covid has held things up a bit.' It struck me then that I hadn't actually seen *any* details of their previous address or their doctor.

Again, he asked, 'Is that unusual?'

'Unfortunately . . .' I began with the lamest of excuses. 'Think IT. Think incompatibility. The NHS is too large and unwieldy for neat and tidy spreadsheets to work. There's too much data. Besides doctors and diseases don't always fit into neat little boxes. Most consultations might start as a tick box exercise but mostly they end in free text.'

'So what' – I sensed Mark had sat up, his interest pricked – 'does this have to do with Nora Selleck? Apart from them living opposite,' he added as an afterthought.

'I don't know but I hoped you might be able to look into it,' I said hopefully.

'Florence . . .' He was getting exasperated now. I knew that tone. 'If this isn't about Nora Selleck, what *is* this about?'

'I think they're hiding something.'

'Aren't we all?' he responded dryly. As soon as he'd said it I sensed his embarrassment, as though Vivian had shot him a nasty look across the room.

'OK, give me their names,' he said, resigned, 'and I'll run them through the PNC.' He couldn't resist a dig. 'Which works a little better than the NHS model. That do you?'

I kept my voice serene. 'Perfectly.'

There was an awkward pause; neither of us could think how to end the call. Eventually Mark said, 'OK, then?'

I said, 'Bye,' and put the phone down.

Then I headed for the cottage hospital.

A wash, breakfast, rehydration with cups of tea, adjusting her medication together with the nurses' attention had brought some improvement in Nora's superficial appearance, but I could tell from the fixed, confused expression in her face that her mental condition was still trapped in confusion.

Jack was sitting by her side, his head in his hands. When I entered he stood up, his face grey with worry. He shook his head. 'Go and get some air,' I said and, after a swift glance backwards he did just that, stumbling out of the ward. I watched the doors swing behind him, then I sat down beside her and waited.

Eventually she turned her head to face me. 'Hello,' she said politely and without any recognition.

'Hello, Nora. How are you this morning?'

'I'm well, thank you.'

I knew I was surpassing the powers of the police but I couldn't resist asking her, 'Do you remember what happened?'

'What about?'

'Do you remember where you've been, who you've been with?'

She didn't even attempt to respond to this but stared ahead and I couldn't decide whether she was refusing to respond to my question or genuinely couldn't remember.

We sat in silence, I watching her for clues as to her mental state, she staring ahead, her face impassive.

I was glad when, half an hour later, thirty minutes filled with silence and the odd glance at each other, Jack returned. His smile was a question. He sat, bent over and kissed his mother on the cheek. 'Hello again, Mum,' he said.

She didn't even turn her head but continued staring ahead, puzzling over something, her fingers pleating and re-pleating the sheet. Occasionally her lips moved in silent conversation but she said nothing.

After a quick, despairing look at me, Jack eased himself into the chair opposite.

For a while the three of us sat like that, occasionally glancing at one another, three people with much to say, but saying nothing.

After a while he looked at me and jerked his head towards the door.

I got the message and followed him out. I began with: 'It isn't my secret,' but he was looking at me, waiting for an answer. I was not going to be able to fob him off.

'Florence,' he said, 'Mum isn't about to give it to me. It has to come from you,' he appealed, and I took pity on him.

'I can't be certain. The police are waiting for the results of the DNA tests but it looks as though Evans posed as a descendant of the child your mother had when she was a teenager. She's now in her late sixties – and in poor health.'

Jack looked stunned.

I felt I needed to spell it out for him. 'There's a possibility that Evans is your mother's great-grandson.'

I had to remind myself – Jack had never met Ben Evans.

He was silent for a moment before asking in a subdued voice, 'And Dad never knew?'

I shook my head. 'Never.'

'Thank God for that. So what . . .?' he began before continuing incredulously, 'did he hope to gain by this?'

'Financial benefit. Leverage?'

'Really? And he really thought that would work?'

I waited while Jack simply looked incredulous.

Two days later I had a call from Mark, and he was laughing now. 'You do pick 'em,' he began.

'Sorry?'

'That couple,' he said. 'What did you call them?'

For a moment I was lost. Then I remembered. 'The Hudsons,' I said.

'Yeah. Those. Sad story really.'

'What is?'

'Their son was murdered by a neighbour. Knifed in what he claimed was a provoked attack.'

'Gosh.' That had not been what I was expecting.

'They appealed against his sentence which they deemed too lenient.'

'And?'

'The neighbour was a young guy named Stanton, who'd claimed provocation. The appeal was successful. The judge threw out the provocation defence and, basically, agreed with the

Hudsons and slapped an extra five years on his sentence. A few of Stanton's mates got together and said they'd get them. At which point the Hudsons disappeared.'

'To reappear in sunny Staffordshire.'

'They obviously want to keep their heads down. Not get entangled with the law and witnessing all over again. And if their names hit the headlines it's possible Stanton's mates would have tracked them down and come for vengeance.'

I was silent. I could never have guessed at this.

After a few moments Mark's voice came over the phone. 'Are you there?'

Truth? I'd run out of words, realizing no one was quite what they seemed. I'd deemed the Hudsons' behaviour suspicious. And it was, but not in the way I'd thought.

And I'd thought of Nora as Caesar's wife.

FORTY-SIX

Monday 19 July, 9 a.m.

The day had a surprise waiting to ambush me.

I had logged on to the computer and was ready to buzz in my first patient when there was a soft knock on the door. Dr Gubb was standing there, his face as pale as death. 'I feel I owe you an explanation,' he said. And with typical politeness he followed that with: 'May I come in?'

'Of course.' I was flustered, wondering what was to follow.

He entered, closing the door carefully behind him.

He dropped into the chair at the side of my desk. His mouth was dry. I picked up that he was about to confide something he was ashamed of. 'This isn't my story,' he said, holding his hand up as though to ward me off. 'When my father . . .'

I was still utterly confused and couldn't see where this was going. He began again. 'When my father aged he became lost in some memories. He felt guilty about something.'

I still couldn't see where this was leading. 'Before my mother.
My father . . .'

I hadn't been brought up in Stone but in the Potteries. I had
never known Dr Gubb senior. I waited patiently but saw out
of the corner of my eye that this was costing me time. Three
patients were now sitting in the waiting room waiting to be
seen by me.

Perhaps Dr Morris Gubb had seen my eyes slide to the right
because now he blurted it out. 'My father believed he might be
the father of Nora Butler's child.'

He looked shame-faced and I felt huge sympathy for this
decent man who had buried a secret.

'This isn't anything to do with you,' I said firmly, but his face
didn't lighten, and after a moment he turned and left.

When Mark rang again three nights later, I'd regained my
equilibrium and found my position. 'Parenting holds respon-
sibilities, Mark,' I said, keeping my voice cold and distant.
'Being a father is . . .' And I couldn't finish the sentence. If
he couldn't see it then I couldn't teach him. But I knew it was
time to let go.

And Nora? I would love to say that with the correct medication, regular meals and the nurses' TLC she returned to The
Beehive and resumed her former life. But she never did. Jack
continued with his filial duty but his mother's long-held secret
had come between them. Scott or Ben Evans melted into the
background. No charges were ever brought. He said Nora had
expressed a wish to see her daughter and he had merely
complied. His half-brother did face charges and was given a
custodial sentence of ten years. Who knows whether he'll
achieve 'good behaviour'. It's very likely he will. To be a
successful con artist one has to maintain a good veneer.

By October Nora was in a residential home and The Beehive
went up for sale.

Sometimes life is never ever quite the same.

And so . . .

Next patient, please.